The Truth it needs no Proof.
Either it is or it isn't
India. Arie

Truth and Proof

By

Jenni Roussell

Dedication

To my dear friend Helen
For your ongoing help and sage advice
Thank You JR

Chapter One:

The air outside hung hot and oppressive, Auckland on a bad day. This February had seen diabolically hot, sultry days. Barbe felt cool, grateful for the air conditioning inside the hotel, as she scanned the guests from the mezzanine floor of the lounge bar. The waiter brought her a tray of tea, silver teapot and fine china cup and saucer. She continued to watch watching as the pot of Earl Grey sat brewing on the tray.

Sitting there at afternoon teatime she tried to guess the occupations and stories of the guests and visitors in the lounge bar. Drawn to a good-looking man of stocky build with thick black hair and a great smile, she watched him enter the room and peruse the guests. He flashed that smile at two old buddies who tittered at him as they enjoyed what appeared to be a gin and tonic. Then he continued to check the room, catching the eye of a big, bald man with a mousey moustache. Mousey moustache beckoned him to sit with him. Now his back faced her and his smile no longer visible Barbe lost interest. She noticed as mousey moustache turned from her; he had a tattoo at the back of his neck. What was it? As she leaned forward, she recognized a spiderweb. Creepy.

An older man, about sixty sat alone. She became aware he sat watching her. When he caught her eye his lips quirked, then suddenly a woman of indeterminable years, bustled up to him, arms full of shopping bags with designer labels which she dropped to the floor, then waved to the waiter. As Barbe's gaze swept the area there appeared to be only one other group in the room. Three men wearing business suits sat in animated conversation. In one corner a lone man sat behind a newspaper, the broadsheet pages covered his face and torso. Long legs protruded, feet dressed in English punched leather black shoes and stripy socks over hairy legs, trousers with wide cuffs. The shoes were Barker Nova's she guessed; her 'ex' had some. Perhaps this man had been something in finance, his clothes looked dated. She noted his hands gripping the newspaper, long boney fingers. On the ring finger of his right hand, he wore some sort of large fraternity ring. For a long few moments, she stared at the ring then movement caught her eye. The dark good-looking one with the smile, walked briskly towards the closed doors of the lounge and pushing one open he walked through it.

Barbe finished a second cup of tea while deciding what to do with the rest of her afternoon. When she walked towards the door on the mezzanine landing a commotion below drew everyone's attention. She turned to look. Bursting through the double doors on the ground floor a lone gunman armed with a semi-automatic weapon sprayed the room with bullets. Screams were heard above the breaking glass and crashing metal, blood sprayed everywhere. Barbe dropped to the ground on her knees as the gunman sprayed the mezzanine with a haze of bullets.

The noise and then the burning pain in her chest were almost unbearable. Looking down at the gunman as she crumpled in slow motion, he stood smiling up at her. His deep-set blue eyes were almost aquamarine below the straight brows, his nose aquiline. Something compelling about his face made her stare at him. She would never forget his eyes. As he turned and fled, she saw it plain as day at the back of his neck, a spiderweb tattoo partly obscured by his suit collar.

THE EMERGENCY DEPARTMENT at the Hospital buzzed with activity.

'We have four theatres currently in use' the head of triage reported to the emergency nurse manager. 'We've sent two other cases to Greenlane hospital who are ready to receive and operate. Three more cases have undergone x-rays and various imaging tests. They're being given bloods and prepped for surgery as we speak. Paramedics are bringing one more in and three have been found dead at the scene.' Suddenly his hand trembled as he picked up a file. Quickly he controlled it. 'I have no idea of the total,' his face was grim.

THE ARMED POLICE PRESENCE at the hospital felt eerily comforting for the staff and frantic families gathered around. Most were too busy to consider anything other than the fate of the victims.

In a separate room away from the hubbub, Barbe struggled to consciousness. An armed officer could be seen standing outside her room. Checking, she could see attached to her arm a carescape monitor and a cannular needle had been inserted in the vein at the back of her hand. Her gut ached. Slowly she ran her hand over her stomach. A surgical patch covering the point of pain just below her sternum. She carefully peeled it back. It felt swollen, she could feel the bruised lump of a small hematoma. The reddened area around it felt sore but no bullet wound. Thinking back, she praised the Lord for the huge gold-plated Saint Christopher medallion she wore around her neck. It weighed a ton and her eldest son had said with his sixteen-year-old sneer, it looked 'fugly.' He claimed she'd be better off with a cocoa tin lid as a pendant, prettier and not so heavy.

Slumping back against the pillows she began to recall the events. The armed policeman she could see standing outside her door reminding her of the gunman who never bothered to hide his face. His smile arrogant, and his gaze hypnotic, his magnetism had been undeniable. *Oh God if he found out I'd survived he'd be after me.*

Panic gripped her; she scanned the room looking to get away. The boy with a gun standing at her door in police uniform, not much older than her son, he didn't exactly fill her with confidence he didn't look like he could knock the skin off a rice pudding. A steel trolley stood beside her bed. On the bottom shelf she found a complete set of scrubs. Quickly she put them on. Next, the cotton shoe covers and a mask, then she watched as the young police officer busied himself talking to another man. Confidently she pushed open the door.

'She's on the loo officer,' she said pointing to the adjoining toilet. 'won't be long.' He smiled and nodded, and as the man with him turned, his vest identified him as police. To her horror she recognized him, The cuffed trousers and shoes, and those black punched leather brogues. She walked off briskly ignoring the intense pain in her upper abdomen. As soon as she could no longer see him, she pulled down the mask under her chin and made her way to the main entrance.

There were armed Police everywhere, she saw Mr. gorgeous smile he seemed to be in the thick of things, gesticulating furiously giving orders. She froze as he looked right at her. Turning abruptly, she walked quickly into the first closed door which on closer inspection looked like a utility room. Slumped against the stainless-steel tub, heart racing and knees weak, her head swirled with unanswered questions. Instinct told her to get away from the hospital as fast as she could. Something did not feel right.

Two plain clothes police officers sitting in the lounge bar of her downtown hotel. What were they doing? one hidden behind a broadsheet newspaper, the other left the room and then in a hail of bullets the others are all gunned down.

Chapter two:

The utility room door swung open and in stepped Mr. gorgeous smile weapon drawn. Horror stricken and weak, she held on to the tub.

'Inspector Don Lancini' he said. Reaching carefully into the breast pocket of his jacket he produced his Police ID. 'Don't be scared,' he said softly, securing his weapon back in his shoulder holster. 'I'm here to protect you Mrs. Anderson.' She almost fainted, he knew her name. He grabbed her with both hands and held her firmly. It took a moment or two for it to register, the smell of his aftershave instantly recognizable, filling her with the gorgeous essence of him and yet a strange sense of foreboding. The sensual aroma she recognized instantly, Pascal Rousseau's signature fragrance for men. At over five hundred pounds sterling a bottle, it would be way above a police officer's salary. She knew there were only a select few clients who bought it in the whole of New Zealand, she shivered.

Barbe worked for Pascal Rousseau New Zealand, as the face of their exclusive brand of French cosmetics and fragrances, a role she had enjoyed for the last three years. At thirty-six when she landed the job, she thought herself too old, but Ricard Beauchene the Managing director thought differently.

'Few women younger than you could afford the products,' he reassured her. 'You have the look we want and the panache to carry it off.'

Barbe loved her work. She never thought of it as just a job, but right now she felt vulnerable with her face plastered all over the up-market pharmacies and department stores promoting her in-store

5

visit and the new range of colours and products. Trapped like a possum in the headlights.

'I saw you at the hotel and the gunman,' she blurted out. Looking directly at her face he recognized her fear. Then he took in her striking good looks, peaches and cream complexion, classic features and huge green eyes. She smelt good too.

'The guy who shot you?' he asked.

'Yes, but he missed. Well, I mean the bullet must have hit my saint Christopher medallion I wore around my neck and ricocheted off somewhere. But what were *you* doing there?' her voice anxious watching as he pulled an exasperated face.

'It makes no difference now, but I went there to meet with a snout.' She didn't understand. 'A police informant, someone who tells me things,' he explained.

Getting another whiff of his aftershave she naively wondered aloud.

'How can a policeman afford such an expensive aftershave?'

He wondered how she knew what it cost. Curious he searched her face for answers?

'Wealthy brother,' he said.

Did she believe him? He instantly realized she didn't trust him, and he felt uncomfortable.

'Did you see anybody else? Trust me please, I need to protect you, did you see anything? Tell me what you saw before the shooting? Did something happen?'

'How can I trust you? You must have seen the shooter; he came in just seconds after you left.' True, he had heard the gunshots from the street, but never saw the shooter he told her.

'I saw him, and he saw me. He smiled at me.' She shivered, watching his warm dark eyes widen. She prayed she could trust him because she felt so tired and weak.

'He had the most extraordinary blue eyes they were almost a green blue like an aquamarine, plus he had a spiderweb tattoo at the back of his neck like your bald friend with the moustache.' She said, praying she could trust this man.

'You didn't miss much, did you? The man you describe is known affectionately as 'the blue-eyed assassin' his name is Carlos Matua, an Australian citizen of Argentinian descent.' The utility room light illuminated her face. He could see beads of perspiration on her forehead, and she had a slight tremor.

'Why are you telling me this?' she wanted to know.

'Because he has connections to the largest and most dangerous drug cartel in Columbia and operates in the golden triangle of the Pacific, and now, he knows your face.'

He needed her to face the reality of her situation. His phone vibrated in his pocket. As he answered it, she noted he wore a bullet proof vest under his suit jacket.

'Don' he answered, 'Inspector what's up?' He indicated to her to be quiet as he put the phone on speaker.

'The woman, Mrs. Barbe Anderson, she's done a runner, can't be too badly injured. She may have seen something. If you see her, it's imperative you get her back here to me.' Don Lancini put a finger to his lips and indicated the need for her silence.

'I haven't seen her, I'm not sure I know what she looks like. Send me a pic. You'll be the first to know if I see her. Do you think she knows something?' he flashed his gorgeous smile at Barbe and touched her arm.

'Not sure, maybe. I'll send you the pic right now.' He killed the call.

'Someone else sent me your pic, but Inspector Powell doesn't know. Stay here while I get you a wheelchair then I'll get you out of here.'

'Wait, you didn't give me up but how do I know you won't? Does this Inspector wear black punched leather shoes, cuffed trousers and striped socks?'

'Damned if I know. Why?' he grinned brows knitted together. 'Doesn't sound like he's got much dress sense whoever he is.' Don thought about her observations. 'Why do you ask?'

She simply said she saw such a man wearing a police vest and talking to the very young constable outside her wardroom door and wondered who he might be.

Don knew the police had a leak on the inside. He would never give this women up. Someone in the department above his paygrade he felt sure was feeding the gang information about police raids and operations and being financially rewarded.

They were called the Griffith Gang because their Australasian base was Griffith in New South Wales. It had been the birthplace of this group importing cocaine from Columbia. Narcotics squads on both sides of the Tasman were working to infiltrate them and trap the kingpins to stop the importation of the cocaine across the Pacific. The only problem seemed the drug bosses were now diversifying into methamphetamine made very cheaply in Tonga. The gang had links to numerous other gangs, the Australian Mafia, the Cobras, Hummer Bees and various Latino gangs in South America according to information from Interpol and the Australian Federal Police.

So 'Teflon Don' Adone Lancini, a kiwi of Italian extraction, worked undercover on the case until a week ago, when his cover had been blown. He believed the leak came from within the Department's own ranks.

SEEING A PORTER, DON flashed his ID and asked for a wheelchair and a blanket.

The porter simply obliged no questions asked. Don thanked him, saying a nurse had been looking for him and pointing in the opposite direction and the man scurried off as the pandemonium continued.

Back in the utility room, Don helped Barbe into the wheelchair covered her with the blanket, then wheeled her out to the car park and his parked car. They were pulling out onto the Southbound motorway when his phone pinged a text. A quick glance revealed the photo of Barbe Anderson. Don blinked, checking it again. A promotional shot for the autumn range of luscious lipsticks and eye shadows. Made up, she looked stunning. The photo he'd previously seen that helped him identify her had been a police security clearance photo. A bland shot for authorized school sports facilitators, HQ had sent it to him. He closed the message and switched on the car's Bluetooth connection. There seemed more to this woman than he first thought.

'Where are you taking me?' she wanted to know. He thought for a moment, unable to answer.

'Not sure, but I need to keep you safe, change vehicles and get you some clothes.'

His honesty surprised her.

'Well, what about my car? It's in the underground car park of the hotel. The concierge has the key, and my clothes are in my room there.'

'Right, I have an idea.' He drove off the southern motorway and rounded a bend and over a bridge to drive on to a northern motorway entrance. 'When we get close to the hotel, I'll get you to lay down on the floor of the vehicle and cover up with the tarp from the back seat. Then I'll deal with things from there.

THE HOTEL AND CAR PARK teamed with police. Don spoke, pretending to be on his phone so she could hear what transpired.

'Yes, I'm just parking now and lucky I have just found a park next to the Anderson woman's vehicle. I'll be about fifteen minutes getting her luggage then I'll bring it in.' He waved to the armed officer guarding the perimeter and showed his ID.

At the Concierge's desk this time he flashed his smile. Various Police staff acknowledged him.

'Sergeant Waddington, will you be a ...' He saved himself from saying *sweetie*, will you be the female officer who packs Mrs. Anderson's bags from her hotel room. She needs them, and she's arranged for someone to collect them and her vehicle. If this charming lady at the desk will give me her keys, I'll load her vehicle.'

Five minutes later the Sergeant returned with three bags.

'Cripes, how long did the woman plan on staying?' Don asked as she grinned. The concierge informed him that it would last four nights and three days.

'She stays about half a dozen times a year. Always gives us samples and gifts. Lovely lady, hope she's going to be okay.' Don took the bags and Sergeant Waddington went off to deal with the forensic team. He opened the rear door of Barbe's vehicle and distracted the police officers with conversation. A charmer clearly told them what a good job they were doing and about the chaos at the emergency department. When he could see she had moved into the back seat of her car as they had arranged, he loaded her bags in the boot. He got in and drove off, remotely locking his vehicle on the way out. Now he took the scenic route to South Auckland. He stopped in a deserted school yard where Barbe managed to grab a dress and sandals from her suitcase. Although she felt less conspicuous, she did not feel entirely comfortable. Something about Don Lancini made her trust him, but she did wonder if it may be it was foolish.

They sat in silence as he drove, listening to the Police Commissioner on the news.

'This shooting bore all the hallmarks of a terror attack. But in the absence of any manifesto or evidence extreme ideology the police are treating it as the random act of a madman. We still have no clues as to the identity of the lone gunman. In the meantime, we will remain on high alert and the public can expect a highly visible police presence. I will personally update the public of New Zealand as soon as we have anything to report.'

Later a report confirmed a semi-automatic weapon had been found empty with no prints and lying in the rose bed of a nearby car park. 'It is believed to be the gun used in the hotel shooting,' the broadcaster said.

By the time they reached Huntly, Don advised he had a plan. He called an old friend, then headed down an isolated country road towards his semi-retired mate's rural retreat. The radio reported the weapon found in the park had been identified as the one used in the hotel massacre. Frank Taylor a Detective Senior Sergeant from head office phoned,

'it appears the weapon jammed and so by the grace of god the death toll currently stands at six, but there were several seriously injured and a waiter with moderate injuries and then there's the Anderson woman who has bolted. We believe she saw the shooter and so she's at risk. So are you Don, the Griffith gang have issued death threats against you. They have come from our Australian counterparts.'

Barbe could see Don's expression. She realized he hadn't wanted her to hear the details, but the call had been on speaker. Soon after they turned down a long winding driveway to a remote cottage, a small Lockwood construction. A lanky, rugged old bloke sat on the veranda in shorts, jandals and black singlet. Don introduced him as Mike Shepperd.

'Shep this is Barbe Anderson.' Don said they would stay here the night and with Shep's help plan their next move.

Barbe had the spare bedroom and Don the couch. The two men hid Barbe's car in a big shed and loaded bales of hay in front of it. Don made a call to his trusted superior at police HQ. Shep and Don talked long after Barbe retired for the night.

The pair had worked together when 'Teflon' Don had been a young rookie in the criminal investigation branch of the police. Shep had shepherded him through his work, his rocky marriage and subsequent divorce. Don's Italian Catholic family had never really accepted the fact he'd never married in the church. They could have accepted the fact his wife was not Italian had she been Catholic, but not marrying a Catholic had been totally unacceptable. In their eyes the marriage had never been consummated by the sacrament.

Don and Shep had stayed in touch especially now in Shep's retirement and the death of his wife three years ago. Their strong friendship had always been unique, forged on the anvil of Don's youthful enthusiasm and tempered by Shep's mature wisdom. One thing the pair both shared was their absolute dislike of being required to be politically correct. They delighted in their private honesty of thought. Neither man felt racist or bigoted and they both loved and respected women.

'But why the fuck can't we call a spade a bloody shovel.' Don had said after a few drinks, the usual time the pair of them would put the world to rights, remembering old cases and old work mates. They had each other's backs for years, two honest hardworking coppers of the old school. Shep delighted in telling any young cop who would listen, his marriage had been a success because he could say the magic words, 'yes dear.' Don pointed out his mother had always been the boss in their home unless his father said different. But he never did. 'Scared of her,' he joked.

NEXT MORNING BARBE woke refreshed and dressed in cutoff
jeans and a tee shirt, hair in a ponytail, she sat at the breakfast table
and suddenly felt alarmed.

'Please can I call my family and tell them I'm, okay? My boys
need to know. My husband, too.' Don looked at her, she seemed
agitated.

'Husband, boys how come you never mentioned them before?
"There is no mention of a husband in the report,' he accused, alarmed
this business had suddenly become more complicated.

'I'm divorced, and the boys are in boarding school, St Benedicts
in Wellington.' Shep listened understandingly, but Don's face
showed barely disguised annoyance as he looked towards the ceiling.

'What else are you not telling me?' His smile vanished replaced
by a bulchy chauvinist. She swallowed hard.

'Must have been shocked. I forgot. I thought the police would
have been in touch but...' she bit her lip. 'But Hunter should know so
he can protect the boys if necessary.' She watched Don's face as the
penny dropped.

'Hunter? not Hunter Anderson, from Holmes Anderson
Chapman and partners?' his voice incredulous. 'You never thought
to tell me your ex-husband is one of the country's leading criminal
barristers?' he almost scoffed. 'No bloody wonder you know the
price of expensive aftershave lotions.' Barbe felt very alone, as though
his support had been suddenly withdrawn.

'Sorry,' seemed all she could muster. Shep called him out to the
veranda and the two wandered off out of earshot, although their
voices were raised, and Don did a lot of waving his hands around and
yelling. Shep's deep drone could be heard placating him.

When they finally returned to the cottage Barbe had recovered
herself and stood up to him.

'The reason I know the price of your aftershave is I work for the company, and just because my ex-husband's a smart lawyer, don't think life has been easy for me. I've had to fight him tooth and nail to get this divorce where it is today. He didn't want a bar of it. Our boys are fourteen and sixteen and were day boys until three years ago. Believe me, I have very tight restrictions on my life. Lawyers can screw you more ways than you can imagine.' Now she had spat it out, her hands were shaking, her breasts heaving with her breathing ragged. 'So, believe me when I say I'm not scared of some Australian criminal or a bulchy cop.' She noted Shep smirk and Don's smile desperately trying to stop his lips from quirking. Shep spoke first.

'Don's been in touch with HQ, and they are happy for him to keep you safe for the time being, because they also need him out of circulation, keeping a very low profile until this case is wrapped up.' Shep looked up to Don who stood beside him as he sat across from her at the table.

'You tell her Don,' he insisted.

'The thing is, well I have good cause to suspect this investigation is being interfered with at a higher level than me. We have a few people we can trust this information with, but we must step back and let them do their job. I have suspicions, but I don't know for certain who they might be or how many of them are involved or to what extent. We are going to a safe house only Shep and I know about. We'll travel in disguise.' She now understood his attitude and why he had trusted her with this information.

'Well perhaps I should tell you something. Before I do, Shep explain to me why you're sticking your neck out for me or him? I mean you're retired.' The two men looked at each other, Barbe seemed a very intuitive woman, not just observant, she had good instincts. They told her Shep had to be something more.

'Undercover cops need a support network to keep them safe and to pass on messages back to the department. I've been Don's support network for years. I took early retirement because my wife had cancer and my situation worked well for the department also. I'm back part-time. I have the security clearances and know not only the job but many of the blokes in it. The most important thing is we trust each other, and I can go wherever I'm needed, no ties.' Shep spoke quietly and with a considered sincerity. Barbe trusted him.

'Okay, I never told you before, but I saw another man in the hotel watching proceedings. I never saw his face, he sat behind a broadsheet newspaper, but he had black punched leather brogues, Barker Nova's I believe. He also wore grey and black striped socks. His legs were long, and his trousers had a wide cuff, making me believe he is older, because they went out of fashion years ago,' she confided.

'This is the guy you said you saw speaking to the young constable outside your room at the hospital?' he asked, his tone serious, wishing he'd probed deeper earlier. Shep suggested the young Constable be questioned surreptitiously, 'he may know the officer who spoke with him.'

Chapter three:

Shep reinvented the pair. Their disguises were grey wigs; hers a permed job of real hair and his, a scraggy affair he covered with a terry toweling hat and sunglasses. The vehicle he gave them had been his late wife's old four-wheel drive Toyota Hilux truck. She used to drive it to the markets to sell her produce, he advised them. Shep suggested Barbe wear an old handknitted pink cotton cardigan over her tee shirt. It had belonged to his late wife. Don had some of Shep's old clothes, a polo shirt and baggy jeans with the wig they aged him. He did not look impressed, it amused Barbe. He had to be the vainest man she had ever met.

Then they talked phones; three burners, all prepaid and preprogrammed with Shep's late wife Sandra's number. A different number for each phone, they had done this before. The phones were numbered one, two and three. Shep also had three similar phones. They used alternate phones on different networks each time. Then they would be dumped. Shep gave them a picnic lunch and they set off. Barbe hugged him, thanking him for arranging head office to get in contact with her husband who would in turn speak to their boys. He had been in touch with detective senior Sergeant Frank Taylor at head office and asked him to inform Hunter Anderson of his ex-wife's situation.

EARLY THAT AFTERNOON Frank arrived at the offices of Holmes Anderson Chapman and Partners, Barristers and Solicitors, on the Terrace. Hunter's assistant, a woman in her sixties ushered Frank into Hunter's office and announced him. Hunter Anderson now enjoyed the role of senior partner in the prestigious company which had been started by his late uncle years ago. He stood tall and bespectacled, his greying hair thinning.

'Thank you for seeing me immediately, Sir. It's a nasty business, I'm pleased to report your wife is safe and recovering.'

Hunter Anderson immediately corrected him, 'My ex-wife,' he breathed deeply, 'but I still love her for my sins.'

Frank frowned and continued. 'The large medallion she wore protected her. A bullet ricocheted off it apparently, she has been incredibly lucky to have just a few bruises. You can appreciate Sir, as a material witness and one with the least injuries, we have taken her into protective custody until the shooter is apprehended.' Frank watched as Hunter Anderson stood thinking one hand in the trouser pocket of his smart pinstriped suit, the other gently fingering a file on his desk. 'Mrs. Anderson felt anxious you be the one to tell your sons, Sir.'

'Yes, yes of course Detective. I've been thinking, Barbe is a very observant woman, she could be a valuable prosecution witness. This situation in itself may have repercussions for our sons, if you understand where I'm coming from, Detective.' Hunter fixed him with a steely gaze; he looked intimidating even when worried.

'And possibly for you too, Sir.' DSS Taylor added.

'I live with it all the time, many of those I have defended have had a history of crime. But it does not mean they are guilty of the crime they are accused of when I defend them.'

His penetrating stare went right through Frank, who felt obliged to say, 'Yes well if I was ever accused of a crime, I'd want you defending me too, Sir.'

'You miss my point detective, so I'll be direct. I visit prisons all the time. I'm told things and so I'm aware what is reported in the media often has nothing to do with the facts of a case. This shooting may not be the work of a lone wolf operator. It could well be the tip of a much bigger iceberg; we may need to work together to keep my family safe. Do you understand?' He narrowed his eyes at Frank who felt like a schoolboy in the headmaster's office being berated for some misdemeanor.

'I think we're all on the same page Sir, so I urge you to be honest with me also, if you learn anything relevant to this case.'

Frank extended his hand which Hunter took, asking with a worried frown, 'you have someone good looking after my... Barbe I hope?'

Frank processed the remark; did he mean good as in a *good man* or did he mean good at his job? 'Yes Sir, rest assured he is the best and good.' Hunter simply nodded he understood the answer.

NOW, LATE AFTERNOON they had been driving for hours and Barbe needed a comfort stop. Don took the opportunity to check in with Frank.

'Don, I gotta say Hunter Anderson surprised me, well for an ex-husband, I think the guy still loves her.' Silence reigned for a moment then a frustrated Don countered,

'hell Frank, I still love my ex-wife too and I'd worry about her if she were involved in something like this. But I'm not *in love* with her.' Frank ignored the remark, he'd worked with '*the Don*' as he referred to him long enough to recognize when he might be interested in a woman. So, he simply reported the conversation, with the parting shot, 'keep your mind on your job.' Don killed the call and raked his fingers through his hair thinking Frank must be getting cabin fever, he'd been in bull shit castle too long.

They were now travelling down a bumpy, rutted, unsealed road. Somewhere along the Whanganui River towards the National Park. The heat felt stifling and with no air conditioning in the vehicle. The road dust tasting dry and peppery as it seeped inside the old truck and caught in their throats. Don mulled over in his mind the phone conversation he had just had with Frank Taylor on his new burner phone.

They drove for another hour. It seemed slow going because the metal road. Don had been there before. He didn't need a GPS and noticing she looked tired, he commented,

'nearly there Barbe. What does Barbe actually stand for? I mean sure I've seen it written down is it short for Barbara?' she smiled as she wriggled in her seat.

'Tell you what, I'll tell you if you tell me how to pronounce your name, because it is not Don, the name on your ID is not Don, you had your fingers trying to cover your Christian name.'

He gave a half eyeroll.

'Okay you go first.'

'My name is Barbe, after the martyred Santa Barbara. It's pronounced Barbie as in the doll. It originates from Macedonia where my grandparents came from. I felt happy enough with it as a child when I discovered the Barbie Doll. But as a teenager, my friends persecuted me relentlessly. What's your story?'

'My full name is Adone Mario Lancini.' He grinned, watching her look him up and down as though judging his worth to own such a name.

'Oh dear, you poor thing. Although I can see some of the traits.' Hearing her say that he sucked in his gut, 'I mean in Greek mythology Adonis was vain, and you touch your hair more than any woman I know. Your fragrance is much more sensual and exclusive than any woman I know and believe me there are plenty of prima donnas in my industry. Don't get me started on your shoes or suit.' She laughed, fortunately he didn't take himself too seriously.

'I'm particular, okay?' he smirked.

Finally, they arrived at the isolated property. An old house circa 1920's, a villa with a separate garage.

'Don't you lift anything; I can't have your wound getting worse.' He took the keys from a keychain telling her he'd open up. Standing back, she let him check the property. Inside the place looked clean, maybe a little dusty. There were three bedrooms, a sunporch and a veranda. Some cane chairs sat in the middle of the open plan living area. Barbe lifted one of the chairs to shift it back on to the veranda.

'What did I just tell you?' he bellowed. She ignored him. It felt very light. He settled the other cane chair and matching café table alongside it on the veranda. An older television set sat in the corner, but reception seemed poor, only good for playing DVD's. The kitchen looked dated.

'The house is off the grid and there's a huge diesel generator here to power everything. Solar panels cover the roof, and we have a septic toilet system,' he advised. In the basic kitchen stood a gas stove. Two huge gas bottles were attached to the house, she could see from the kitchen window. Two large water tanks on stands gravity fed the internal taps.

'Adonis,' she facetiously called, 'can you get the fridge to work?' He gently pushed her out of the way with his hip. 'No problem, Barbie Doll,' he replied, 'I've just started the generator.' He pulled off her wig.

'You don't need to wear your wig here, unless you're on the road or out in public. It's safe here.'

As soon as the groceries were packed away, she turned on a transistor radio dialing up the National program. It needed an Aerial. she'd get a wire coat hanger and improvise. Don busied himself fixing the generator, switching to the battery storage system. Barbe fiddled with the TV and managed to get TVNZ although the reception was poor. Seeing a news flash about the shooting she called to Don. Immediately he came running, her voice sounded anxious.

'Look I got channel one, look.' They gazed at the screen horrified, posters of Barbe flashed across it, they were promotional photos. They featured beautifully made-up face to promote their expensive cosmetics. The tag line on the poster read: Any woman can feel beautiful with Pascal Rousseau. The voice over said this woman pictured had been in the hotel at the time of the shooting and was now missing.

'Shit, what a fuck up! How the hell did they get this?' Don immediately pulled out his phone calling his Auckland counterpart. 'How did it happen?' He found himself sweating profusely, he puffed up his chest indicating testosterone-fueled anger. 'It's hard enough trying to do my job without this. Yeah, I know you told me to bring her in. But would either of us be alive if I'd brought us both back? Well fortunately, I got the message straight from the old man himself, telling me I'm on their hit list so from now on I take my orders from him alone.' He killed the call. 'Bastard, if I didn't know better, I'd say Inspector Bill Powell authorized those photos himself.' Don sighed and sat down beside her as she told him, 'don't be mad at him, there were posters galore in Smith and Caughey's department store and a few upmarket pharmacies. This was bound to come to light after the shooting. But how do they know I'm missing? To me, that is the most disturbing part of all this.' he agreed with her and sat thinking for a moment.

'I'm starving, but I need to think logically about this situation and plan ahead. Can you cook?' he asked as though he expected she had someone to cook for her.

'I think I can manage to rustle something up. The list you had at the supermarket looked very precise. I'll check the cupboards.' From a draw in a sideboard, he took out an I Pad and attached a keyboard while she moved off to the kitchen. From the kitchen window she observed a decent lemon tree and picked a few for lemon cordial. There were a few staples and condiments in the pantry and all the basics were on his list. She made some pasta, noting he had purchased triple O flour, a foodie she suspected. 'Can I cook? Patronizing Adonis I'll show you.'

Half an hour later she announced, 'dinner will be another half hour, fancy a drink? I see you bought a couple of bottles of wine.' She gave him a wry expression, 'either you don't drink much or we're not staying long.' He shook his head. She appeared to be so laid back, maybe she didn't fully understand her position.

'Thanks, a glass of pinot would be great.' Returning with his wine she set down a plate of crusty bread brushed with olive oil and baked and two smaller bowls, one with pesto and the other looked like grated zucchini and feta. Raising his eyebrows in faint surprise he said, 'great thanks' and started tucking in.

'Tell me why you don't seem to be as alarmed about your situation as you should be?' he asked. 'Most people in your situation would be panicking about their family.' He sipped his wine watching her shrug.

'Ah well I'm not most people. Besides, I had scheduled to be away from home for three weeks travelling around the country with this new promotion. My boys are in boarding school, and I had arranged for their father to have them in the weekends till I return. We co-parent.' She ran her teeth over her bottom lip as though there might be more, but she didn't say.

'What about a partner?' She shook her head as he asked, 'a boyfriend then?' She shook it again and looked away. There definitely had to be more to this. It was not his business, still he pushed it. 'Do you expect me to believe an attractive woman like you has no one, no love interest?' He studied her face, she looked stunning even without makeup, perhaps she still loved her husband?

'No, I don't expect you to understand but it's the truth,' she told him; he pushed her one step further. 'Do you still love your husband perhaps?' She shook her head again.

'No, I stopped loving him like a wife years ago, but it's complicated.' He wished he had a dollar for every time he heard that line. But this time his gut told him something in this situation was different. 'Is it because you're catholic?'

Inhaling deeply, she sighed.

'Partly, but no, not really.' She stood up from the table and went to check on dinner. 'Looks good.' She returned with the wine bottle and offered it to him. He topped up their glasses and she set the table. Noting his pleasure as she set down the food, she passed him a serving spoon and sat back sipping her wine as he tucked in. Then with indescribable pleasure she watched him eat. Smiling, she watched his eyes half close as he savored the sauce with sensual enjoyment.

'Glad to see Adonis enjoys his food,' she said as he took a second helping of her three cheeses Cannelloni.

'Where did you learn to cook like ...?' he licked his lips mopping the last of the tomato sauce from his plate with fresh crusty bread.

'Like what? Cook like what?' she goaded him. 'Like a Mediterranean?' He noted the hint of sarcasm in her voice.

'Like my Nonna actually,' he sounded surprised.

'My Baba taught me.' He flashed her his beautiful charismatic smile and instantly she felt something, a warm connection, a buzz. 'Thank you,' she whispered, her cheeks flushing, her teeth nibbling her lip again. Instinctively Don felt this mission would be different, it had all the hallmarks of ... something new. He wanted to ask if her Baba had told her the way to a man's heart is through his stomach, because his Nonna had told him, and she had always been right.

Chapter Four:

Father O'Connor ushered Hunter Anderson into his small private lounge where Nicholas and Ryder Anderson were waiting. The three of them joined in a hug. 'She safe boys, she's safe.' Immediately Ryder broke down sobbing. His father comforted him as the priest stood in the doorway not wanting to invade their private moment. Hunter told him to come in so he would understand their situation.

'Listen to me boys, your mother was very lucky, the bullet intended for her ricocheted off the gold St. Christopher medallion she sometimes wears. She's a material witness and she's helping the police. They have her in protective custody.'

'She's helping the police with their inquiries and she's in protective custody? helping police with their enquiries isn't that code for she's under arrest?' Nicholas lashed out, his apprehension making him cantankerous.

Hunter shook his head. 'No, it's very real and if she didn't co-operate, we could all be in danger.' Ryder asked him to explain.

'You know how we've discussed things as a family when I've had a big case. We need to keep ourselves safe. We can't speak to the press, and we can't post or go on Facebook or Instagram or any social media until the case is resolved. And we never comment on a case. Father O'Connor has your phones. All communication with the outside world must be through him.' Hunter watched as Nicholas lifted his lip, about to say something. His father pre-empted him.

'Nicholas, this lone gunman, may not be alone. What say? he is part of something bigger and the only thing in their way is your mother? they could try to get at her through you. The police may need to have someone protect you, too.' Hunter's stern look told the boy he meant business.

'You mean like Woolly V?' Ryder asked. Wooly V had been the nickname they gave to a certain Polynesian Prince. A student at the college at the time of a Military Coup in his home country had been provided police protection and some younger students thought it very cool.

'Yes, exactly, I'm sorry to say.' The idea appealed to the less worldly Ryder, but annoyed Nicholas and he lashed out.

'This is all because of her job, she should have listened to you, she didn't need to work.' Nicholas looked more like eighteen than sixteen. He didn't want his mother working, she'd been there for him most all of his life, and he expected it.

'We've had this conversation before Nicholas and I told you then, your mother is entitled to do something for herself.' He sighed, sounding so reasonable. In truth he had been anything but reasonable. He had reduced her allowance but refused to sell the family home which he tied up neatly in a trust. Also, he refused to give her money to buy her own home. No lawyer she consulted wanted to deal with her at the time. They all feared Hunter Anderson and his watertight exit agreement /come divorce settlement, she had willingly signed. He couldn't do it to her forever but until Ryder turned sixteen, he had the upper hand. It had all been written into this agreement he had her sign when they divorced.

'Dad, can we come home this weekend?' Nicholas felt constrained already.

'Yes, but you will wait here until I pick you up tomorrow afternoon and you'll stay with me.' He looked to the priest for confirmation.

'Gees dad, I wanted to stay at home not trussed up in your apartment, all my stuffs at home.' The boy groaned, his father sighed, sounding tired. He could do without this drama complicating his life.

'Okay, we'll stay at home, but you have your things at my apartment as well.'

Listening the priest could see how difficult family life became when the parents divorced. In fairness to this family, they always provided a cohesive face to the school although he knew they were divorced and neither had remarried. But then a Catholic marriage is indissoluble.

'Nicholas, keep an eye on your brother and Ryder, you try not to annoy him.' He turned to the priest. 'Is there a game Saturday?' Hunter raised his hand to silence his son.

'What time do you want us all to be there on Saturday?' Polite conversation ensued and as a parting shot, he added to the boys, 'take no notice of the news on TV or anywhere, their sources are not as reliable as mine, and behave.' Hunter always told the boys to behave, as if they could do otherwise with an authoritarian father. Nicholas, a typical lippy teenager, had already set his sights on a career in law so being argumentative had been seen as an attribute when it suited his father. Ryder, a sensitive loving child whose father loved him deeply, came across as bright and caring. He had no aspirations for law but at fourteen he still had years to choose anything. However, being a little secretive and the rebel of the family, his father thought Ryder reminded him of his mother.

DEEP IN RURAL WHANGANUI the unlikely pair sat facing each other across the breakfast table. Barbe with her dark hair pulled up in a scruffy ponytail, dressed in a soft floral sundress dropped off one shoulder. Her offsider in board shorts, boat shoes and a tee shirt sat grumbling about his lack of aftershave.

'My God, you are such a prima donna. Are you sure your name is not some wicked curse? How does your wife put up with you?' She poured another cup of tea. She enjoyed winding him up and he bought it, although it seemed to amuse them both. Then the wife remark.

'Wife, what wife? I have no wife.' Face deadpan he buttered his toast. 'Bugger, I forgot to get some marmalade.' He stood up and rifled through the pantry, found some marmite and sat back down.

'I don't believe you. I've seen the way you look at women,' she accused.

He harrumphed, 'I rest my case; I wouldn't be checking women out if I were married.'

'Who's Shelly? I heard Shep ask after Shelly and your face lit up, full of love. You said she's gorgeous, simply gorgeous,' She questioned with quiet curiosity. Again, his face lit up like a neon light. He flashed his trademark smile.

'Yeah, you don't miss much. Shelly or Michelle as she likes to be called now, is Daddy's little darling, my daughter. My only child actually. Michelle lives with her mother, my ex-wife,' he proudly explained.

'How lucky you are. How old is she?' Barbe sounded genuinely interested.

'Thirteen going on twenty-one.' He topped up his coffee. 'A copper's life is hard on kids.'

'Well, yours is anyway. All careers have their tribulations. Kids are more resilient than you give them credit for,' she advised, 'but I know what you mean. Tell me about her.'

'She's taller than you,' he indicated, waving his toast. 'Dark hair and quite a beauty. She's interested in Graphic Design.' He smiled proudly, 'a great sports woman too, netball and wind surfing.' Barbe nodded warmly.

'What about your boys?'

'Nicholas is the oldest and he's a mini me for Hunter, tall, handsome and very intense. When he and Hunter are not arguing they get on well. He wants to join the firm of course. He's ambitious and driven in everything, sport included.' As she fingered the handle of her cup, he asked what sport. 'Really you need to ask. Rugby of course, first fifteen. A very serious business at St Benedict's.' She looked up at him.

'I know, my older brother went there. He still talks about the three Rs he learned there; Rugby, Religion and Rough housing in that order.' His voice a tad derisive.

'Sounds like you don't have much time for the place. Didn't you go there too?'

'No, the old man died, and the money ran out.' Now she understood why he seemed so cynical.

'Where did you go then?' she didn't really mean to ask, he seemed obviously hung up about it.

'The local high school, what about your younger boy?' briskly he changed topics.

'Ryder's fourteen a fourth former, or year nine and he's more like me both in looks and demeanor. He seems quiet but he doesn't miss a trick and just when you least expect it, he socks it to you. Already, he doesn't always agree with his brother or his father. I just know one day he will rebel. I only hope he chooses the right moment, because neither his brother nor his father like to lose and those two are so dogmatic, they can argue their way out of any situation. Ryder cares about people and is very loving. The humanities are more his strong suit. He reads all the time.'

'They sound so different. How old is Nicholas?' Don asked.

'Sixteen, going on twenty-six, just one more year of school, then off to University,' she started to clear the table.

'Cripes you don't look old enough.' He knew her age but needed to get it into perspective. 'How old were you when you married?'

'Almost twenty-two, twenty-three by the time I gave birth to Nicholas.' She wiped the table and shrugged.

'Hunter had turned thirty-six when we married.' She heard him gasp.

'Cripes a good fourteen-year gap. What did your parents think about the age difference?' he frowned at her.

'They were fine with it. They had an almost twenty-year age gap and it worked for them. My father doted on my mother. I really loved Hunter and he'd been touted as a good catch too, a partner in the firm. I felt so grateful for how lucky I had been. He told me it would be a forever thing, no divorce. I thought so, too.' Unable to look him in the eye she looked away. 'Don't ask.' She read his mind.

Chapter Five:

They locked the house and set off for a short bushwalk so Don could check the boundaries. The property, set on ten acres, had been stocked with a few cattle, five or six just, keeping things from turning feral he had told her.

'How long will we be here?' she wanted to know.

'How long's a piece of string? I've got no idea; my guess is a week or so.' He watched her face. She did not look happy. 'Do you have other family you need to contact, your parents?'

'My father died years ago. My mother's overseas visiting her sister in Europe. Hunter will get in touch with her if necessary. She and he have a great relationship, she loves him and believes the divorce is all down to me. It's sad when you can't be honest with your own mother. But I can't destroy her belief in him by telling her the truth about his ...affairs,' she covered her mouth.

'Please I can't talk about this.' The pain in her expression told him there was definitely more to this but he liked her so didn't push.

'I'm going to have a Nonna nap after lunch but then I'll forage in the garden and weed it a bit and do a planting.' He liked gardening, 'we try to have something growing here regardless of who is or is not here.'

'Fancy a sandwich?' she asked back at the house. He said he'd get it, so she scoured the bookshelves for something to read. In her bags she had a book somewhere too. Searching through her work sample bag she found more than the book.

'Found these,' she pushed a full-size bottle of Pascal Rousseau's exclusive men's fragrance and a moisturizer at him. 'Samples' she said.

'You beautee!' he whooped. Pleased, he thanked her, and she went to read her book.

ONE EVENING ABOUT FIVE days later she came out of her room, showered and freshened up, to watch the news. Having prepared a salad earlier she had no more to do. Don agreed to cook on the BBQ after the news. He had showered and smelled like Pascal Rousseau pour homme as he sat down next to her his hair still wet. The news had started, neither spoke. Tonight, the shooting had been relegated to the number three slot behind some Trump antics and a rugby player's sex scandal. The announcer said the network could now report Mrs. Anderson, who had been involved in the hotel shooting, had been located visiting friends at a secret hideaway on Waiheke Island in order to recuperate out of the media spotlight. The announcer said the network regretted any inconvenience caused by their misinformation.

'Fake news,' Don said jubilantly. 'I love it, don't you just love it,' he said as a rhetorical question, obviously someone had fixed the story. Barbe felt relieved even if it were untrue because the press were off her case.

The next item on the news had been the body of a man found dead in a boat shed just north of Auckland. The victim suffered several stab wounds thought to be the cause of death. Police were investigating. He turned to face her. His eyes widened as if seeing her for the first time. But he said nothing, drinking her in. She looked good, so did he. But they were business, pure and simple. No arguments. He had been about to suggest a drink, when a dusty covered black Ford Ranger swung into their driveway. Don disappeared into his bedroom and came out wearing his wig and pulling his shirt out to conceal his weapon stuffed down the back of his shorts.

'Stay here. I'll deal with this,' he told her brusquely, then he called over his shoulder, 'Don't be a slack arse Jack, I did it all last night.' Barbe realized he had been trying to make out they were not alone. She stood up and went off to the kitchen where she could observe proceedings covertly from the kitchen window. There were two blokes sitting in the Ford Ranger. In seconds Barbe worked out if they shot Don, she would be on her own. The weapon Don had stuffed down the back of his trousers didn't look like the same weapon he wore in his shoulder holster. Living with two video game mad teenagers, had taught her to notice these things. The shoulder holster gun had a curved black handle, the one down his shorts looked straight plastic and smaller. She went into his room and opening the bedside drawer she saw the gun in the holster. Removing it, she went back to the kitchen and sneakily peeked out of the window. One of the blokes slid out of the vehicle. Don looked busy pointing back down the road. She heard him say,

'Sorry mate, I have no idea who you're talking about, a bunch of us have hired this house for a week and a couple of them went into town to get some grog, we ran out. There's a house about fifteen clicks back, they might be able to help. But my mate said to be careful you get lots of cops around here, looking for weed plantations, bastards, still he might know, don't know how long he'll be though.' Barbe froze, why on earth did he bring up weed? Her heart beat a tattoo, and her hands shook. The guys in the vehicle said something and now they were backing out and turning. She watched as they drove off.

Shock suddenly made her drop to the floor. 'Barbe, where are you?' He called, she didn't answer, she couldn't move. 'What the hell?' he saw his weapon on the floor. Bending down to get it he noticed it still appeared to be clipped secure. Helping her up he could see she looked afraid. But there were no tears.

'Why did you spin them a yarn about cops and cannabis?' she accused.

'Come on Barbe, sit down we need to talk.' He sat her down on the couch. She looked fragile, her sundress had dropped off her shoulder again and humidity had caused her hair to become all wispy around her face.

'Those two guys were stoned I could smell it and I saw it in their eyes they were on something. I knew they'd be scared if they thought they might get turned over by the police. It was a strategic thing; trust me I've been there before.' She wanted to cry. The shock, her pent-up emotions the endless questions about her ex-husband, the effects of the shooting. He could see it too, she looked uptight.

'You need a drink; would you like a limoncello over ice? It's very moreish.' He had a secret stash he told her. The stuff hit the spot and tasted very moreish alright. She had a couple and felt so much better, more mellow, less strung out.

'I have a recipe for this stuff did you make it?' she asked. It had been his Nonna's own recipe he told her. By the time they had dinner it had gone eight thirty. As soon as he'd cooked the steaks, he secured the house and closed the windows. It had still been hot but, 'just to be on the safe side,' he told her. Then he sliced the steaks thinly and folded them through the salad and dressed it with his own sweet chili sauce and served two platefuls. Barbe was grateful for the food and being slightly squiffy, it felt so good.

'You fancy a coffee?' he asked after dinner. Telling him she'd prefer another limoncello he smiled.

'Then you shall have it.' Don sat on the couch sipping his coffee, raking his hair as he thought.

'I reckon that black Ford Ranger they were driving is stolen, I got the number, but we are not here for stolen vehicles. Still, it is far too expensive a vehicle for a couple of weed heads,' he said talking to himself she had stopped listening, instead she sat giggling at him.

'Adonis you're at it again playing with your hair,' she giggled and teased him, flicking her own hair. No one had ever called him on his affectations before. He found it highly amusing, and he gave her his charismatic smile. 'Oh gee, I love your smile, it's beautiful like you Adonis,' her breath hitched, and she sighed. He leaned over her, his smile now subtle and seductive. She closed her eyes not wanting the moment to end. The smell of his aftershave, now it would always remind her of him. The feel of his breath on her lips nearly tipped her over the edge.

'Please,' she said he didn't know what she spoke about, but he didn't wait to find out. Gently moving his lips over hers he kissed and nibbled softly, teasing her lips with his own and she responded. She put her hands under his tee shirt. He got the idea and stripped it off and then, still kissing her, pulled the other shoulder of her sundress down. He kissed down her neck to her breasts, she groaned. Picking her up he carried her off to his bedroom where he set her down on the bed and stripped off his shorts. Gently he resumed kissing her, as his lips softly navigated the curve at the top of her bosom. Her back arched and she moaned.

'I want this, but I'm scared, I haven't had sex in years.' He continued kissing her then stopped, helping her shed her dress.

'How many years?' he asked not really registering what she'd said.

'Fourteen, mmm fourteen years three hundred and five days...' Suddenly as he stood up and pulled the curtains across to darken the room and rechecked the locks it hit him like a ton of bricks. Fourteen years and how many days? It posed so many questions. Minutes later he put his arm around her and continued kissing nuzzling into her neck slower and more tenderly. Then he became aware, she no longer responded, he looked at her. She'd fallen asleep, surely, she hadn't passed out. No, she'd just dropped off to sleep while he pulled the drapes and rechecked the locks. He shook his head so grateful he didn't take it further. Just as well he never did kiss and tell because he'd never live it down, this stunning woman fell asleep just as he was about to make love to her.

In the half dark he saw a huge bruise on her abdomen about the size of a saucer. Lying next to her frustrated, he processed what had just happened. Okay, he knew she had too much to drink so perhaps, no informed consent there. It had been the reason he didn't proceed, he told himself, and the admission she hadn't had sex in how many years? He hadn't realized she had been divorced so long. Little wonder she felt scared. Surely it couldn't be right her youngest son would turn fifteen in a couple of months. He just didn't understand. Watching her sleep, he had to admit she looked gorgeous, everything about her appealed to him. She had a great sense of humour; she seemed brave, fun, and bright, she could cook, too. As he looked at her lying there, he admitted he found her curves very sexy, the bulge at the top of her bra, the voluptuous body.

What the hell is wrong with Hunter Anderson? Lying on the bed next to her, he remembered facing off with him in court, he could see the man now. He came across as an arrogant prick. Barbe seemed lovely, he scanned her curvy figure again, very feminine. He hadn't ever had a woman like her. He couldn't imagine cheating on her. Is the guy a deviant into kinky stuff? Visions of the tall, wigged and gowned barrister in women's underwear made him wince. Surely there is a simple explanation, perhaps something had gone wrong after the birth of her youngest child and the impatient bastard went elsewhere? He wondered if he'd given her coffee instead of giving her another drink, things may have been different. It had not been too difficult to imagine she lay right next to him in her bra and knickers. Trying to fight these images and get some sleep he rolled over. She snuggled into him, it felt natural. Feeling comforted, his frustration shrank away, and sleep claimed him.

THE CELL PHONE BUZZED on the nightstand. Don grabbed it getting up to take the call in the kitchen, so he didn't wake Barbe. He grunted into the phone.

'Don, it's Tim Paxton.' Instantly awake, he acknowledged the Superintendent.

'Sir.'

'I've had a call from Hunter Anderson, he's had an interesting phone call,' a pregnant pause stretched out between them.

'The caller insisted he takes on a certain case.' Don interrupted him, thinking ahead.

'Not the murdering crack head, Matty Thomas?' Don stood raking his hair, working out the ramifications.

'Yeah, well he has connections to Carlos Matua,' the Super enlightened him. 'The bigger connection is Tonga, and the internal corruption over there. Both men recently travelled to Tonga, Matua from Australia, and Thomas from New Zealand. Spent a week there at the same time. Two weeks later on your tip off Don, our Navy intercepted an Indonesian-registered fishing vessel carrying over a hundred kilos of crystal meth, worth fucking millions on the street. Almost one hundred fucking million to be exact. Imagine what it would do to small town New Zealand?'

'Remove the need to cook it here?' it tritely tripped off his tongue, without thought.

'Don't be flippant Don this is a bloody nightmare, because the suppliers simply cook up another few batches. It's not like they have to wait a year for the next poppy harvest or batch of coca leaves,' he scoffed. 'It's easier to get the ingredients into the islands on smaller vessels. There are too many little islands to police for customs. The crew on the fishing vessel reckon a man fitting Matua's description visited the vessel before they left for New Zealand.'

As he listened Don put a coffee capsule in the machine. Paxton went on, 'the caller said Hunter Anderson must defend Matty Thomas, who's accused of murder on the high seas. The absence of a body makes it difficult for the prosecution. We've locked up the crew for importation, but we're keeping them separate from Thomas. They're doing a deal giving evidence against him in exchange for a lesser charge. They claim Thomas shot the captain and tossed him overboard.'

'What's Hunter Anderson going to do about it, if anything?' he asked, pouring himself a coffee.

'I've told him to visit Thomas in custody but to stall. We'll make sure the court dates clash with another of his cases, he said the dates might not work for him. If so, he'll offer to advise the court appointed defending counsel in a stalling tactic.'

Don sat, thinking aloud, 'the guy had been caught red handed with over a hundred kilos of meth, why are we even having this conversation? I mean he'll go down for quite a few years regardless of any murder charge.' The caller fell silent for a moment. 'Super do you think Matua has made the connection to Mrs. Barbe Anderson?'

'Yes, that is the reason I'm calling you Don, I believe so. When you visited the hotel the day of the shooting, did you learn anything?'

'Apart from the fact the hotel security cameras were not working, there appears to have been another police officer in the hotel lounge bar the afternoon of the shooting. The other guy must be working for Matua.' He sipped his coffee listening to his Super spitting tacks,

'who else knows about this Don?' his voice brusque.

'Only those who need to Sir and as soon as we know who he is you will too Sir. In the meantime, I have to keep Mrs. Anderson safe.'

'What sort of witness do you think she'll make?'

'Very credible and observant, brave too.' Don struggled to be rational.

'Mmm well, her husband is concerned, particularly for his kids. You take care out there and is there anything else I should be aware of?'

'He's her ex-husband Sir, Hunter and Barbe Anderson are divorced.'

'Yes, well neither has remarried and they spend a lot of time together, it works better for some people not living together full time. Then there's their children.'

Don made no comment, instead he gave him the registration number of the black Ford Ranger and a brief description of the event.

Don peeked around the bedroom door. Barbe appeared to be deep in sleep. After finishing his coffee, he showered and dressed then took a mug of tea into her and set it down. He watched her for a moment, guilt creeping in. She was a witness in a mass shooting, and he almost compromised the whole operation by sleeping with her. Well, he did sleep with her but fortunately he didn't have sex. He knew why. Never in his twenty plus years of policing had he ever done anything this incredibly stupid. But then never before had he felt like this about any woman, even his ex.

Gillian, his ex, worked as a real estate agent, moderately successful, attractive and a drama queen prone to an overactive imagination. Fortunately for Don, she kept a relatively low profile in his life and had been a good mother. Five years ago, she remarried and apart from constantly reminding him he had always been a 'shit father' she left him alone. Although they started out co-parenting their only child, it had not always been possible for Don to be present at the various school concerts and sports games or to have his daughter every second weekend. So, he paid child support and had his daughter when he could. Gillian failed to understand what the life of a senior undercover police officer could be like. Don had long since given up any hope of her ever understanding, to the point where Gillian just believed he had been some sort of senior detective who worked out of Wellington. The guy never seemed to be there and often missed important dates. It hurt him to have his daughter continually told he didn't care about her. Now she had turned thirteen and being a bright girl Don found himself able to explain he really had been working, not skiving off when he missed things like her school play or a sports match. But Gillian had ingrained the child with her own prejudices, so it felt like an unrelenting struggle.

Don watched as Barbe started to stir, he stroked her arm.

'Wake up Barbie doll,' he traced her face with his finger.

'Mmm, have I slept in?' About to sit up, she realized she looked half naked, so she pulled the sheet around herself. 'We didn't' she pointed her finger from him to her and back again. 'Did we?' she bit her lip embarrassed.

'What do you think?' he asked, passing her the mug of tea. 'Don't be embarrassed sweetheart.'

'I know I wanted to, but I didn't think we did, except I had a great night's sleep.' Her face flushed with embarrassment and taking the mug from him she drank it thirstily.

'I wanted you too. Have a great night's sleep I mean. But no, we didn't, not last night.' He shook his head and tenderly continued tracing his finger around her jaw line. 'I didn't want a case of limoncello drinkers' remorse.' Relieved, she nodded.

'We just cuddled,' he pushed up his lip he felt torn, wanting to say, perhaps tonight? But then knowing he couldn't allow himself. Also, he couldn't tell her about Hunter phoning the Super and the ramifications it had presented. The last thing he needed now was for her to get stressed out and worry about her family.

Chapter six:

Barbe sat on the settee blow drying her hair. The phone rang and Don picked it up, grunted and then acknowledged DSS Frank Taylor.

'Don, the old man has just informed me the car number you gave him for the black Ford Ranger is registered to a company called Autam Auto Supplies limited. But we believe it's a cover for Carlos Matua. Autam is Matua spelt backwards, Regardless the old man wants you out of there pronto. It's plan B, I'm sorry. Also, he forgot to tell you Hunter Anderson said his caller sounded Australian with a Latino accent. Does it make sense to you?'

Don half closed his eyes and groaned in frustration.

'He could be Carlos; I'll be in touch.' He looked across at Barbe. 'I'm sorry Bebe, but we have to leave... right now.' The look she gave him felt strange yet warm.

'What did you call me?' her voice hitched.

'Bebe, I called you Bebe, it's a term of endearment like babe.'

'I know what it is,' she blushed and nibbled her lip. 'I'll be packed in fifteen minutes.' She packed up the food they had purchased and her bags while he switched off the power and set the solar system direct to storage mode. How could he not have feelings for this woman? But once again it became strictly business.

Disguised as 'Grey Nomads' they set off.

'I've never known a woman who can pack so fast and still manage to get the kitchen sink in there,' he joked.

'I live out of suitcases quite a lot with my job.' They bounced along the rutted dry road. The heat became oppressive, the humidity had built up.

'I think it's trying to rain; I won't be sorry to be back on the tarmac,' he explained 'so I can get us away from here a bit faster.'

Never once did she complain, instead she sat drinking him in wondering how after all these years with no man in her life, suddenly this prima donna in the form of a stocky middle-aged Kiwi of Italian descent, called Adone, had touched her. Touched her, yes literally and metaphorically. Trying to analyze how it happened, she could see a warm hard-working, fun-loving guy who loved to eat. He enjoyed fine things, and still spoke affectionately of his late Nonna. Thinking about it, he spoke affectionately about everyone even his ex-wife. What is it about him she had felt drawn to? They enjoyed some sort of chemistry between them, yet he seemed so different compared with Hunter.

Tall, lean, Hunter had always been an ambitious driven man whose name suited him. Barbe remembered the first time they met. It had been the Christmas holidays of the year she finished her arts degree. As the only child of older parents, she intended spending Christmas with them in the Marlborough Sounds. Her father, a retired senior civil servant, had been invited to a party at the elegant holiday home of a golfing friend. Naturally, his delightful daughter would accompany him too. Edmund Anderson, the senior partner in his law firm and his nephew Hunter, a junior partner, were at the party. Barbe noticed any number of young women, also guests and to Barbe they all looked so sophisticated and elegant and seemed to hang on Hunter's every word. She noted he appeared to be not in the slightest bit interested in them. Instead, joining in with the crusty old men, talking law and politics. Barbe drifted off through other parts of the beautiful house studying the artwork. The lady of the house, a stylish looking older woman asked her what she thought of a particular painting. Barbe knowledgably told her it was a self-portrait of the late Rita Angus. From there she went on to describe the idiosyncrasies of the particular artist unaware Hunter

Anderson stood back surveying her from a distance. Then he stepped forward.

'Aunty it's very naughty of you, particularly as Rita Angus was a family friend of my great grandparents. I'm Hunter Anderson,' he offered his hand

'Barbe Brunner,' she blushed.

'You certainly know your stuff.' Hunter seemed impressed.

'Barbe has just completed her BA, majoring in art history,' his Aunt advised him, suggesting he show her around their art collection and then she left them.

'Let me show you my favourite piece,' guiding her down the hall he opened the door to a study and putting on the lights he pointed out a portrait of a man dressed as an Arab. 'It's by James McBey. Tell me what you know about it.' Barbe remembered this tall handsome man called Hunter standing too close, invading her personal space. She felt intimidated.

Stepping back from him, she told him, 'This is a fine example of his work, painted in 1918 the subject is TE Lawrence, you know Lawrence of Arabia.' Hunter looked clearly delighted, and then went on to give her the minutiae of the Arab Revolt from the British perspective.

'The revolt had been a relatively minor part of the war in the Middle East, involving just a small number of British military liaison officers, supporting a loose army of disparate tribes. But I just love the romance of the white robed, camel-mounted warriors, led by the enigmatic 'Lawrence of Arabia,' Barbe remembered looking up at him staring into his grey eyes.

'I can imagine you dressed up like a tall Lawrence of Arabia.'

He seemed absolutely smitten. Everybody noticed it and both sets of parents encouraged it. Hunter invited her to join his tennis party the next day. The following day they enjoyed a picnic. By the holidays end, they were in love. Looking back Barbe had often wondered whether the whole 'holiday' had not been engineered to get them together. She liked the fact he knew what he wanted in life, and he did not continually paw her like the boys her age had done. He talked of a future with her, took her to exciting places and showered her with gifts and of course he was Catholic. The same religion made everything so easy. Not simply their shared values but the culture of Catholicism was way of life they both enjoyed. Belonging to their Catholic community, which started with their education, gave them the lifelong bonds of friendship and belonging. Barbe loved Hunter's large extended family because she had been the only child of older parents. Within six weeks they were engaged and within six months they were married.

After securing her first real job in a private gallery on Featherston street, she felt reluctant to give it up when she married, as Hunter had wanted. But she did agree she would give up the position before the birth of their first child.

DON AND BARBE WERE driving on the tar sealed road again now and Don had been watching her surreptitiously as he drove towards Bulls, a small town on the way to the city of Palmerston North. They had hardly spoken for the last two hours.

'Penny for them?' he asked, watching her deep in thought and chewing her lip.

'I've been thinking about Hunter, he will be so cross with me,' she sighed. 'He did not want me to take this job in the first place.'

'What business is it of his? I mean he's no longer your husband.'

'Well, he forced me to look for a job, when he cut my allowance. He's still miffed, and I got the job three years ago,' she volunteered.

'How long have you been divorced; I mean decree Final?' He could see her thinking.

'Ryder turned seven, it came through on his birthday,' her face forlorn. 'Naturally, I didn't tell the kids. Hunter had an apartment in the city. He's got a bigger one now. But he made me sign this agreement to expedite things. I still live in the family home, it's in a trust. Hunter said it would be better for the boys. He told me I would never have the ability to earn enough money to provide for them the way he wanted even if he paid half of everything.' She shrugged in acceptance.

'A bit high handed, isn't he? You would be paid pretty well now though; I would have thought.'

'Yes, but nothing like him and without his financial support the boys could not have the life they do.'

Listening to her he wondered what she had been expected to sacrifice, to achieve this.

'Well, it's what fathers do, support their kids. What does he expect you to do in return for living where he tells you; I mean you could have moved out and let him stay there surely?' He surveyed the storm clouds gathering and wondered if they'd make it to Palmerston North before the weather broke.

'No, I couldn't move out, part of the settlement contract stated I must stay in the family home. I have even been known to host a party there for him. Not in the last couple of years though. When the kids were young, he didn't want me moving out or working. He joins us for Christmas and holidays. We all take three weeks together in January,' she admitted.

'Believe me it's been hard. When the kids were young Nicholas was a clingy toddler, and Ryder got every childhood bug imaginable, so the arrangement worked well for them.' Hearing her talk about her strange marriage, well divorce... He could not have imagined his ex-wife being so agreeable and not ending up back in bed together.

'You didn't really want this divorce, did you?' he questioned. It had started to rain by now and the rain became heavier the closer they got to Bulls.

'Yes, I definitely wanted a divorce. But I never wanted to be in this situation. No woman who loved a man would ever want it either.' He thought she talked in riddles, not wanting to come right out and say, the guy cheated on me.

'So, he wasn't honest with you then.' He blew air out of his mouth in a 'whew' sound. 'Why didn't you just kick him into touch years ago instead of prolonging the agony? I can't believe it's because of your boys. Kids are a lot more resilient than you give them credit for you told me.' Thinking about it ticked him off, the arrogant prick didn't want to let her go so he tied her up legally. She did say lawyers could screw you over more ways than anyone else.

'You're right, kids are very resilient. I did it for Hunter mainly and the boys of course. But when I tried to get out of the arrangement or change things, I found I'm screwed until Ryder is sixteen.' She pulled up her hair under the hot wig to keep it off her neck, the humidity felt oppressive, and the air conditioning did not work.

'Did this agreement dictate the terms of any future relationships you might have? I can't see how it could be legal?' he pointed out.

'You're probably right, but until three years ago I never had the opportunity. Since then, it's been a huge learning curve and I haven't really had any reason, until...' she didn't explain.

He understood.

'Same here, work and time poor. Nothing meaningful so haven't bothered.' He looked at the dashboard. 'Cripes, look the temperature gauge is up.' He pulled over off the road, 'we'll have to sit here till it cools down, bugger it, I didn't want to draw attention to ourselves.' He seemed annoyed.

'We still have some sandwiches left, fancy one?' she asked.

'Good idea' he told her and leaned over into the carton of food in the back and picked up the container. While they ate, he regaled her with stories of his Nonna, 'she always cooked heaps of food. If there were no leftovers, she didn't think she'd prepared enough. If we left anything on our plates she would accuse us, *you no lika my food?*' Don was such a character putting on a woman's voice with an Italian accent. She enjoyed his company.

Half an hour later he carefully put two litres of water into the radiator and returned to the driver's seat, drenched. 'Thank God for this bloody awful terry toweling hat.' He wiped rain from his face.

'I'll get this vehicle seen to in Bulls.'

THE MECHANIC AT THE garage in Bulls could not get the vehicle fixed and on the road until the following morning, when he could get apart from the local wrecker's yard. They borrowed the courtesy car and booked into a motel. The only motel with a vacancy, as a huge Golf tournament in the district had caused all others to be fully booked. After unloading the vehicle Don complained he felt hungry.

'We can't be seen out together. I'll get us a takeaway. I bet they don't deliver in this tin pot town,' he moaned.

'Inevit-a-bull' she quipped.

'Un question-a-bully' he rejoined, smirking, every shop in the town of Bulls had some 'bull' in it. The Baker had been Delect-a-bull, the china shop was Break-a-bull, the grocer Ed-a-bull and so on. The town had become famous for it.

Don returned after about half an hour with fish and chips, a bottle of wine and a pack of cards. The cards he found in the glove box of the courtesy car, an old blue Toyota Corolla and quite 'un-remark-a-bull' he joked. They shared their meal and the wine, neither mentioning the elephant in the room.

They only had one bed, a table and two café style chairs. After a few games of cards which he always won, she accused him of cheating. He took it in good part. She had cabin fever, locked up with a stranger with whom she nearly had sex whilst intoxicated. He understood and wished things were different, but it is what it is 'unaccept-a-bull,' he told himself.

'Let's watch a movie, you can choose,' she said bored with cards. He chose some die-hard detective movie during which Barbe once again fell asleep.

Her parting salvo to him being, 'you're too old to be sleeping on the floor,' then she turned over and went to sleep. Sitting on the bed in his shorts he sat staring into the TV with the sound turned down, thinking about this woman next to him. Wishing things were different he wondered how long they would need to hide from Carlos. He lived with the reality he had become the target of the drug bosses. Police corruption in New Zealand had not been something he could fully grasp. Sure, it happened in Tonga, the cause obvious poverty, he believed. Australia, they had seen cases of corruption and at the highest levels in various states. That had been pure greed. Still, they had cleaned it up and worked hard to prevent further cases. But New Zealand had learned from other countries, also the ethos of law enforcement officers here in New Zealand was innately good, morally strong. There had been the odd bad apple over the years, soon weeded out and dealt with but nothing that caused Don to worry his work had been sabotaged, until now.

The rain had brought the temperature crashing down and Don switched the TV off, covered Barbe with a blanket and got in the other side of the bed in his clothes, like her.

Chapter Seven:

The smell of coffee woke him. He'd been dreaming about it. Putting the fresh coffee down on the nightstand she smiled at him, 'morning Adonis' she teased.

He groaned, 'what day is it?' she told him Tuesday. 'No, I mean what's the date? I miss my own phone and electronic diary. Michelle had the school cross country, I think it's today,' he said frustrated. 'I couldn't phone her. Not till I get the clearance from HQ,' he sighed. 'Now I'm definitely a shit father. I'll have to make it up to her.' He looked over at Barbe, in her robe sitting at the table reading the morning paper, sipping her tea, hair still wet. 'I seem to spend my whole life playing catch up.'

'Don't beat yourself up. Have you ever thought of getting someone to cover your back? Like a friend or colleague, who could send cards or messages on your behalf when you can't?' she suggested.

He scoffed. 'What delegate my parenting to rent a dad?' he didn't sound very impressed.

'Men with secretaries often delegate their husbanding to them, you know birthday gifts, the I'm sorry flowers, and so on so why not?' she added, and he scoffed again.

'Yeah, no wonder they have marital issues. If I'm going to be a crap parent, I can do it without help.' He sounded upset and she felt for him knowing how Hunter would lay a huge guilt trip on her about this shooting and causing her family grief. Hunter always made her feel guilty when he had another agenda, like wanting her to accompany him to the Law Society's annual ball or change his particular weekends for having the boys. He enjoyed playing the aggrieved spouse and she didn't want to be part of it anymore.

'I'm sorry, I understand much better than you think. Get a shower and I'll cook some breakfast.' Whenever food came up, he didn't mind who became the boss.

Barbe dressed and had been about to dish up breakfast when he returned showered and dressed.

'There's a lot of hurry up and wait in these covert jobs, isn't there? Do you ever get bored?' she asked. He flashed her his smile, gone were the pre-food grumps. He looked happy again.

'Yes, but not this mission. Thanks for your concern.' Watching him tuck into a hearty breakfast cheered her. Time had begun to drag for her, he sensed it. 'As soon as we get Carlos, you'll be able to go home.' He knew it wouldn't be so simple but wanted to give her hope.

By the time they got the old Toyota truck back on the road half the day had passed. They were headed to a comfortable safe house in the Wairarapa, he told her. They were to wait there until cleared to return to Wellington.

BARBE HAD SPENT TIME in the Wairarapa as a child and knew the remote rural property where they were holed up would only be about two hours from home. It unsettled her; she missed her boys, one week had stretched into two. Sometimes Don went off, replaced by other officers for a day or just a few hours at a time, but it didn't feel the same. Although she had a comfortable room and there were books to read and a television, she missed her life. Being isolated away from people had taken a toll on her. Don had been fun, and a friendship had developed between them. But it never got back to where they had been the night, she almost had sex with him.

Gradually she felt bereft, as though she had delayed shock from her trauma. Her health began to suffer, she started to lose weight, had difficulty sleeping and she didn't cope well. Don had been replaced for several days by a female officer, who had relieved him once before several days earlier. Detective Helen Couch had been shocked to see how pale and fragile Barbe had become since her last visit. Helen insisted on some fresh air and exercise, which only served to make Barbe tired as well as stressed. She stayed in her room for hours. Unbeknown to her, Helen had reported her concerns to Detective Inspector Lancini.

When Don returned to the property, Barbe had been out enjoying a walk. He had arranged for DSS Frank Taylor to have Barbe's sons write a letter to their mother which the detective sergeant collected from their father, and the letters were passed to Don. Recognizing the strain of the past few weeks Don felt anxious for her to get the letters and seemed surprised to learn Helen Couch had allowed Barbe to wander around the isolated property alone. He sent her on her way back to HQ with a flea in her ear, telling her it was simply unacceptable she left their witness alone and unprotected.

It took him a good hour before he found her sitting almost covered in the long grass of early Autumn. He called to her; she ignored him. As he approached her, he could see she didn't look happy.

'What's wrong Bebe?' his voice echoed his concern. She turned; her eyes welled up with tears, something he'd not seen before; she had never been teary.

'I'm sorry I don't want to do this anymore; I want to go home.' Shocked, he wanted to know why.

'I miss my boys and I'm scared,' she sobbed. He tried to comfort her.

'You're safe with me, nothing will happen to you.' Putting one arm around her he patted her arm. She pulled away. 'I'm not scared of any blue-eyed assassins, mine is a selfish fear.' She chewed her lip. It's nothing to do with the shooting. 'I'm afraid of losing their love, I don't think I can continue as things are. They need their mother,' she said thinking about her boys.

He frowned and raked his hand through his thick mop of hair.

'I'm just a bloody copper Bebe, don't talk to me in riddles. I can't deal with that shit. Just tell me what the problem is?'

She sobbed harder. 'I'm sorry I've never told anybody, so don't expect me to tell you now. The truth is, it's not new.' She breathed deeply. 'I've had too much time on my own to think about things, I want to go home.' Shaking his head, he told her, not right now but soon.

'There has been a breakthrough in the case, and it may well be over within days.' He pulled a manila envelope from the inside breast pocket of his smart linen jacket. 'Here're some letters from your boys.' Thrilled, she grabbed the envelope, eagerly tearing it open. There were three letters inside. Sitting beside her in the long grass he watched as she opened the first letter. The tears ran down her face as she read it.

Dear Mum,

I hope you are all right. Dad told us the story and we understand. Dad has picked us up every weekend and taken us home to Kelburn. We've had good fun. Although Fortnite screen time has been restricted to one hour per weekend, hardly enough time for anyone. But I have been painting my new models. I hope they are looking after you. I miss you.

Love Ryder. Xoxox

'Here read,' she thrust the handwritten letter at him. Then she opened the next.

Dear Mum,

So, they have you in protective custody helping them with their enquiries. Smarmy words for under house arrest. Bet you like that like a hole in your head. Oops poor choice of words. We do miss you; Ryder blubs sometimes. The first XV are ahead in the tables and the season has just begun. I've scored a few tries. Dad took us shopping only because we ran out of gear, so he left the washing for Mrs. Nelson. The Rector told him to send it all back to school with us. A first for Dad. Speaking of firsts looks like I'm headed for another first this year if this term report is anything to go by. Definitely miss your cooking. Come home soon.

Love Nicholas.

'See how different they are. Read this,' she thrust a second letter at him.

Then she tentatively opened the third letter.

My Darling Barbe,

Don't fret too much. I know things are beyond your control. I understand how traumatic these situations can be. If all is resolved by the school holidays, I think we should all take a trip somewhere warm and sunny where we can relax together, a tropical island maybe. You decide where you'd like to go. Also, I've been thinking. If you are tired of being in the public eye and everything it entails, maybe we can come to some arrangement whereby you give up this role. If you must work, then maybe you do something for a local gallery or charity. Think about it and we can talk on your return. Whatever happens do not do anything rash. Life is too short, and we love you.

Take care my love.

Hunter.

'Here you might as well read this so you can be properly confused.' She stood up 'I need a drink. Do we have any alcohol or am I reduced to getting shitfaced on your over proof limoncello. At least that had been fun.' Don folded Hunter's letter into his breast pocket, he'd read it later. Now she sounded positive and ticked off at the same time. Very interesting.

'I bought a bottle of bubbly. I intended saving it till we had something to celebrate, but now seems like a good time.' He looped his arm around her as they headed back to the farmhouse. 'Ryder sounds sweet, Nicholas on the other hand let's just say typical teenage boy.'

While Don found some crackers and cheese Barbe had a quick shower and changed from pedal pushers to cotton dress. He handed her a glass of bubbly. 'You're right I'm totally confused having read Hunter's letter; it reads like the guy still loves you.'

'You're right he does love me, he never stopped loving me.' Her voice hitched. He wondered what the real problem might be. she didn't call him a cheating scumbag, but they were still divorced and neither appeared to have honestly moved on.

'I thought you were a compassionate woman; can't you find it in your heart to forgive him?' Don began to think she might be spoilt and privileged and perhaps Hunter was busting his arse for her.

'I do love him, I've forgiven him,' she shrugged. 'Well not for everything.' He felt disgust, she recognized the look. 'You don't understand,' she struggled, not wanting to betray Hunter. 'I don't give a dam he cheated only why he can't be honest with me,' she spat out with venom. 'I'll get dinner.' Looking at him she could see he looked confused. 'Men, you're such a boys club.' She sniffed, taking her glass to the kitchen.

His police mobile rang and taking it, he walked off to talk.

'Frank, you got something for me?'

'Don, the body I told you about looks like Carlos. The spiderweb tattoo, it's there on the back of his neck. The hands were cut off so no fingerprints. We can't find his dentist so no dental records, and still working on the details we need to check his DNA. But he has blue eyes, and all the other boxes are ticked, height, weight etc. We need the DNA to confirm otherwise we may be setting Mrs. Anderson up to be a target. You got the letters? Hunter Anderson has been great, doing everything we've asked. I've got nothing else at present, except...' he laughed, 'bit of gossip trivia for what it's worth, did you know Carlos was gay? His partner identified him; flew in from Australia to make the ID and he bought the guy's comb for the DNA so we should have it soon.' Listening, Don felt pleased, and confident they'd soon wrap the case up then Barbe would be free to go and no need for her to give evidence in Court, just a statement.

Don put his mobile on charge on a small table. Then hearing a bit of banging and crashing in the kitchen he asked what he could do to expedite dinner. He felt hungry but didn't tell her. He sensed all was not well. She dismissed him saying she had it under control and looked up at him. Pausing for a few seconds she warmly thanked him, immediately going back to nibbling her lip. Something inside him skipped a beat. He wondered why she had never remarried and why she seemed so unhappy.

While sitting in a planter's chair on the veranda he mulled things over in his mind and sipped his wine. He liked Barbe. He'd like to ask her out but at present he felt it neither appropriate nor wise. Seeing more of her would be the only way he'd understand her. In his gut he liked her. She seemed like a good person and cops learned to trust their instincts. Don found it had saved his life more than once.

The pair sat down to a tasty meal of pork chops with apricot glaze, savoury potato bake and a medley of steamed fresh greens. For dessert Barbe had made a fresh plum cake with lashings of whipped cream. Don tucked in enjoying the food, then he became aware she was watching him eat.

'My boys like plum cake too.' She laughed, 'they like food actually. Is there something bothering you?' Suddenly she became aware he had hardly spoken during the meal.

'No nothing is bothering me at all. you go watch TV. I'll clear away then I'll tell you what's on my mind.' Doing as he suggested, she didn't bother with the TV, she found her book more interesting.

After a few minutes he gave her a mug of tea and himself coffee. His face expression appeared enigmatic she wondered what he wanted to say.

'I feel confident we'll get the call tomorrow permitting us to go home. My colleague, Frank Taylor, told me Carlos Matua's partner, well his husband actually, identified him. I got to thinking, then I realized why the guy left the rest of his family in Argentina to start up a branch of the gang in Australia. Why do you think he did it?'

Chapter eight:

Without hesitating she told him.

'Well, he couldn't marry his male partner in Catholic Argentina, could he? Even if it were legal, his family would not have approved.'

'Is it is the same between Hunter and you? His high-profile Catholic family would not understand. So, he lives a lie and expects you to do the same?' He watched her face flush, her eyes welling up. He put his arms around her and pulled her gently to him. Holding her firm he whispered into her hair, 'your secret's safe with me. How did you learn of his... predilection?' He heard the sharp intake of breath and watched her face.

'I knew very early on in our marriage something did not seem right. Exactly what, I had no idea. Until one day I came home a day early with the kids from visiting with mum. He and this young man were at it naked and in our bedroom. He pushed me out of the room and locked the door.' Don sat next to her gently rubbing her arm in support.

'It felt awful, I know what I saw, Hunter refused to discuss it, let alone admit it. He denied what I saw and became nasty. he stormed out of the house and didn't come home until the next day. Looking back there were warning signs I ignored. But then he is the only man I've ever been with, so you don't know what you don't know. Do you understand?' she asked, her eyes like sad green saucers.

'Do you think anyone else suspected?' he frowned.

'Looking back, I think quite possibly. I remember comments made to me when we divorced. Nothing definite just inuendo suggesting I should have seen what he was.' Her voice soft sounded fragile. 'I felt too scared to ask what they thought that might be in case they told me, and I couldn't handle it.' Don listened, asking how she dealt with it. 'Frankly, I didn't handle it well, I claimed not to know what they were talking about, and I defended him saying my marriage was not their business. I mean what he does is not illegal. I have argued the facts in my mind hundreds of times. I think his family had suspicions, but his father had been on the bench. His uncles one was a well-known barrister, the other a Catholic priest. I needed to protect my sons from gossip; The thing is, you couldn't get a better father than Hunter. I often wonder how he'd react if one of our boys were gay. I would want my son to find someone who loves him as he is, and pray they be allowed to be happy together.' Don agreed, holding her close. 'When we got engaged, I remember his family members being so relieved Hunter would finally marry they joked about it. I reckon they were stupid enough to believe with prayer he would be *cured*. I have never told another living soul about this.'

'Not even your priest?

She started to shake; Don wrapped a throw around her.

'I tried to talk about it with the priest, he told me I must be mistaken. It seemed a strange thing, he covered his face with his hands and said, 'Oh dear Lord, poor Hunter.' Then he stated 'you have two children; homosexual men are impotent with a woman. You're mistaken.' I told him there is a difference between emotional impotency and the physical kind. The priest seemed out of his depth, I felt totally alone, inadequate and unworthy. You know there are no women priests to talk to. Since my marriage I hadn't allowed any girlfriends into my emotional secrets. The stories they told me were so different from my own experiences. I felt shame as though it's my fault I'm not attractive or desirable enough.' Swallowing hard she controlled her tears. Don took her face in his hands stroking her cheek with his thumb.

'You are an extremely desirable woman. I understand how you've protected your family. It was wrong of Hunter to marry you when his needs render him incapable of being a real husband.'

'The thing is Don, he's inherently a good man. But I expected more than occasional perfunctory sex from the man I married. Is that too much to ask?'

Lost for words, he raked his fingers through his hair.

'Bebe I'm sorry, it's not your fault, if a man takes a woman as his wife, he should desire her as a woman, it's the natural order of things.' She felt his warm breath on her cheek. Her skin smelled gorgeous; he'd been fighting it for weeks. Gently he grazed her face with his lips and then he nuzzled her neck. Both knew once his lips covered hers there would be no going back.

Chapter Nine:

The early sunlight woke him, he lay quietly watching as she slept soundly, occasionally emitting little kitten sounds in her sleep. He couldn't feel sorry he'd crossed the line, he enjoyed it. Eventually he got up and showered. He took his phone into the bathroom with him as he expected a call anytime. The case would now be wrapped up easily and he'd be back working in the Central Investigation Section now his cover had been exposed and his details were in the public arena. Once dressed he made himself coffee. His phone vibrated; he answered it walking out onto the back porch to speak. He grunted his usual non-committal greeting.

'Don, its Tim Paxton. You can bring Mrs. Anderson in so we can get her to sign another statement, just a few new questions. Then she's free to go home.' The Chief Superintendent cleared his throat. 'I need you to fly to Tonga and liaise with their investigation team for a few weeks as an advisor. You should only need about eight to ten weeks max; the Government has approved a small New Zealand contingency of police to help clean up their methamphetamine and corruption issues. Your job will be to set things up and run the advance party. The whole undertaking will be at least a two-year operation. Their police numbers are small so it shouldn't take you long to get things started. The meth situation in Tonga is dire. I need you to fly out tonight. The sooner they get on top of this investigation the better for all of us.'

Sipping his coffee on the porch Don could see the cycle starting again. It would be the same old thing in a different setting, and it would be relentless. He didn't know if he wanted this life anymore. Regardless, it could take him months to get a transfer. He heard

Barbe in the bathroom and before long she sat across from him in jeans and a tee shirt, her abundant dark wavy hair hanging below her shoulders. Each sensed the other's unease.

'What's happened?' She wanted to know, watching him butter some toast. 'Something's wrong?'

'I've had word from my commander. I have to take you to the CIB in Wellington to answer a couple of new questions, then you're free to go.' Blinking at him she didn't understand.

'What do you mean exactly? Is the DNA is a match for Carlos? Will you come with me and check if my house is safe? You're off on another case? Is that it, we're done?'

Listening to her verbalize her thoughts he could hear they were close to the mark apart for one thing. Reaching across the table he covered her hand.

'We're not done, I want us to keep seeing one another. Is this what you want?' she nodded.

'The DNA is a match; someone will come and check your house. Regrettably, I have to fly out to Tonga tonight. Here's my mobile number.' He pushed his card across the table as he stood up, then taking her hand he explained, 'come here let me kiss you. Bebe this is the nature of the beast with me, and it makes relationships difficult at times.' As he kissed her, she could taste a mixture of coffee and marmalade. She felt loved, yet apprehensive.

'I'd like to apply for a transfer out of the section. I'll even drive a desk, I'll do whatever it takes, but we will make this work.' He flashed her his trademark smile and she melted.

On the way to Wellington, he explained how long he expected to be in Tonga. He suggested they plan a weekend away, somewhere they wouldn't be recognized. She sat there miles away in thought not looking forward to seeing Hunter, feeling like she had betrayed him.

'You're not having regrets about last night, are you?' He wanted her but felt annoyed with himself he hadn't managed to get her out of his care before he made love to her.

Pulling a silly face her breath hitched and she surprised him, 'how could I possibly regret something so...wonderful. I won't deny how I feel,' she whispered. he reached out and took her hand and squeezed it as he drove.

'So, what are you worried about?' As soon as he asked, he saw it again, a certain fragility. Before she could answer he said, 'whatever it is we'll face it together. Go home, deal with life there. Reassure your boys you're fine, get your job sorted and start testing the water with Hunter.' He watched her frown. 'Tell him you've met someone. If you'd rather not tell him just yet, we can wait.' Immediately she agreed, although the thought of telling Hunter troubled her.

'Okay, in three months' time we'll do it together. Remember he no longer has the title husband, regardless of how he couches it with the Church. I doubt whether his personalized divorce agreement can be legally enforced either. I'd like to read it sometime just to know what we're up against.'

Barbe had no doubts about it. Adone Lancini inspired confidence, he connected empathetically so Barbe felt safe. His brand of humour buoyed her, and his stories were great. Unlike Hunter Anderson, the autocratic authoritarian who told people what to do and how to do it. His manner intimidated some, this style he had developed over years in Court fighting for the marginalized minority who were often criminal. In her mind Don couldn't intimidate anyone, it had never been his way, but break the law or push him and you'd know who was in charge.

They arrived at Police HQ and Don found a car park nearby. Together they walked to the building. The front office staff greeted him as they proceeded to the lift, using the barcode at the back of his ID to operate the lift doors. On the third floor he asked for DSS Taylor, who led the pair to an interview room.

'Don't be nervous,' Don whispered. 'Do you fancy a coffee, or a comfort stop?' his voice conspiratorial.

'Coffee please, nothing else,' she told him. In came Detective Senior Sergeant Frank Taylor. Barbe watched as he warmly acknowledged Don. She stood up and offered her hand confidently. I'm a witness for the prosecution not a criminal nor a suspect, she told herself.

'Mrs. Anderson, I'm DSS Taylor. I'm the officer who apprised your husband of the situation.' With an amused smile she corrected him.

'My ex-husband. Yes, thank you,' as another officer arrived with their coffee. Don said nothing just watched, amazed at her confident articulate manner, knowing Frank Taylor would be stunned if he knew just how sexy Mrs. Posh ten hours had been earlier. Don would never kiss and tell; he wanted this woman and would never do anything to jeopardize their relationship.

An hour later Frank Taylor had two statements. The shooting and what she had observed, Then another about seeing Mr. Barker Nova's wearing a police high vis vest at the hospital and talking to the young constable. When they had finished, Frank Taylor offered to get her a ride home.

'I'll drive her, Frank.' Don jumped up from his chair, 'I have some business I need to attend to before I meet with the Commander.'

Frank agreed knowing Don would be off to Tonga that night.

Arriving at 43 Latta Crescent Barbe got out of the vehicle and punched a code into the gate lock, it opened. Don drove in and she activated the closing lock and then walked towards the front door. Turning, she watched Don surveilling the property. Impressed, he expected nothing less. The imposing nineteen thirties double storied house had white painted weatherboard with a tiled roof and triple garage attached.

'Welcome to my home. Well, Hunter's really. I've spent years thinking of it as temporary.' She opened the door and disarmed the alarm. Don had noted the surveillance cameras on the property perimeter.

'May I check out the security system and your general security,' he asked professionally. She pointed to a small walk-in cupboard under the stairs where all the up-to-date technology had been housed. TV monitors, the extra fast broadband, lights system and security cameras. Don felt relieved she seemed secure, but also alarmed at her lack of privacy.

'Who deals with this stuff?' he asked as she shrugged.

'Hunter has a company monitor it remotely, unless there's an issue then they send a tech. I don't have anything to do with it.'

As Don walked around this elegant home of substantial proportions he asked,

'Who did the decorating?' Barbe pointed to herself, a little curious.

'You don't like it?' she asked about to agree it would not be to everyone's taste.

'It's very tasteful, very nice.' Everywhere he could see little touches of a sophisticated homemaker. Interesting art groupings, handmade petti point or embroidered cushions, eastern floor rugs, expensive drapes together with elegant traditional furniture and antiques. The house did not look minimalist but nor did it appear cluttered. Chic and eclectic he thought.

'Show me around outside,' he said opening the French doors off the family living room on to an outdoor entertaining area and a good-sized pool.

'Where's the pool house?' he wondered. Instinctively she led him to the small, shed housing the filter and cleaning products. He closed the door behind them and pulled her to him.

'Bebe I'm going to say goodbye here, no cameras or microphones. If we talk on the phone, will you take it outside, please?' His voice soft, his lips covered hers as he held her firmly their tongues meeting and greeting. he whispered, 'you are the most desirable woman I've ever met. I want you in my life and I want you to be happy.' Then he raked his thick hair for a second while he thought. Immediately she laughed.

'Adonis, you funny man you make me very happy. Text me when you can. Otherwise, I'll worry.' Together they walked back to the house, neither wanting to leave the other.

After Don left, she phoned Hunter at his office.

'Barbe you're home at last. When can I see you, we need to talk?' He sounded slightly agitated. She could hear activity going on in his office.

'Come for dinner, what time suits you?' They agreed seven, as he told her he had started preparing for a case. When Hunter worked late, he often missed meals. His secretary Stephanie Maxwell had worked with him for over twenty years and became accustomed to his driven, sometimes manic, work methods and she acted as the perfect foil. Stephanie, a paralegal a good ten years older than Hunter, had learned how to keep him from going overboard.

Chapter Ten:

Hunter arrived about seven fifteen in his black Mercedes four-wheel drive. Although he no longer lived at 43 Latta Crescent he came and went as though he owned the place which technically, he did. Having parked his vehicle in the garage, he used the internal door. As he walked down the hall to the family living area, he could see Barbe working at the bench. Seeing him approach she held out her arms. It wasn't a hug or barely a kiss, just an awkward acknowledgement. He couldn't even give her a hug.

'Barbe' he offered. 'I'm so pleased you're safe.' He sounded sincere in his sentiments at least. 'Food smells good, what are you cooking?' He watched as she set down two wine glasses, 'just a half, top it up with soda water' he insisted.

'Dinner is chicken breasts stuffed with apricot, red onions and cream cheese, pistachio nuts and rolled in bacon.' He gave her a tender look and sadness filled her. 'I phoned the college and spoke to the boys; I'll pick them up tomorrow afternoon. Do you want to join us for the weekend?' she asked. He told her he couldn't, he needed to finalize his opening address for the Tara Reed murder. Barbe remembered the case when it first happened. A young prostitute found dead near the Basin Reserve. Last seen on a street corner in Vivian Street talking to a man in a silver sedan. A man whose DNA had later been found in her underwear. A man not unfamiliar with the inside of a prison. Yet her ex-husband had been working frenetically to ensure he received the very best representation. It took a great deal of money, but Hunter would be worth every penny of it.

Sitting together in their family home Hunter considered Barbe, impeccably dressed in a fitted green silk sheath dress, the creamy curve of her bosom showing teasingly at the neckline. Beautifully made up, her face enhanced by her thick dark hair softly falling below her shoulders. Didn't all women dress this way to have an intimate dinner with their husbands, sorry ex-husbands, he continually reminded himself. He'd been celibate for more than nine months now, a long time for a man with a strong sex drive, even Barbe tempted him. Did she do it intentionally or just to show him what he gave up?

'Thank you for cooking for me tonight, I appreciate it. In two weeks, the school holidays begin, and I thought, well my case will be finished, maybe we could take the boys and go somewhere in the Whitsunday's, the weather will be perfect.' He watched her sitting sipping her wine and occasionally nibling her lip. He knew the look well; she had something on her mind.

'A lot of water has passed under the bridge since our divorce, I don't want to discuss it tonight. but maybe in a few weeks we could have a serious discussion about where we're both going,' he said. Once again, he watched her face. Suddenly it lit up. She immediately thought, he's met someone and he's being sweet. Perhaps he's coming out. He'll be amicable about me moving on, maybe even moving on with Don. God knows I want to but who knows?

Barbe stood up and fetched the dish from the oven. She put it straight down on the rustic family room tabletop. It smelled good. Then she brought out a salad from the scullery and set it down and Hunter sat down at the head of the table as was his habit.

'I'd like a family holiday; the boys would love to go sailing around the islands and swimming and fishing. You're right, it's time we revisited conversations of the past. Life's too short, don't you agree?' Hunter smiled the soft warm smile of self-confidence. He believed maybe the shock of the shooting had her thinking she could live with him again. He wanted to try, having not been with a man for almost a year. He would be prepared to try being with this woman again and Barbe was a beautiful woman. He didn't feel in the mood for the discussion tonight, but he'd put his mind to it and maybe on holiday he could soften her up and if it didn't work out for him, they could go back to the way they were. The feeling of being trapped by his Catholic roots inhibited him when it came to coming out. He'd spent years keeping up appearances and he could never admit his homosexuality. Life would have been so much easier for him had he been straight. The first few years of his marriage he felt sure he could cope with it, but when Barbe didn't immediately conceive Ryder it all became too much. Now they were both older, surely her expectations could be managed. He served himself some of the chicken set in a dish of roasted potatoes and then added some delicious green salad. Barbe had always been a great cook, and she even did baking for him which he simply loved. Stephanie ensured the other partners didn't snaffle it all. None of them could understand the strange relationship of Barbe and Hunter, or so he thought. But then perhaps they noticed things and never commented. Who knows? They would never offend him, too afraid of alienating him, the highest earning partner in their practice. Hunter brought in so much business, he kept them all busy.

After dinner and a coffee, he took his leave of her not before surprising himself by giving her a hug, and saying very honestly 'thank you Barbe, thank you for my greatest gift.' She frowned and he added 'our sons, I feel truly blessed. They're a credit to you.'

'And you, they're a credit to you too,' she added. He left. While loading up the dishwasher a feeling of joy and warmth washed over her. Perhaps Hunter would finally let her move on.

STANDING OUTSIDE THE dorms where the parents waited to collect their weekly boarders, she looked more like one of their girlfriends rather than their mother in her designer jeans and stilettos, hair swinging in a high ponytail. Barbe acknowledged the other parents and wondered if they had the faintest idea what she'd been up to in recent weeks. Nobody mentioned it and she didn't mind. They all had their private worlds.

Ryder had to be the first out of the door and he didn't care who saw him hug his mother, he'd worked out an answer if they dared tease him. In her four-inch heels they were the same height but give him a couple of years and even the heels wouldn't help. He had his father's genes making him grow tall and lanky. A few minutes later the cooler Nicholas arrived and gave her a smile then checked to see who watched them.

'Let's get the hell out of here,' he told her, 'I'm starving. Why are you driving my car?' Nicholas was all about image and his car didn't cut the mustard. A small Japanese import only had a one point three litre engine. Nothing to write home, about no bragging rights there. She explained her car was still in Auckland.

At home they wanted to know all about the shooting. What sort of gun did the gunman used?

'It just looked like a 'nerf gun' on TV,' Ryder commented. Nicholas rolled his eyes.

'Like a nerf gun would kill anyone. Can we play Fortnite?' when Barbe frowned, he added, 'you can earn big bucks gaming you know. Don't worry, it's still probably easier to earn it as a barrister like Dad.'

Ryder gave him a look of astonishment, even he thought Nicholas sounded pathetic.

'Mu-um,' he exaggerated the word in a whine. 'Dad said we're all going to the Whitsundays for the Holidays; did he *tell* you?' Barbe smiled, Hunter always assumed he never asked never asked.

'Actually, he did last night when we had dinner, he can't come home this weekend. He's got a big case starting next week.' She watched them tucking into the baking she'd just finished this afternoon. Hollow legs.

Ricard Beauchene from Pascal Rousseau phoned she recognized his number.

'How are you my dear?' he wanted to know. 'I told Hunter when he rang me about the school holidays, I always insist you take them off with your boys, he forgets I think.' Before she could get a word in edgewise, he went on, 'Shep, a long lean lanky cowboy; boots, Stetson, belt complete with silver buckle, dropped your car off to me. He said you'd explain when you were able.' She giggled, wondering what Shep was involved in now. 'I'll drive it down to Wellington on Monday and we can talk Tuesday, better you're away from Auckland. I'll bring the new samples for when you work in David Jones.' She gasped, having forgotten about beauty week. 'Don't fret my dear, I would even understand if you didn't want to do it. I mean it's a snake pit we all know, and the vipers will be out to get you, because we have had so much free publicity since the wretched shooting business. If lives were not lost, I'd say any publicity is good publicity.' Barbe smiled. She did love this man his over the top French accent, exaggerated gestures, and flamboyant clothes. he looked exotic and dangerously heterosexual. However, he always treated her like a lady, nothing about his behaviour had ever been untoward. They arranged to meet in Wellington on Tuesday.

Chapter Eleven:

O n the plane to Auckland Don felt pleased they'd booked him in first class. A big boy hated flying cattle class. Stretching out he replayed in his mind the conversation with the Commander. The shooting was still an ongoing case, but now it had a different focus. Who killed Carlos? The man had been linked to the amphetamine trade in Tonga. Don would need to be careful. He liked the comfort of his own weapon, not some standard issue he didn't like the feel of. He had been issued with two pistols of his choice, one a Smith & Wesson Bodyguard .38 a hammer-fired, double-action, semi-automatic, effectively his service revolver to be used in accordance with police regulations. The plastic trigger could pull roughly 9.5 pounds. It felt smooth and easy to use with its small J-frame and shrouded hammers. But the weapon he wore completely hidden, his weapon of concealment, a Glock 19, this weapon had been preferred by many police and military officers around the world. He used it as his backup weapon, small and deadly. Fortunately, Don disarmed more people with his smile than any weapon. He'd never fired a single bullet in the line of duty in his entire career, only in practice at the range. He'd been shot at, and he always said he felt too bloody old to take risks. The process to get the weapons to Tonga on a public passenger plane required a mountain of paperwork and a formal procedure. The necessary permits for exportation and importation were issued, and the weapons broken down and given to security, but they were useless without the part he held with his documentation. Don had each weapon's parts tied in a different sock and security covertly handed the useless parts to the captain to be secured in his locked cabin with their necessary paperwork. From there they would be handed to the Police in Tonga. All this would be done directly from Wellington.

Don had just enough time between flights to change to the international airport and check in the required two hours prior. He planned on getting some food and a paper to pass the time. He'd sleep on the flight. Arriving in Auckland at the priority check in, he learned his plane had been late flying in from Tonga. After about an hour the passengers were advised their flight to Nuku'alofa had been delayed overnight due to technical issues. On ringing his contact in Tonga, he learned the plane had not left the tarmac in Nuku'alofa it had a problem with the engine.

This delighted Don. He phoned his brother Tony who insisted he stay over with him and his family. Antonio Gabriel Lancini pulled into the passenger pickup at Auckland International airport. The brothers hugged and kissed each other. 'Where's your luggage Bro?' Tony asked. Don shook his head. 'Buggered if I know, somewhere in the system,' he gave a little laugh. 'I've got a toothbrush in my cabin luggage, I'm lucky I suppose.' The two men had a strong brotherly likeness. Their unique family genes were kind to them. Both stocky men, Tony being the oldest, seven years older than Don then came a sister, the middle child. The pair of them chatted animatedly, smiling, laughing and joking with one another.

'How's Mumma's boy? You still living at home? When you gunna move back into your own place,' Tony quizzed his brother.

'I had to rent it out after my divorce to pay the mortgage, you know I had to pay Gillian it's only fair.' Don moaned.

'How many years ago did you do that? Mumma tells me you're hardly ever home anyway.' Tony shook his head. 'You gunna end up a lonely old man if you don't get your act together.' Don smirked; he had no intention of ending up lonely.

'How's the beautiful Beth and the kids?' He skillfully changed the subject.

'Good, they're all good. Ed's at Uni did Mamma tell you he graduates this year. The company will have its own Architect. Mia, she's doing accounting and has a serious boyfriend, Beth has to hold her tongue, he's not Catholic.' Don shook his head, thinking poor Mia.

'Cripes, what's the big deal, it's not like you and Beth are bothering God every week at Mass.' Tony ignored Don's comment. He liked to believe he attended more regularly than he did.

'You know I have a team of builders working in the Wellington Diocese on the Churches we need to bring up to code after the earthquakes.' Don rolled his eyes and arm punched his brother.

'Buying our way to heaven, are we?' he laughed, but knew Tony to be a very generous man and wealthy. 'How's Lancini Construction anyway?' he asked casually.

'You asking after your shares or for some other reason?' They pulled into his driveway on Paritai Drive, Orakei the most coveted street in New Zealand and drove into his ground level four car garage.

'Gees Bro, you've done it again, have you got this place on a refurbishment loop? You know, redo it every five years.' Don looked amazed. It had only been about six months since his last visit and Tony had started on a makeover, but this looked like a rebuild job.

'I might sell it when Mario finishes his education. What do we need in the family? A lawyer, maybe we can talk him into becoming a lawyer? He's too interested in rugby, sailing and girls at present,' he joked.

'He gets that from you Don, I told him you're just like your uncle Don.' Tony switched off the ignition and turned to his brother. 'Before we go upstairs, I need to tell you I'm thinking of selling the company. What I mean is I'm considering floating it on the stock market, you know, give Fletchers a run for their money. They've had a bad few years, simply mismanaging all those huge contracts after the earthquake. I dunno you know, me bit of a control freak, don't want to take my hand off the tiller. But I'm fifty-three, too bloody old to be working on my tools and I don't. But I'm hands on everyday even if it is in a flash suit. Speaking of which, I have several for you. I've been put on a strict diet, pre-diabetic apparently.' Tony shrugged and Don raised his eyebrows. No one in the family had diabetes. Their father died of a heart attack after a boating accident, while out fishing. 'You know little brother everything I enjoy is either no good for me or a sin.' Don smirked at his brother.

'I won't tell Beth; she just might have something to say about that.'

The pair sat in the vehicle and Tony said 'I don't think so but look at you, I worry about you, why don't you settle down? The criminals aren't gunna keep you warm at night, or keep you company in your old age, are they? Beth's always trying to match you up.' Don laughed at him but remembered family parties and knew his brother meant it.

He hesitated, 'don't worry about me I've met someone. It's all pretty new but its real, and I'm determined to make it work.' Tony's face remained impassive, he motioned with his fingers.

'Photos?' Don got out his phone, pulled up the promotion pics of Barbe and showed Tony.

'Wow, I think I saw her on telly, just a few weeks ago. Were you involved with the shooting? Is the shooting how you met her? God that is new. She's a beauty, but hang on a minute, it said on the news she was married, I remember they called her Mrs.... ah Mrs.' Don interrupted him.

'Mrs. Anderson and she's divorced.' Tony's face looked a little disapproving. 'But hell, so am I.' Tony shook his head as Don made excuses.

'You're not privy to the facts, believe me she's special and she's Catholic.'

Don watched his brother's let down expression. 'So being Catholic makes it all right then.' Tony pursed his lips as he got out of the vehicle.

'It must be serious; you've never tried to justify your position to anyone before.' He looked over at his younger brother.

'Frankly I'm not worried about justifying myself now, but I want it to work this time.' Don said. Tony pulled a stupid expression for Don's benefit.

'It's just between us don't talk about it in front of Beth, okay?' They agreed.

The huge open plan living room had magnificent harbour views that ran the full length of the first floor.

'How's my favourite brother-in-law?' Don embraced Beth, a short curvy woman about his own age.

'What do you mean favourite? I'm your only brother-in-law.' She laughed, kissing him.

'Details, you cops are always hung up on details. Sorry all the kids are out tonight maybe at breakfast you'll see them.'

ON THE WAY TO THE AIRPORT next morning Don casually asked Tony if he remembered any boys from St. Benedict's and his college days.

'Like whom?' Don never asked empty questions.

'Like Hunter Anderson.' Don said. Tony sat thinking.

'Yeah, I remember him; he had tickets on himself.' The answer came automatically without consideration, then suddenly remembered.

'He did come and speak to me at school after Papa died. I guess he had some humanity after all. Why do you ask?' Before he uttered the words, Tony had joined the dots. This woman you're serious about, don't tell me she is Hunter Anderson's ex?' Don sat motionless. He said nothing. 'I can't believe he's divorced, his family were very devout Catholics, his uncle's a priest. It must have been a very grave matter. His sort never divorce.' Still Don said nothing. 'What's she like this woman? She's way younger than him or she's had work done.' Don laughed.

'No, she's a natural, and a bit younger than Hunter.'

'Quite a bit, by the looks of her.'

'Fourteen years actually.'

At the airport, the brothers hugged and kissed each other's cheeks agreeing to keep better contact. As Don checked in his extra bag of suits and brotherly hand me downs, he thought about how drawn Tony looked, his hair now almost completely grey, his face lined and tired. The strain of running his empire showing.

BARBE ENJOYED A NORMAL weekend with her boys. Rugby had started properly now, and they both had a game at different venues and different times. Hunter had allowed her to use his vehicle so she could take a few extra boys to the game. It always helped to take turns with the other parents ferrying the kids to and fro. The boys invited their friends over after the game. On the Sunday, they went out for brunch after Mass. By the time Sunday evening rolled around the boys were happy to be back at school.

Sitting amongst the detritus of life with her teenage boys, sipping tea Barbe felt flat. She realized the boys were becoming independent, which made her sad, but she wanted it. She had repeatedly told them; I'm bringing you up to be independent. Hunter had said they were her greatest gift to him, and he felt proud of the way they were growing up. Her phone pinged a text, *can you talk if I phone you now? D.*

Excited, she heard his voice and asked. 'How's the weather in sunny Tonga?'

'It would be better if you were here?' she could hear the smile in his voice.

'So, you're all settled then?' they chatted in this vein for a bit and they each spoke of their weekend and their plans for the coming week. They decided to talk on Sunday evenings and text in between, each on a high after their conversation.

Chapter Twelve:

R icard Beauchene proved a delight to work with. Although they met at his hotel, he had a suite with a sitting room where they could work. They talked through the sales figures for the month and of the classes booked to train the store staff in the new application techniques and products.

Barbe worked part-time, but Richard paid her as a full-time equivalent salary counting all the travelling hours involved and the nature of the business. Being required to represent the company at the cosmetic trade fairs over various weekends up and down the country might be fun, but it proved tiring.

'Barbe, you know after the school holidays Beauty Week in Sydney starts. I need you to cover for us in David Jones. It's a big affair, they'll love you and we have the most fabulous gift with purchase promotion,' he enthused. 'It's so exciting. An exquisite designer evening bag filled with lipstick, mascara and moisturizer.' Barbe studied the beautifully presented products. He always gave her a personal sample to use and keep.

'The Pascal Rousseau School of Beauty in Paris is offering a scholarship to some young woman from Australia. The accommodation for the winning student is at a Convent near the school in Paris. It's a very valuable scholarship offering a great future as a beauty therapist and cosmetician. We need you to assist the Australian company manager, Mark Wood, interview the young women we have selected from the applicants.' Ricard seemed slightly embarrassed. 'It's simply I trust your judgement to choose a young lady of elegance and er... refinement, we have an image to maintain. It's not simply looks you understand.' He fiddled with his pen. She

understood completely. Mark Wood had become a young hot shot in
the beauty world. A great salesman with an MBA and an overinflated
ego, not to mention his reputation with women. Barbe being a bit
older than him, Pascal thought her a lot more mature. She could
handle him for sure. Some of the applicants were only two or three
years older than her son Nicolas and she had a parental view as well
as business.

'I'm happy to do it for you. I know what you're looking for and
we only have to get the choice down to two. Mark and I should be
able to agree, worse case there could be his choice and mine then
you get the final say.' She laughed. Being the face of Pascal Rousseau
presented all manner of opportunities. In the afternoon, the pair
visited a couple of clients and at five thirty she drove him to the
airport for his flight back to Auckland.

NOW IN FULL SESSION, the Supreme Court in Wellington
looked busy, with the public gallery loaded to the gunnels. The court
orderlies were turning people away. In the number one court the
Crown versus James Yee in the case of the murder of Tara Reed.
The jury had been chosen the previous day and the prosecution had
commenced with their opening address.

Hunter Anderson desperately tried to keep his wits about him.
He was still reeling from another phone call from the mystery man
with the funny accent, this time on the Court's own landline. He had
the same message.

'Take the Matty Thomas case if you know what's good for you
and your family.' Hunter had difficulty concentrating on the case
in hand. During the luncheon recess he phoned the Governor of
Remutaka Prison and asked him to set up a phone call with Matty
Thomas. Then he called Detective Senior Sergeant Frank Taylor to
get a copy of the evidence against Thomas. Frank offered to deliver

it in person and Hunter agreed to phone when the court adjourned around four thirty.

As soon as Hunter commenced his opening argument, his attention became focused entirely on the case. Everything else he locked away in the back of his mind while he gave his all to the defense of his client. By the time Justice Harvey Banks called for an afternoon tea recess Hunter appeared in fighting form. On their return from the tea break the Crown would present their first witness. Hunter's cross examination seemed tame, but he lined up all the Crown's ducks in a row to be bowled over when he ran the defense argument. At day's end DSS Frank Taylor arrived at the office on the Terrace and Hunter patched him up to his floor and greeted him at reception.

'Fancy a drink?' he asked, and Frank said he'd like a coffee.

A tired looking Hunter suggested. 'I'm having something stronger,' Frank could see he needed to talk. 'We've both finished for the day, haven't we?'

Frank agreed and they settled into the comfortable club chairs, each nursing a whiskey.

'I've had another call from the voice. I don't think he's got anything to do with the accused, Matty Thomas, because the way he spoke I'd be taking the case pro bono. However, I spoke to Matty earlier in prison and I checked what he told me. He wants me to take his case, he has the funds to cover the costs, to ensure he gets the defense counsel he wants. I spoke to his lawyer who confirmed it. On examining the evidence, he presented to me, I believe he has a case.' Frank couldn't believe what he heard. Thinking for a moment he wondered if the voice had said more and threatened more. There had to be more to all this. He decided not to comment so he nodded in agreement.

'I met your ...er...Barbe Anderson last week. She's a confident, articulate woman.' He looked to Hunter for his reaction.

'And beautiful too,' Hunter added in a calculated statement. Frank agreed, pushing him even further.

'Women, can't live with them and can't live without 'em.' Frank eyed Hunter cautiously. Shaking his head, Hunter laughed heartily, Frank had struck a nerve, but never understood exactly what nerve. The two men chatted about their kids and Hunter mentioned after the Tara Reed case, he would be taking the boys and Barbe to the Whitsundays for a couple of weeks. When Frank expressed surprise, Hunter smirked and raised his eyebrows up and down suggestively, muttering.

'Hopefully she can't ignore me when we're alone together on a tropical island.' A tad embarrassed, Frank muttered back.

'Good luck mate, and thanks for the drink.' He stood up and took his leave.

FRANK TAYLOR COULD not erase his conversation with Hunter from his mind. First there had been the phone call from *the voice* as Hunter referred to him. Then he had agreed to take the Matty Thomas case, and he also attempted to justify it. Everybody knew they were caught red handed with a cargo of amphetamine. Not to mention, there were witnesses to Matty Thomas committing murder. Then he remembered the bizarre comment about taking his ex-wife on a holiday to a tropical island. Did the man suspect she had met someone else and if not, why tell him?

He needed to talk with Don, and he wanted to do it face to face to get the guy's reaction. When he interviewed Barbe Anderson, Don had stuck to her like glue. His gaze on her seemed intense. Frank could swear there seemed something between them.

THE HIGH COURT TRIAL now, in its second week, progressed well and the prosecution were summing up. Hunter felt nervous, like an actor before a big performance. He always got like this before his final summing up. Prosecuting counsel seemed so confident the case looked cut and dried. In his condescending pompous voice, he droned on.

'The defendant James Yee picked up Tara Reed in Vivian Street and drove her to a bushy area near the Basin Reserve. He does not deny he had sex with her. The Crown contends an argument ensued and he strangled her. He simply left her body at the scene. Not only does the DNA link James Yee to the crime but also his vehicle. Members of the jury, you heard the witness, Nigel Blunt, say he recorded the registration plate number because he didn't like the way the defendant had been driving. Then you heard the forensic evidence revealed an inspection of the vehicle confirmed Tara's presence in the vehicle. The timeline also served to confirm the evidence.' Listening to his learned colleague's tedious monotone Hunter studied Justice Banks. The man looked pained and quite grey. Experience told him as soon as the prosecution finished albeit before noon there would be a recess. The prosecution had barely finished when Justice Banks called for counsel to come to his chambers and called a luncheon recess of two hours. Hunter knew something had to be amiss.

He looked questioningly at his opposing counsel, Thomas Nelson, the prosecutor who opened his hands, and shrugged; he didn't know what was happening either.

In the judge's chambers it soon became apparent as Justice Banks writhed in pain.

'I'm sorry gentlemen, something is acutely wrong. My doctor will see me immediately, worst case scenario we'll have to resume tomorrow morning. I'll make sure he patches me up so we can see this case through. I'm not sure what the problem is.' The man grimaced in pain and stood up. They all knew the ramifications of a trial judge falling ill mid proceedings. The jury would have to be dismissed and a new trial called at great expense and inconvenience to everybody.

The judge's associate said she'd keep them informed and they left. Hunter needed some fresh air and decided to get a coffee. He took a short cut through David Jones to look at a new fountain pen he wanted. Hearing his name called, he turned.

'What are you doing here? I thought um, is your case still proceeding?' Barbe looked gorgeous. Just about to have an early lunch she waved to her fellow consultant's from beauty week in David Jones.

'Recess' he announced, 'fancy a coffee?' She agreed, and they headed to Waring Taylor Street where they knew of a discreet café.

'I'm sorry our flight out on Saturday is at such a horrendous time, still we'll have the weekend in Brisbane before we head off to the Whitsunday's. The boys can catch up with their cousins.' He ordered their coffees and some wraps before they moved to a quiet booth at the back.

'I thought if you didn't mind, I'd stay over at the house on Friday night, I mean it would be easier.' For some unexplainable reason she felt uncomfortable, but it made sense, and he always used the spare room when he stayed.

'No, it makes sense,' she shuffled about awkwardly. 'You do remember tomorrow evening is parent teacher interviews?' She looked at him.

'Oh, blast I forgot. Look, if the jury is out, I may not make it. Also, I did promise the team, you know we usually have a drink after a case like this.' She understood. He normally entertained the team after a big case. Perhaps he had someone he wanted to celebrate or commiserate with. Good, then he wouldn't be so needy. Their coffee and wraps arrived, and she looked up to see two men move into the booth opposite them. Not taking too much notice she sipped her coffee. Hunter sat watching them intently and soon her curiosity became roused when he acknowledged them with a nod and a smile. Turning she saw the detective who interviewed her in relation to the shooting, DSS Frank Taylor. He acknowledged her and she smiled. They all resumed eating and drinking.

'You know him?' she didn't seem surprised. Wellington is a boutique city, and the cops knew the lawyers. Hunter asked her about her week in David Jones.

'Ricard calls the beauty department the snake pit.' She smirked, 'he's such a drama queen, but there's an element of truth in it.'

When they left Hunter passed a few words with DSS Frank Taylor and his colleague. Barbe hung back a little, she watched Frank eyeing her intently.

Back in the Court House the court orderly advised the session would resume again but only to call another recess for the day. This time a senior Court official announced they would resume tomorrow morning at ten am as the Judge had some other business this afternoon. Hunter realized the man must be ill and conferred with the opposing counsel. He learned the judge had been admitted to hospital, but that was not the official line. Hunter and his second, a bright young woman barrister, went back to their offices on the Terrace.

Chapter Thirteen:

N ext morning at ten they all rose in court for Justice Banks
presiding. Hunter's closing address sounded impressive; he
took the jurors on a journey with him. Agreeing with all the evidence
presented as a fact.

'Yes, my client had sex with Tara Reed. He knew the woman,
and he looked out for her in particular. She had been kind and
sweet towards him and he had been fond of her. Although James
Yee had at one time been a client of the deceased, it did not mean
it had only been business. He cared for her. She listened to him.
His was not the only DNA found on her underwear, but none of
the other DNA had been sufficient to identify and no one else had
come forward like James Yee. I suggest to you they had something
to hide, maybe one of them murdered her. The Crown have failed
to prove beyond reasonable doubt my client actually killed Tara
Reed. If they had done, they would have produced the other men
whose semen left a partial genetic fingerprint. I suggest my client
became the easy option, a simple man, not particularly bright, whose
driving attracted the attention of a man who admitted under oath
he called the defendant, 'a chow, the yellow peril of the road.' The
witness seemed surprised to learn James Yee is a fifth generation New
Zealander, unlike him. Hunter Anderson claimed, 'his prejudice
allowed him to make a snap judgement of the man. Ladies and
gentlemen of the jury, each and every one of you has a duty to decide
this case without fear or favour, without prejudice or bigotry. Just
because my client sought the company of a prostitute does not make
him her murderer, just like it does not make the other man or men
whose DNA had been found on her clothing murderers. But we will

never be sure about them and so we will never be sure about James Yee. Therefore, you must find the crown have failed to prove their case beyond reasonable doubt.'

After lunch, Justice Banks summed up addressing the jury and directing them in matters of law. Asking whether a fair and honest assessment of the facts could convict the man? He raised the question of other DNA cells, and he couched his words in the same direction as Hunter had suggested. Did it raise doubt for them? The jury of seven men and five women returned a not guilty verdict after two hours deliberation. James Yee was free to go. Justice Banks thanked the jury and discharged them.

'I want you to know yesterday I suffered from a kidney stone. Fortunately, my doctor shattered it with a laser beam.' He advised the Court looking much happier today. 'After a good night's sleep, I could return to my duty in relative comfort.' He smiled, adding, 'a miracle of modern science.'

The case finished early, and the results were on TV. The newscaster interviewed Hunter briefly. However, he did not attend the parent teacher meeting. Neither Barbe nor Nicholas had really expected he would. They were used to this sort of thing happening and Nicholas's teacher understood. In fact, he believed it to be the reason the boy enjoyed an excellent work ethic.

'Dad said he'll celebrate my good marks on holiday,' the ambitious boy said proudly.

FRANK TAYLOR RECEIVED information via an informant, a member of the King Cobras gang. This was a largely Polynesian group heavily involved in the illegal amphetamine trade. The usually reliable informant claimed Carlos Matua is alive and well and hiding out in the far north of the country. Discussing it with the National Commander of the narcotics squad, Superintendent Tim Paxton, they voiced their long-held fears the body they had identified as Carlos Matua had been someone else. It posed problems. One, Matua's so-called partner had conspired to pervert the course of justice, by providing the DNA of a corpse he tried to pass off as Matua. Number two, they had another unsolved murder on their hands. Then there remained the death threat against D.I. Don Lancini. Not to mention, the eyewitness to mass murder being at risk, and possibly police corruption having an involvement.

'Actually Sir, Mrs. Anderson, the witness may be safe. Matua and his cohorts don't know the ruse with the corpse hasn't been completely successful. But also, the Anderson family are off to the Whitsunday Islands for the school holidays.' Frank pointed out.

'Lucky for some,' Tim Paxton sniffed 'should have been a barrister. Strange relationship going on holiday with the ex.' Frank agreed, and Tim sniffed again. 'Well, I suppose she's out of the country at least, making it a bit easier for us. Still, you better tell Hunter Anderson and Don Lancini when you next talk to him. The internet and the phone lines in Tonga were accidently cut by some shipping vessel apparently.' He gave a knowing smile at the last revelation.

'You think they did it on purpose?' Frank could see from the look on Tim's face that he did.

'GET THE PHONE WILL you please Nicholas,' Barbe said, busy dishing up dinner. 'Turn TV off Ryder and wash your hands, then get your father, he's busy in my office.' It had become a mad house trying to tick off the to do list and get the boys packed.

'Dad, phone!' Nicholas yelled at ninety decibels as his brother dried his hands on the kitchen tea towel.

'Ryder,' his mother cautioned him 'tea towels are not for drying hands.' Nicholas heard his father pick up the office phone and he set the kitchen phone back in its cradle.

'Hello, Hunter Anderson,' Hunter said, surprised to get a call on the house phone and Frank Taylor heard it in his voice.

'Sorry to call you at home Mr. Anderson. The Super suggested I call you. Can you talk?' Hunter stood up and called from the office door for Nicholas to hang up the phone, saying the call is business. Nicholas roared back he had already hung up. Then Hunter closed the office door.

'Yes, all clear now what can I do for you Detective?' he breathed deeply slightly concerned.

'We've been reliably informed Carlos Matua is not dead. He is the man Mrs. Anderson saw shoot a dozen people, eight now dead. He saw her face as plain as day and he knows who she is.' Hunter froze. 'Before we panic, let me tell you what we're doing. There's a plain car outside your home and we will have you covered until you fly out tomorrow. As far as Carlos knows we think he's dead, but we're still tracking him down. At least he can't leave the country without us stopping him.' Frank Taylor spoke slowly, giving weight to his words. 'You can tell Mrs. Anderson if you need to, but she seemed quite traumatized by the event, and you may just want her to enjoy her break away without this added stress. By the time you return, we should have him in custody.' Frank had his fingers crossed as he spoke, knowing they had a leak within the department.

'Thank you for telling me this. Just one thing Detective, my wife mentioned the officer who kept her safe had also been threatened. What is his name?'

why does he want to know Don's name? Frank thought with curiosity.

'Sorry I can't tell you; they sometimes use alias's anyway he's overseas at present.' It became obvious to Frank, Barbe Anderson had not told her husband about Don Lancini he wondered why. He also wondered why he thought of the man as her husband and not her ex.

The boys had finished eating their spaghetti Bolognese by the time Hunter sat down at the table.

'I'm glad we're flying out early in the morning. It's been a hard week' he told Barbe quietly. She could see he looked pale and drawn. They had barely finished their meal when her cell phone pinged a text. *Can I ring you on your mobile? D.* she replied while she made Hunter a coffee, then she excused herself to go upstairs, and scurried off before her phone rang. Shutting herself in her ensuite bathroom she greeted him.

'God, it's a mad house around here. You know I'm off for two weeks to the Whitsunday's then the following week I'm in Sidney for the whole week.' She gave him the dates. He asked her for the name of the resort where they were staying.

'We can talk on our mobiles,' she told him then added, 'you couldn't join me for the weekend when I'm in Sydney could you?' He said he the department owed him leave and he'd try, she felt elated. They agreed to discuss it over the next week.

'Bebe, I've missed you. Hiding out felt easy compared to this.' She laughed at him. Imagining him raking his hair the way he did.

'I know it's hard for me too. But it will be interesting. I think Hunter is gearing up to tell me he's met someone.' She sighed, 'then I'll be free.' They said their goodbyes and she flushed the loo, turned off her phone and washed her hands. Already she had forgotten Don's instructions about taking mobile calls outside. When she unlocked the door and walked into her bedroom Hunter stood there, she froze.

'You, okay?' he asked. She had her suitcase on the bed and clothes everywhere.

'Yes, I just need to get sorted and then I'll check the boys bags. They have the list I gave them.' She sounded full of business, and he stood filled with thoughts about his conversation with Frank Taylor.

'DON, GOT YOU AT LAST.' Frank moaned 'you've been on your phone.'

'What else are phones for Frank? What's up?' As soon as he asked, he realized they had an issue.

'My snout reckons Carlos is hiding in the Far North, alive and well.' He paused for Don to take it in.

'Is he reliable?' Don didn't need to be told Barbe was in danger. He assessed the situation in his mind.

'I don't get much from this guy, but he hates Carlos because he's competition. Big competition. He wants him out of the way and death by cop is the cleanest.'

'What about my witness? Who's looking after her?' He called her his witness now.

'We have an unmarked car outside her home, her husband's staying over tonight, and they have a three am check in tomorrow morning for an international flight.'

'Ex-husband' Don sounded irked. Frank wondered why he didn't ask more questions. He realized Don didn't know what was happening when he asked. 'Does Barbe know Carlos is not dead?'

'I don't believe so. Don't you think you should trust me, Don? Tell me what's going on between you and Mrs. Anderson?' Silence reigned for a minute and Frank thought he'd lost the call.

'Okay, I care about her very much. We both agreed to see each other outside of work when the time is right. We only phone once a week. I want to do this right. We have agreed we'll tell Hunter together in three months or so. In the meantime, it's business as usual.' Don sounded measured.

'So, you know theirs is an odd divorce?' Frank didn't understand the relationship at all.

'They don't hate each other's guts. It's not unheard of for divorced people to care about one another. But not want to live together.' Don heard Frank mutter something then he clearly said.

'Well, I think I better warn you I had a drink with Hunter the other night after work. I dropped the Matty Thomas file off to him. He said to me he couldn't wait to get her alone on a tropical island. The way he said it indicated he wanted to get her back in his bed.' Don said nothing. 'I just thought you should know.' Frank heard a deep labored intake of breath.

'Hunter's aspirations may be one thing, but I'm telling you it's over. They're Catholic, it's complicated.' Don sounded frustrated.

Chapter Fourteen:

Detective Senior Sergeant Taylor stood in a briefing room on the Whenuapai military air base ready to address the elite team from the Special Weapons Assault Troop. He looked at the wall clock, midnight. He studied the SWAT members, all appeared ready for this mission.

'I need not remind you this operation is strictly on a need-to-know basis. Shortly you will split into three groups and board one of the three Navy Seasprites out there on the tarmac. I'm DSS Taylor, I'm your field commander for this operation. We have information Carlos Matua, the shooter in the Auckland Hotel massacre, is hiding out in a fisherman's hut along the coast near Herekino. We believe he's been waiting for a shipping vessel of some kind with a load of cocaine on board. We haven't seen the vessel but some of the cocaine has washed up along the shoreline and of course the press were all over it.' He saw an expression of surprise cross several faces.

'The body previously identified as Matua has been formally identified as Ray Wilson, a member of the Griffith gang.' Frank Taylor said grinning and raising his eyebrows. 'Yes, we were never one hundred percent convinced because a body with the hands cut off, is suspicious, a sign we were being duped. The Australian federal police went through every tattooed criminal associated with the gang till we matched all the corpse's tatts with the gang members on record but with no dental records to confirm his identity it proved difficult. If they had his DNA on record, it would have saved us a deal of grief. But we must operate within the law. Carlos Matua is still alive and well and we want him captured the same way. We can't avoid the choppers being heard along the coast, but we'll drop you off at three different locations.' He pointed to three positions on the map. 'From there you will need to search and keep in touch. There are only three huts we know of, and they are marked on the maps you each have. As soon as we check each of them, locate Matua and extricate him, we can be on our way back to Auckland. We have five hours of darkness at most. A naval ship is sitting off the coast if he decides to move off out to sea. Okay team, take care out there.' Frank stood back as the squads divided into three and boarded the choppers. He noted with interest Constable Liana Duckworth, the country's best sniper, had been allocated to his team. With a nod of the head, he acknowledged her, he knew she may well be needed on this operation.

THE ANDERSON FAMILY travelled by taxi to the Airport to get there for their three am check in. The only person who knew they were being followed by an unmarked police car had been Hunter. After very little sleep the four of them were fairly subdued. The boys soon stretched out on the bench seating at gateway forty-five waiting for their early boarding call.

Once the plane had taken off Barbe and the boys went back to sleep while Hunter's mind raced, still in overdrive. He shuffled about restlessly in his seat, his long legs uncomfortable even though they were flying first class. He wondered whether they had an air marshall on board. DSS Frank Taylor had promised to keep him in the loop regarding Matua.

DON LANCINI STAYED in a serviced apartment of a hotel in Nuku'alofa, definitely not his favourite place, but it beat the police barracks and felt comfortable and private. Not to mention, he had the use of the great swimming pool and comfortable indoor airconditioned gym. As far as the locals were concerned, this New Zealand Government accountant had been sent to Tonga to oversee a Govt audit. His charismatic smile and charming manner meant before long, he became privy to tit bits of gossip and local information he cultivated and valued as he knew it would come in handy down the track.

Instead of wasting his leisure time he spent it getting fit and thinking about the new woman in his life. He owed it to himself. Plus, his routine fitness level check would be due in a month, and he didn't feel confident about it, having done a lot of hurrying up and waiting which involved sitting around and eating while undercover. He'd only been in Tonga a couple of weeks and now each day he looked forward to his workout and swim. The hotel's owner, a retired professional rugby league player from Brisbane, really hit it off with Don. Sione Fifita loved to work out in the gym, and he devised a program for Don. Two big, sports-loving men they spent time together. Sione, a devout Mormon, proved a fine example to his staff. Don never really told Sione about Barbe, he just mentioned he had someone in his life.

Don worked with the Tongan Minister of Police to agree on a framework for the New Zealand police contingent to operate within. This agreed framework would take several weeks to complete. In the back of his mind, he felt concerned for Barbe and her safety. Frank Taylor would keep him up to speed.

The amphetamine trade in Tonga, had been wreaking havoc on family life, with increased poverty and violence. Don could see it all around and felt in no doubt about the seriousness of his mission. Users became addicted very quickly and seemed to gain a superhuman strength when in the grips of a violent outburst. Busting the kitchens and cooks where the drug was being produced, required planning and resources to outwit the gangs behind the illicit trade. The backing these gangs seemed to have at their disposal appeared limitless. The street value of the drugs sounded like a king's ransom and the gangs had international connections.

Don had his work cut out organizing the narcotics squad and ensuring they would not fall prey to corruption. The time he spent with Sione seemed unique. Sione took him to meet his family and eat with them. Don envied the life of family and structure Sione enjoyed. He now aspired to do the same things before it became too late. Don joked cradle Catholics like him did not enjoy the same piety Mormon boys aspired to.

'We don't need to give two years of our life to a mission service.' Then he laughed, 'perhaps if we had clearly defined expectations, we might be a little holier.' Thinking about it he realized his own family dynamic had dramatically altered with his father's early death. His godfather also lost in the same accident and so his elder brother had needed to shoulder a lot of responsibility. Tony had proved his worth to the family and when Don spoke to him earlier in the week, he had been shocked to learn he had been having tests for cancer. Little wonder Tony had aged when he saw him in Auckland.

Chapter Fifteen:

F rank Taylor surveyed his crew all on high alert and filled with anticipation. The chopper took off. There had been little or no conversation between the team members. They sat in silence listening to Frank and the Pilot discussing the mission. Each member of the exclusive special weapons assault troop was wearing protective clothing including body armour, helmet, night vision goggles and assault webbing. Some of the older members wore knee pads, gloves, and harnesses. They all had weather-proof tactical pants, shirts, and jackets. Through their headphones the captain's voice could be heard 'ETA five minutes.' Various team members started adjusting their night vision goggles and synchronizing their watches.

'I'll land in the clearing over there, Commander and I'll wait there till I get your orders.' Frank's team silently followed his hand signals and surrounded the old fishing hut. On Frank's signal they stormed the hut… voices screamed 'Police' as they broke in to find it empty. Realizing there were only two other options they boarded the chopper and Frank called ahead.

'Target one clean papa bear over.' They heard crackling on the line before a reply came.

'Target two clean, mumma bear over.'

'What the hell's happening?' Frank called out. Team three did not respond, using his cell phone he called team three leader.

'What's happening? Targets one and two all clear.' Frank broadcast the message to the rest of the team.

'Team three have just entered the premises Sir and we have secured the two occupants. Repeat we have the suspect and one other in custody.' A cheer went up amongst the group. Frank worried, it seemed too easy.

Back in Auckland Frank phoned Don Lancini.

'Don early wake up call. Matua's in custody, you can relax.' For a few seconds he made no response.

'What time is it?' Don groaned.

'Six am same as here in New Zealand, no time difference.' To Don it felt like the middle of the night. Frank explained how straight forward the procedure to capture Matua had been.

'Don't look a gift horse in the mouth, it's not over till the bastards are sent down,' Don berated his colleague. 'Anyway, Barbe's safe, thank you.' After Frank finished his call Don couldn't get back to sleep and took off down to the gym for a workout and swim.

THIS HOLIDAY HUNTER had organized came completely out of left field. Sure, they all enjoyed Christmas together and then around the twenty seventh of December, Barbe, her mother, Hunter and the boys joined the rest of the Anderson clan in the old homestead in the Marlborough Sounds. The house had been the very same house, where Hunter and Barbe first met. The bedroom arrangements had never been an issue after their divorce.

The old villa had been added on to several times and a bunkhouse out the back with a huge bathroom meant they had no shortage of accommodation. The family usually stayed in the Sounds until Wellington Anniversary Weekend at the end of January when Hunter went back to work after what he referred to as the *illegal holidays*. Hunter knew he was privileged to have so much time each year and the family had established holiday rituals they all enjoyed. BBQ's with friends and neighbours, tennis, fishing, water skiing, reading, sleeping late, board games and so on.

Thinking about this island holiday, Barbe imagined Hunter may be getting ready to say they would do their own thing from now on while still co-parenting. That would be fine with her. In the past every time she wanted to move on, he laid a guilt trip on her. Looking across at her boys occupied watching a movie she noticed Hunter, in animated conversation with a beautiful young flight attendant. The young man looked about twenty-seven. She shivered, she always felt anxious when he was around young men.

WITH CARLOS MATUA AND his henchman safely in custody in Auckland, Frank Taylor texted Hunter Anderson who had been about to land in Brisbane. As soon as he landed Hunter switched his phone back to roaming and received a text as he waited at the luggage carousel. '*Shooter in custody. Enjoy your holiday. Frank Taylor.*' Feeling like a huge weight had been lifted from him, Hunter relaxed.

AFTER A WEEKEND IN Brisbane their aircraft flew directly to Hamilton Island. The boys were anxious to go sailing around the islands, swim and even try parasailing. At the Resort check-in they were given an activity sheet of what activities were on offer and how to book. Hunter oversaw the arrangements and insisted they also did family things.

On the beach one afternoon during their second week away, the boys were swimming and occasionally lounging around chatting with their parents. Barbe noted the boys' interest in girls, particularly Nicholas. He overtly ogled bikini clad girls. Ryder seemed a little more circumspect about it coyly noting his mother's unease. With Hunter the females never registered on his radar. But his neck ricocheted in the direction of any young males. She had seen it before many times when they were married. In those days she felt wounded and small, now she knew this was his norm. But why did he keep up this charade, a facade? Refusing to admit his sexuality.

In a few days Barbe would turn forty. She did not look forward to it. Not because she would be marking a big milestone but because she had wasted so many years 'keeping up appearances.' It had not all been sadness though because within days of each other, Nicholas would turn seventeen and Ryder fifteen. Hunter had planned a special dinner and a shared birthday cake with all their names on it. Sensible enough to realize if he drew attention to the big four O birthday, Barbe would be less than impressed, so he ordered a family birthday cake for Ryder's day, the middle birthday.

The evening of Barbe's birthday they all dressed up and went to the resort's exclusive a la carte restaurant. Unbeknown to Barbe, Nicholas and Ryder wanted to go to the Island's disco. The resort put on a fortnightly disco for the under eighteens. It would be alcohol free, and the event would be supervised. The boys planned to be out of the restaurant and down to the beach by eight pm. Hunter suspected something. By the time the main course had been served it had gone seven thirty and Barbe also realized something might be afoot. Noticing the boys check their watches every few minutes and exchange looks, she asked,

'Am I keeping you from doing something else?' Ryder couldn't stand it any longer and came clean.

'Gee Mum, you don't mind, do you?' She shook her head realizing they were growing up so fast. As soon as they finished their meal, they were good to go.

'Both of you be back in our suite by eleven pm.' Their father laid down the rules only to be told the event finished at ten thirty. 'Good you'll be back by ten forty then.' Smirking at Barbe he gave a half eyeroll. 'They're growing up fast, I expect they won't want to go on holiday with us much more,' he sounded wistful.

'I thought you may have planned this as our last hurrah as a family,' she quietly told him; he covered her hand with his.

'I don't want to talk about it just yet, soon but not yet.' He had trouble saying what he wanted to. If he persisted in this vein, she would force the issue.

'Push the boat, out have dessert,' he insisted picking up a menu she perused it but the knot in her stomach felt too tight to allow food.

'No thank you, a liqueur would be nice, but not limoncello.' He ordered two baileys' over ice and took a sip.

'I know I've been a disappointment at times,' he said to her surprise. Not knowing whether to agree or not, she reassured him.

'You're a good father Hunter, the boys couldn't ask for better.' The awkward moment broke when a couple from a neighbouring suite stopped by their table and chatted about nothing in particular. They were from New Zealand and Hunter confided,

'I think they know me, or of me.' Barbe said nothing simply agreeing. They could have recognized her from the telly of late, but she hoped not. They left the restaurant and walked back to their suite, it had not even gone eight-thirty, they were not arm in arm or hand in hand, just two lonely separate people. It made Barbe ache for Don. He was a tactile man she mused, forever touching, even if just flicking his hand against her arm to get her attention, nothing inappropriate. His fingers touching her hair, or her face, his arm around her, rubbing her arm. Not Hunter, but then his needs lay elsewhere.

Once inside Barbe put on the jug,

'Want a cuppa?' she asked. He shook his head, she wanted to scream it's my birthday, I'm forty. I want a real life where somebody values me as a woman. Instead, she said curtly 'I can't do this anymore, this playing happy families. We're divorced and I want my own life.' He gave her a look of pure annoyance, as though she were a petulant child having a tantrum.

'Barbe, don't.' His voice sharp. 'I have something I want you to think about,' taking her mug of tea she sat opposite him.

'This life we live, it's unnatural, isn't it?' she said completely out of the blue.

'Personally, I hate going home to an empty apartment every night, with no one to talk about my day with. It's bloody lonely at night, you're right its unnatural,' he paused, watching her face. She sat agreeing with him and he watched her eyes well up. 'I'm sorry I never intended you be unhappy. The boys are, well in three or four years they could fly the coop,' he said. She interrupted him.

'Don't wait till then Hunter if you want to do it do it now. The boys are more mature than you give them credit for.' Suddenly he took her hand and set down her tea mug.

'So, you wouldn't mind, I mean it makes sense we can never marry anyone else,' he pulled her to him and started kissing her, she tried to pull away, confused by what he had just said. Still holding her firm, he gave her an annoyed look. It didn't feel loving, more like he felt irritated and wanted to punish her. Mustering her strength, she pushed back harder.

'Oh, for heaven's sake Barbe,' he hissed, 'you're forty and you've had two kids, sex isn't so important, is it?'

what did he say?

'I beg your pardon. What is it you're trying to tell me?' His words rang in her ears. The acrid taste of bile filled her mouth.

'I thought we could get back together legally. It would be so much easier.' still she didn't fully comprehend what he meant. Pulling free from him she sat stunned.

'Are you suggesting we remarry?' he half smiled, nodding. 'Are you mad? What would I have to gain from that arrangement?' Her voice incredulous, she watched his face change. Hunter did not like to lose, he had been thinking about this for a while, but only from his own perspective.

'You enjoy a very good lifestyle Barbe.' He said cold and threatening. 'And it need not change.' He tried to soften her up, but this was all about him.

'You would be free to give up your part time job.'

'I happen to like my job' she insisted.

'You could join an art group,' he said becoming annoyed.

'I could have joined an art group years ago if I chose.' She couldn't believe him.

'Look you could play golf or play ladies or whatever.' He didn't understand why the idea didn't appeal to her. She shook her head as he watched, telling her in a poisonous tone. 'I can never satisfy you, why do you have to be such a bitch?'

'So, it's all my fault. I only ever wanted for my husband look at me the way he looks at young men,' she watched his face turn bitter.

'You're being ridiculous, pathetic, can you hear yourself?' his voice hostile.

'Why do you think we divorced? You can't admit the truth. I understood it years ago. You prefer men.' Hunter lashed out and slapped her face. Immediately she stood up, shocked. This was a new low.

'Barbe, I'm sorry I didn't mean...' he had even shocked himself. She stood in the doorway of her room about to shut the door.

'I think I'll have your divorce agreement checked by a specialist lawyer.' Putting her hand to her face she could feel the heat from it as she locked her bedroom door. Then she heard him storm off, slamming the door of their suite shut on his way out. It was just past nine pm and she quickly changed for bed. Upset, she remembered how good she felt earlier when she got ready to go to dinner, just a couple of hours ago. Now she understood what Hunter had on his mind. He could be an affectionate father but.... it would be no good. He is who he is. nothing would ever change.

Unable to settle to anything she'd been dozing on and off she noted the time now eleven forty-five pm. Getting up she quickly pulled on a robe, opening her door she checked for Hunter, he was not there. The boys had a two-bed unit next door. They had a separate entrance, but they also shared an interconnecting door, which she opened and found Ryder in bed but not asleep.

'Where's your brother?' she asked watching him guiltily pretend to be asleep, 'Ryder,' her voice sharper this time.

'I dunno he was with a girl last I saw.' Barbe sighed.

'Just when your father's not here either,' she exhaled, frustrated.

'Dad's in the beach bar with a man,' he announced as a matter of fact.

'What bar? What man? Where's this?' She felt utterly confused.

'You stay there, I'll go down to find him, the beach bar you say.' She knew it stayed open until after midnight all the young ones hung out there. She turned to go back through the interconnecting door and Ryder called her.

'Don't go mum, you'll only embarrass yourself.' She didn't stop to ask what he meant.

'Goodnight son.' In a minute flat, she had put on a sundress and pulled her hair up in a scrunchie. Sliding her feet into her scuffs she grabbed her keycard. Barbe almost ran to the beach bar. By the time she arrived breathless, heart pounding Ryder's words were ringing in her ears. The bar looked almost empty. Glancing around she couldn't see Hunter, the barman asked if he could help.

'I'm looking for my husband, he's wearing chinos and a check shirt' (he's not your husband hasn't been for years) 'he might be with my son.' The young barman eyed her cautiously.

'A very tall guy? Greying?' She nodded, noting, he looked uncomfortable as he wiped down the bar. 'I don't think he was with your son; I mean the guy he's with looked too old to be your son. Anyway, they left about half an hour ago.' She understood and thanked him.

Barbe would not be going to look for Nicholas, she had no idea where he had gone. Did he see his father too? He may well have and decided he could do what he liked.

The cool sea breeze made her hurry back to her suite. When she arrived, she checked on Ryder who had fallen asleep. Hunter hadn't come back nor had Nicholas. She didn't assume for one minute they were together. For the rest of the night, she tossed and turned. Sick of pretending, she wondered what the boys knew. Lying in her bed, it dawned on her being forty had meant a huge change. It had been foisted upon her.

Barbe had not been arrogant enough to presume she might be the only woman in the world who had ever been in this situation, and she would have felt absolutely desolate had it not been for Don. Having no idea of the time in Tonga didn't stop her from texting him.

I turned forty yesterday, shittiest day of my life. I miss you so much. xoxo

He replied almost instantly.

Would U like a call. Don

'Yes please' B

The pair chatted, she told him the whole sorry saga, never mentioning Hunter slapped her and she felt ashamed. He had never ever done anything so desperate before.

'I couldn't tell him about us. Like you say we'll do it together in a couple of months.' Her voice sounded lost. 'I wish you were in my bed,' she told him.

'I'll make up for it in Sydney promise,' she knew he would.

IN THE PRESENCE OF the children Hunter maintained a thin veneer of civility, but whenever they were alone, he either gave her the cold shoulder, not speaking at all or he eloquently delivered veiled threats. Intimating as only solicitors can her comfortable lifestyle was about to be terminated.

On their return to Wellington Hunter made his excuses at the airport, hugged the boys and took a taxi back to his apartment, a busy man. They simply accepted what he said.

On the Sunday after dinner Barbe returned the boys to school. Driving home alone she remembered her fortieth birthday. Hunter had refused to discuss where he spent the night returning back to their unit at breakfast just ahead of Nicholas. He told Barbe he would deal with Nicholas, and she was not to discuss it with him. You didn't argue with Hunter.

Chapter sixteen:

When Don telephoned, he warned her she needed to get a legal opinion. He asked her to scan their divorce agreement and send him a copy. He advised he'd read it and talk to her the following evening. Barbe told him Hunter would wipe the floor with any Wellington lawyer and she would ask Ricard Beauchene to recommend someone in Auckland and have him make an appointment for her; she would be there Thursday before flying to Sydney.

Studying the divorce agreement Hunter had her sign years earlier, Don could see it had not been an equitable arrangement. Barbe would never have seen it for what Hunter really intended. A gag order made to look like he had been generous. The document looked restrictive. The family home is held in a trust. Don learned Hunter is the sole beneficiary. Barbe is permitted to live there until the youngest child turned sixteen. It stated she would pay her fair share of the expenses, but he had prevented her from working, not physically but other ways, with inconsistent access times due to his enormous self-imposed workload.

Generously Hunter had provided for the boys one hundred percent and given her a small allowance, which Don felt sure she could not have survived on. Barbe said she had a little inheritance from her father, she used it to top up her living expenses. Running a large house cost money. Three years ago, Barbe could see her inheritance running out. When she got the job, Hunter had cut her allowance barely providing for the boys, claiming the boarding school fees were more than his fair share. After her inheritance ran out Barbe had been forced to make economies, fortunately the job provided a company car, rare in a part time position but her arrangement with Pascal Rousseau New Zealand Limited, had been unique and flexible. It worked for both of them, she had increased the company's sales by fifty percent in the three years she had been with them. Don felt sure Hunter had hidden assets but he would never be so foolish as to defraud the IRD so a decent lawyer could find those. Hunter had not been in touch since he arrived back from Brisbane. Barbe felt it ominous. He could be nasty when it suited him, and she felt intimidated wondering what he planned.

On Thursday morning she flew to Auckland and Ricard met her at the Airport. They returned to the company premises in Francis Street where the executive team held their monthly meeting from nine till twelve thirty and then Ricard drove her downtown to meet Simon Perry, a suave divorce lawyer, in his forties. The man appeared impressed with Barbe. An elegant beauty, the face of Pascal Rousseau and he knew of her ex-husband, the renowned criminal lawyer. Their divorce agreement had been a simple two-page document. Sitting behind his huge desk in the glass tower of his office block, Simon Perry tried to understand why she would have signed the agreement in the first place. How come she had never sought advice before this? He reread the agreement then he put both his beautifully manicured hands on the desk and leaned over towards her.

'What am I missing here, Mrs. Anderson?' At first, she didn't understand the question. 'Do you still love the man?' This time he put his head to one side as though he were questioning a child. Barbe said nothing, feeling a tight lump in her throat.

'What do you mean?' she finally said.

Simon Perry gave a sad little smile and added, 'you've never remarried.' He said it as a statement.

'We're Catholic,' she told him blinking away tears. Studying her closely he observed her impeccable dress, a navy raw silk creation, with contrasting accessories and flawless makeup. Her fragrance gently making him want more, as it occasionally wafted his way.

'Why did you want this divorce in the first place?' He stood up and walked around his desk coming to a halt just in front of her.

'I couldn't live with his ...continued infidelities.' She bit her luscious red lip and looked up at him through her wet lashes.

'So how come he has never remarried?' She looked out of the window.

'I told you we're Catholic.' The look he gave her appeared to be one of disbelief. She felt uncomfortable.

'In my experience when a man like Hunter Anderson wants something, he usually gets it.' He wanted her to tell him what she felt he had guessed. But she couldn't. Instead, she inhaled deeply, her breath hitching.

'Are you telling me he has never had a serious relationship in all these years?' Simon Perry perched his backside on the edge of his desk, with his arms folded and legs crossed.

'What about you? Have you never had a serious relationship either?'

Barbe smiled at him and nodded.

'I've recently met someone, it's serious but we don't live together. In fact, he is not even in the country.' Now Simon understood and unfolded his arms, putting his hands behind him on the desk.

'So, this new relationship precipitated this consultation?' he asked knowing it to be true. 'Does he know about your ex-husband?' He spoke quietly now as though he just slipped the comment into the mix.

'Of course, he knows.' She watched the lawyer's slightly irked expression as he pursed his lips.

'So, you tell your 'new love' about your ex-husband but not your lawyer,' he stared at her.

'Are you going for an annulment then?' He seemed strange this Simon Perry.

'What makes you think I would be granted nullity. I don't think infidelity is grounds for Catholic annulment.' She stood up the man, had been all but invading her personal space. She gazed out of the window wishing she'd never come.

'Because when God joins a man and a woman in holy matrimony, he expects the sacrament will keep them strong. If one party were unfaithful, then their needs were not being met for whatever reason. So, to make the marriage work the other party would need to offer forgiveness, because to forgive is to truly love. The parties would then agree they were too committed to let the marriage fail. They would work together on the physical intimacy so they each had their needs met and there would be no infidelity.' Staring straight ahead out of the window, the tears silently rolled down her face.

'I know you are a warm loving mother, Ricard told me. I can see you are a very attractive woman. I know you love your husband, or you would have quickly told me you hated his guts. You did tell me he has been unfaithful. The kind of woman who would want a man like Hunter Anderson is the kind of woman who wants commitment and a future.' He followed her to the window and casually, without comment, handed her a box of tissues.

'Therefore, I believe your husband must have some impediment to making your marriage work. So, you divorced but now you have met someone, and you're torn.' She blotted her eyes and cheeks and even managed a smile.

'I didn't think lawyers were priests too,' then she blurted out, 'perhaps you should give them instruction on marriage. You have a better handle on the situation than my priest did years ago when I tried to talk about it.' Simon gave her a sympathetic look and then very earnestly asked 'Did you tell him you thought your husband may be gay?' This time she breathed deeply and controlled the tears, not usually a weepy person. She told Simon about finding Hunter naked with a man, and all the nuances of her troubled relationship. 'I look at my outside façade and wonder why inside I feel crumpled, ugly and unworthy. For years I watched the man I love look at men in a way he never looked at me. Then I met Don and when he looked at me, I knew what it truly feels like to be desired. No one has ever made me feel that way before.'

'I believe you should apply for an annulment. You see sexuality is on a continuum, so imagine if you will a band of zero to six. Zero is unequivocally heterosexual and six is absolutely homosexual. Then there are ranges along it and I suspect you are a zero and Hunter maybe somewhere along it because when you first married things seemed normal, then after a couple of years they turned to custard,' he shrugged. 'Chances are he had relationships with men prior to your marriage, but the pressure to conform.... in a Catholic marriage there is one man and one woman. You believed it to be a love match. Chances are he does love you, but not in the union of one flesh. I'll help you where I can.' He went back to sitting behind his desk.

'Are you Catholic?' she asked wondering at his grasp of the sacrament. He gave her a strange look as though the question were too personal.

'I was brought up Catholic and I have sent some people to the Catholic Marriage Tribunal, but each case is individual and whether your husband will cooperate is another matter.' He looked at his watch and stood up. She knew her time was up.

'But as far as the agreement goes, don't worry about it we'll get you a very fair settlement,' he told her. 'Schedule another appointment for six weeks.'

Ricard drove her to the airport he always said he could keep her up to speed with events while driving. But also, he liked her and often wondered what her life was really like. Sitting with her in the airport café he suggested,

'I think you have met someone, non?' His French accent thick with concern he eyed her with interest.

'Yes, I have but it's early days, and it's been so long I'm new to this.'

'How delicious Ma Cherie, just do what is in your heart.' He waved a flamboyant hand watching her blush. He just wanted her to be happy and he watched her face light up when she spoke about Don. They shared stories about their families and Barbe appreciated this colourful man with his greying curly mane turning up on the collar of his designer shirt.

Chapter seventeen:

F riday in Sydney:
　　Busy with Mark Wood, Barbe had been interviewing the young people who had applied for the Pascal Rousseau beauty therapy scholarship. She felt delighted a young man featured amongst the candidates. Ricard had short listed the applicants and they had nine candidates they needed to whittle down to two. By noon they had interviewed five and the young man looked to Barbe like a strong contender. A well-presented fellow with a polite disposition, his personal presentation and quiet confidence seemed extraordinary. However, his sharp wit and killer smile convinced Barbe. After his interview she wistfully told Mark he would be her choice.

'We would be mad to ignore him. Brad Murphy will go far in this world and he's my number one candidate.' Mark didn't agree, and his words proved he had no argument.

'We can't have him. The accommodation is in a Convent. So, he won't work. Everyone knows these scholarships have always been for girls, pretty girls. Sure, he's impressive, at twenty-one an arts graduate from Monash. Why would he even want the job?'

'Get a grip on yourself Chauvin,' she chided him. 'This guy has style.' Barbe suggested they put him aside and interview the remaining candidates after lunch.

A member of the hotel concierge desk informed Barbe her guest had arrived. Leaving the meeting room, she hurried to reception. Don stood there in his Armani suit carrying a huge bunch of flowers.

'Bebe,' he enveloped her kissing her lovingly. 'You look gorgeous.' he offered.

'So do you, look at you.' She could see he looked noticeably trimmer, and his naturally olive skin looked tanned. Thanking him for the flowers, she admired him. 'Tonga is good for you; I can see you're looking great.' He enjoyed her compliment.

'Exercise is good for me, thank you.' He dropped his voice, 'do I need to get a room?' She shook her head.

'Please give my ... Mr. Lancini his key.' She looked to the receptionist, who took care of the details. Soon Barbe introduced Mark Wood, who didn't know what to make of this big fit-looking guy in a designer suit with a charismatic smile.

'Nice to meet you, Mark. Are you breaking for lunch?' Mark said they were. 'Great because I haven't seen my lady for weeks so I'm whisking her off for a brief catch up. What time shall I return her?' Don took the wind out of Mark's sails he had other ideas.

'One thirty for our next candidate's interview.'

Don winked. 'I've organized sandwiches and coffee so we can talk, only if it suits.' He shot her a glance. When she hesitated, he added, 'in the dining room. I couldn't do you justice in forty-five minutes,' he flashed his megawatt smile.

'You're incorrigible Adonis,' she laughed.

The last four interviews after lunch didn't compare to Brad Murphy. Mark didn't agree and Barbe told him she would look forward to Ricard's final interview to see whom he chose. Don waited for her in the hotel lobby. He had enjoyed a Nonna nap while she worked. He hated long haul flights. Don wanted to go somewhere and talk. They had so much to talk about. At lunch they hadn't even discussed family, they were just so pleased to see each other. The time flew.

'Let's go upstairs and talk, we've had some of our most interesting discussions in small rooms.' She told him. He took her hand, and they went off to the lift.

'What did you say to his nibs to get rid of him?' he wanted to know. She looked at him coyly.

'I told him we were going upstairs to have an interesting discussion.' She raised an eyebrow.

'Funny thing I don't think he believed me.' They grinned at each other. Then he kissed her.

It had become dark outside by the time they came up for air. Cuddled up together they sipped the bubbly he'd chilling in the fridge. Don told her about his brother Tony having been diagnosed with colon cancer, and about to have an exploratory operation.

'A Cooks tour' he called it. 'I knew something worried him when I visited, he didn't look good and then he kept nagging me to settle down like it's as easy as.... I told him I would work on it. He's Michelle's godfather and I think he had an attack of guilt. Beth arranged for Michelle to spend a week with them during the holidays. She had a ball. When I called her, she was buzzing. I shopped online, bought her a new phone for her birthday so I'm flavour of the month.' He seemed pleased with himself. Barbe felt she knew his family, though they had never met.

'Bebe, have you spoken to Hunter or the boys since the holidays?'

'No, but I didn't expect to,' then she told him about Simon Perry and his suggestion she apply for an annulment.

'Does he know they're as rare as rocking horse shit?' Don raked his hair.

'Well, he said he had been brought up Catholic.'

'Him and half of New Zealand,' he chipped.

'And he knows of Hunter,' she added watching the look on his face.

'Ah, the other half of the country. I don't mean to be cynical, but I don't want you to set your heart on this and then get mortally wounded when it doesn't happen.' He gently rubbed her arm in support.

'I understand what you're telling me, but I've given this a great deal of thought and no matter the outcome, I must try. I went into the marriage with honest expectations. If I had known or had the slightest inkling Hunter had this predilection, as you put it, I would never have married him in a million years. I don't understand it except I know it is not something you can choose. But you can choose to marry or not to marry. It's like infidelity, at the outset. Its rubbish to suggest if he abstains from sex with a man then he's cured.' Tired of trying to rationalize the situation, she simply wanted to distance herself from it. But it seemed impossible.

Don could see, 'Bebe, I think homosexual attraction is as compelling as alcoholism and just as dangerous for people like Hunter. Here we are in the twenty-first century. It's illegal to discriminate on the basis of sexuality. But if you are taught from childhood your natural instincts are wrong and deviant, and the people all around you, your family, can't accept what you are intrinsically drawn to and no matter how hard you try they simply will not allow you to be yourself, it must be bloody torture.'

Don felt sorry for Hunter, but it still annoyed him. Barbe continually defended him, even after his huge deception prevented him from loving her the way every wife wanted. He is such a good father, she would say. Don felt his own moniker of a shit father had probably been warranted. Putting those thoughts in his pocket he decided he would have fun this weekend and suggested they take in a show. Dressed casually for a Friday night dinner in an Indian restaurant he had the concierge desk recommend a live show and book the tickets for Saturday evening.

Sitting opposite him in the restaurant, Barbe had not laughed as much in years. He regaled her with stories of his early life as a police officer. She watched his charismatic smile grow before her eyes as he recounted how one of his team, a naïve young detective, literally shot himself in the foot while cleaning his weapon.

'A good case for following procedure' he quipped, adding, 'I choose only to remember the funny stuff.' Then he grinned, 'I got called to this pub fight. We are taught to run to a fire but walk to a fight, so I felt put out when it had turned into a brawl by the time I got there. Anyway, I got stuck in and cuffed this big dude who wanted to flatten me. I took him outside and cuffed him to the patrol car door. We were a bit short-staffed due to a nasty accident. I went back inside; tables and chairs were flying everywhere. I worried about my partner, a female officer, because I thought she might be pregnant. I pushed her into a cupboard and locked the door, then I shoved an overturned table against the door. Fortunately help arrived and as I dragged another couple of scrappers to the paddy wagon, I could hear my partner yelling at me from the cupboard. Outside I saw my big guy had gone and so had the back door to the patrol car.' She could just picture it his face told the story.

'My whole career flashed before my eyes. I imagined I'd be filling out forms and 'please explains' for years. Saturday night is always busy, and I had to get this lot I had in the wagon processed, swap cars and get back out on the street. The boys at the Station were giving me shit, I knew I would never hear the end of it. Someone else let my partner out of the cupboard and boy was she hot on me. I don't know why I did it except my ex was expecting Michelle at the time and I became overprotective towards Jenny, she could look after herself alright but still... Later we agreed she would tell me if she got pregnant. As luck would have it when I went back on the street several hours later, I saw this kid no more than eighteen or nineteen running along the road with a laptop under his arm. He practically ran into me. Naturally, we took him home to search his place and guess who I found tucked up fast asleep complete with patrol car door attached, yeah, his old man.' Don laughed and pointed to heaven, 'he had an eye on me.' Curious, Barbe asked what became of Jenny? 'Yeah well, she did eventually become pregnant. She and her husband were transferred away but we keep in touch. In fact, I'm godfather to their son,' he said, full of pride.

After dinner they walked around the streets, crowd watching, arms around each other, chatting about their families. 'Does Gillian like to cook?' she asked as he hesitated in front of a patisserie window full of sweet delicacies. He stood licking his lips, his hand patting his stomach, and she covered it with hers waiting for him to answer.

'Nah. A good cook is definitely on my list for next time,' he smirked. She ignored his remark watching his face light up. 'But Gill could order up the best takeaways ever,' he grinned at her asking, 'Hunter?'

'He wouldn't starve, but he's not flash. The boys tell me he's worse than boarding school. In fact, he's not domesticated according to him cooking is woman's work.'

'Ouch! I suppose he has someone clean his apartment too.'

'Not often enough according to Ryder who's a little more fastidious than Nicholas or their father,' she pouted, amused.

They arrived back at their hotel around ten thirty. While Barbe stood perusing the guests in the lobby lounge Don started chatting with a couple of staff working the front desk. In the lounge were a group of American guests, their loud voices sounded animated. Then she noticed it and shuddered as the memory came flooding back. She stood motionless, wondering how come she had forgotten such a vital piece of evidence. In the background she could hear Don's unique laugh, it sounded like his smile, special to him. Almost paralyzed she watched the Americans. Don joined her.

'The New Zealand economy has just taken a nosedive,' he advised, 'bloody All Blacks were trounced by the Aussies forty-six to sixteen,' his voice even but his eyes were smiling. He frowned.

'You okay Bebe?' She pointed to the Americans.

'What do you see there?' she asked. He realized this must be important.

'A bunch of half-pissed old soldiers probably Vietnam vets,' he said innocently.

She nodded half agreeing, 'Why Vietnam vets?' she wondered.

'Their accents, their age, their bearing, even their clothes and some are wearing military corps rings.' Frowning he wanted to know why she asked. Taking his arm, they walked towards the lift.

'Mr. Barker Nova wore a big ring like those men. I completely forgot. He had boney fingers too.' she bit her lip.

'How come you forgot such an important detail?' he said flabbergasted. She shrugged. He opened the door to their room and once inside locked it. Then took his phone from his pocket and googled English military rings.

Barbe looked over his shoulder as he sat on their bed.

'Why English military rings?' she asked. He told her it made sense if Barker Nova's were English, to start there. It soon became apparent the rings could be custom made, so he asked her to draw what she remembered. Struggling, she did draw one image he recognized, a grenade complete with flash. The symbol of the engineers. He decided to put it aside for the moment while he processed the information because he knew the only person, he knew who would be entitled to wear the engineers, emblem was Inspector Bill Powell. He and the son of a bitch were at each other's throats all the time. Don refused to believe the guy was bent. Bill, an older pom came from Scotland Yard to join the department in New Zealand. He did everything by the book. Barbe could see Don looked unsettled, seriously unsettled.

'I need to make this call in the bathroom.' He waved his phone, 'sorry its classified.' he shut the door. Barbe became concerned, he'd never been agitated before.

Don called Superintendent Tim Paxton at midnight New
Zealand time on a Friday night, as soon as the number started
ringing, he thought better of it and killed the call. This time he called
Frank Taylor.

'Frank, yeah, okay I know what time it is. I've just been talking
with Barbe Anderson, she remembered an important bit of
information. Mr. Barker Nova with the trouser cuffs and striped
socks, yeah him, he wore a military corps ring. I had her draw a
picture of it. It is a flaming grenade. She described the man's hands
too, long boney fingers. For chrissakes Frank, what the fuck was the
bloody Pommy smartarse doing spying on me because he was spying
on me, unless he's bent but he's too frigging anal to be bent.' Don
sighed.

'Don, let me talk and don't interrupt. The super has been
worried about your safety. He had Bill follow you just to keep you
safe, because he thought the Griffith Gang would set you up
especially after the big bust when the navy intercepted a huge cargo
of cocaine. Bill left the hotel seconds after you. He had literally been
in the men's room of the hotel foyer when Matua let off a volley of
shots. He called it in, but he never actually saw the shooter. As soon
as there were death threats against you and it became obvious Matua
had both you and Barbe Anderson in his sights, the team decided
you both had to go into hiding until Matua had been apprehended.
Bill had been recalled to Auckland and Shep and I took over. The
Super knows you and Bill irritate the snot out of each other. But you
are still on the same side.' Silence dragged on for a moment.

'Yeah, makes sense now. I thought he'd been breathing down my
neck a few times. You know what he's like a bloody glory seeker
always there at the kill. I should have worked it out. I mean Paxton
would never have told me, but you, you could have,' he accused
Frank.

'No, I couldn't, you know how it works,' Frank growled, knowing how fixated Don could be.

'At least you're in Tonga and Barbe Anderson's in Wellington. I know you're keen on her.' He heard a chuckle. 'No Frank I'm not, I'm not in Tonga I mean, I'm on leave and spending the weekend with Barbe, we're an item. Get used to it.' Don heard Frank suck in a deep breath.

'You enjoy living dangerously. I won't mention it, the Super would go ballistic if he knew.'

'Frank you better keep mum. It's after eleven here now so I'll ring you next week.'

Don felt a great deal happier when he came out of the bathroom.

'Have you seen the size of the shower in there?' Flashing her a sultry smile he said, 'let's christen it.' He took her in his arms and kissed her slowly. 'I've been dreaming about this for weeks.'

Chapter eighteen:

Having slept in they missed breakfast and decided to go for brunch later. The Sidney Morning Herald weighed a ton and came in about ten different weighty sections. Don fancied the crossword; the paper featured a whole page of them. The first few he got out in no time at all. The code cracker today drove him demented. Barbe had showered and shampooed her hair while he sat muttering about the crossword clues, until he became distracted watching her blow dry her hair in her hotel bathrobe. His phone pinged a text. *Dad its nearly noon and you haven't phoned me yet. M.* Immediately he called her.

'Hi sweetheart, sorry, forgot about the time difference. Whatcha doing this weekend? You're gunna watch the rugby? Is this your college first fifteen? Who are you going with? Well, you and Mia stick together. Who are they playing anyway? St. Benedicts,' he sat up 'aren't they a bit old for you? Yeah, I know they're the same age as your college, first fifteen. Still too old. So, the game's at your school. Why? Is the whole college going to be there? Does your mother know you're going to the movies afterwards? I'm not fussing, it's a dad thing. Okay, love you sweetheart.' He sat on the bed in his underpants, looking a bit flat.

'I used to be Daddy, now I'm Dad. I wonder how long until I'm the old man?' Hearing him talk about being an old man made her smile.

'You do realize she probably calls you various names but not to your face. Hurry up and get dressed. We're going to the Haymarket then China town and you said there's a gallery you want to check out.'

The day had been relaxing. The show, the musical of Muriel's Wedding, Barbe thought the characters were a bit hapless, but it seemed fun. She enjoyed it. They had decided to forgo dinner in favour of supper at their hotel room.

They walked back towards the hotel at almost nine forty-five. The city buzzed with excitement. It took several seconds for it to register with Don that the noise he heard had not been a car back firing, it sounded more like gun fire. Single shots but more than two. They had walked through a public car park and an open area across from a green space. There were several vehicles parked in the car park and he felt sure three shots had been fired. Don reacted instantly, pulling Barbe to the ground beside a parked car. He didn't need to tell her to pray, it came automatically for both of them.

'God help us, please' he said into her hair as he protected her body with his. There were several more shots and Don held Barbe firmly under him. No gun, no fucking gun, he could think of nothing else. Then he heard Police nearby calling to the shooters to drop their weapons. This time the exchange of fire went both ways. Vehicles were hit and bullets ricocheted around the area. The sound of metal and glass shattering could be heard as male voices shouted. They heard a pained shriek. Don realized he had called out in pain; he'd been hit in his left thigh. One shooter took off on foot, the others in a vehicle. They heard the screech of wheels and burning rubber then more gunshots. Don stayed on the ground with Barbe while the bizarre event played out. Then they lay still in the quiet blackness.

'Sir, police, can you get up sir, are you okay?' A bright torch shone on them. Don rolled off Barbe who scrambled to her feet, dusting off her knees as he replied,

'No, I'm not bloody okay, I've been shot.' Blood oozed steadily from the rip in his moleskins. Sirens could be heard in the distance getting closer all the time. Don reached for his ID and stopped when he heard the familiar click of a Glock.

'Okay officer, you get it out of my breast pocket, my ID. I'm a Detective Inspector in the New Zealand Police.' Barbe eyed the young officer, would he have shot Don? He looked so young, had he even left school? Fortunately, he was soon joined by an older grey-haired officer. The pair tried to help Don to his feet, but his injured leg buckled under him. Shortly an ambulance arrived and took them both to the hospital. The older police officer accompanied them. Don said nothing, taking Barbe's hand. He realized the gunfire had come from three different groups, the Police and one other group and a lone shooter who took off on foot.

'You witnessed a gang gun fight in the car park,' the officer quietly said.

Don asked, 'which gangs?' He knew it had only been one gang and one other person. He had been trained how to keep track of gunfire. The officer said he didn't know for sure which gang.

The doctors at the hospital x-rayed Don's leg. He had been lucky, only suffering a flesh wound. the bullet had sliced through his thigh.

'The way the bullets were bouncing around, I doubt whether they would have hit anything intentionally,' Don commented to the doctor who told them there had been one fatality. Barbe said nothing, simply holding Don's hand and listening. As the triage team cut the leg off Don's trousers, he didn't seem at all put out. In truth he'd been there a couple of times before. He'd been stabbed in the leg and the chest, but his stab proof vest had paid for itself, saving his life. This latest debacle had been more of an inconvenience; a painful inconvenience but it brought home the reality of what might have been. Fortunately, it had was only a flesh wound. The triage team cleaned him up, sutured and dressed his wound then discharged him without ever being admitted.

The police wanted him to go to the station for a statement. He told them he felt knackered, and they could wait until tomorrow, but they insisted. The doctor gave him some pain killers to take as required. After taking their statements the police dropped them off at their hotel and arranged to interview Don again the next day.

ONCE LOCKED INSIDE their hotel room Don held Barbe close.

'I think I've made a huge error of judgement, I'm sorry. I never intended to put either of us in the firing line.'

'What are you saying?' she didn't understand.

'I believe somebody knows we are here. What better way to get rid of both of us and make it look like a freak accident?' Holding his face in her hands she looked up at him, recognizing his angst.

'My darling Adonis,' she grinned, trying to lighten his mood. 'Don't blame yourself, technically you are in Tonga. If the police thought, it so dangerous for me to be here why did they not warn me?' Gently he bent to kiss her, his tongue teasing hers. She deepened the kiss.

'You are a very clever woman. I realize I'm in love with you. I could never imagine life without you. The answer is they didn't know we were here, until... yesterday.'

He took out his cell phone and called the only person who truly knew what was going on. Don put the call on speaker and sat on their bed with Barbe next to him.

'Frank, are you alone?'

'No, I've just arrived at the office, at two a.m. thanks to you and the Australian Federal Police. The only other person who knows what's happening is the Superintendent here.' The echo of Frank being on speaker disguised the fact Don was also on speaker phone.

'What the fuck do you think you're playing at Lancini?' the superintendent bellowed. 'I should bust your arse back to polyester blue. The Anderson woman, are you shagging her? It's a rhetorical question, of course you are. How could you be so fucking stupid, compromising this investigation? You know this is bigger than bloody Mr. Asia.' Barbe sat listening in silence. She could practically taste the venom in Tim Paxton's voice.

'Sir, the only error of judgement I made was in thinking that on my leave I could see whomever I please. I didn't need your permission, just because I met somebody special, a woman I care about. As far as I knew Matua was dead, until Frank told me yesterday. If you didn't treat me like a bloody mushroom, I wouldn't have put my arse on the line, or hers. As it is, we're holed up in a hotel room and I've got another bloody hole in my thigh.' Don sounded frustrated. 'I did nothing to compromise this investigation Sir, you know I would never turn up to a fire fight without Horace or Gaston.' It was a standing joke; Don called his pistols by the christian names of their inventors. 'So how come Matua's goons know I'm on their home turf?' Nobody spoke. The silence stretched out for a good thirty seconds.

'Buggered if I know Don,' Frank commented. 'The chief and I are here trying to figure out where the leak might be coming from.'

Don wracked his brains. He told them to look at everyone who had anything to do with him or Barbe.

'Don, you are not alone by the way. Check the peep hole in your door, there are two armed officers outside your room. Phone us again in the morning.' Don agreed and killed the call. He and Barbe sat in silence looking at each other.

'How's your leg?' she asked. He stripped off telling her it felt fine, and he needed to road test everything to be on the safe side. She smiled, knowing him well. Instead, he took some blank paper from the hotel compendium and quickly wrote a list of names. He sat, studying the list, staring at the names. Slowly he crossed off various ones until three remained and then around one name, Hellen Couch, he put a big circle.

'Go to sleep Bebe. I need to do this. I won't sleep till I know who I'm dealing with.' Suffering a kind of delayed shock, Barbe lay down between the sheets and tried to sleep. It felt comforting having him sitting there close to her even if he seemed a million miles away in his mind. Eventually she drifted off. Don quietly eased off the bed. Then from the bathroom he called Frank in New Zealand.

'This may be nothing, but I've had reason to tick young Detective Hellen Couch off on several occasions. Just for being a slack arse. What do you know about her? loose lips sink ships. She seems to know a hell of a lot of gossip about various criminals.' Frank said he'd do a background check in case something had changed since she joined the CIB.

'We're desperate, everyone is squeaky clean as far as we can see, but it doesn't take much. This is New Zealand, everybody knows somebody who knows somebody else,' Frank trailed off.

'Yeah, but let's be honest, we don't mix socially in criminal circles so we're just getting intel second hand from untrustworthy sources.' Don had hardly finished his sentence when Frank emitted an expletive.

'Hellen Couch's husband works for corrections at a senior level. The file doesn't say what he does exactly but rubbing shoulders with scumbags everyday could he be a step closer to finding out stuff. No wonder she gets some good gossip. I'll dig deeper and get back to you as soon as I have something.' When Don returned to bed Barbe up.

Don claimed to be starving, and suggested they get some food sent up. To his surprise the first edition of The Australian came hot off the press and accompanied their meal. Accepting the food, he acknowledged the two officers outside their door and with an exaggerated limp he accepted the tray and once again locked their door. On the front page he read a couple of paragraphs referring to the shooting in the carpark as, 'an altercation between rival gangs, with one person shot dead.'

'More fake news, is it?' she asked.

Don quickly replied. 'It's the truth this time, but it didn't mean they knew what they were talking about,' he laughed and turned straight to the crossword. Barbe noted he took more pain killers and after several cups of tea they snuggled down to sleep this time.

Chapter Nineteen:

Downtown in the offices of the Federal Police Don felt comfortable, knowing they would never have been allowed to move out of the hotel had it been dangerous. Detective Inspector Mike Carney shook Don's hand and greeted Barbe.

'If we'd known you were visiting us, we'd have been better prepared. Your customs declaration said civil servant.'

'My passport number should have been enough for your security; well, it would be in New Zealand.' Don needed to get a dig in about being more efficient than the Australians after the All-Blacks epic defeat.

'Let's not go there Mr. Lancini. In this matter we are both on the same side. The good news is the deceased from the shooting is Matua's girlfriend.' The cogs in Don's brain took a bit of cranking up.

'Hang on I thought Matua was gay.' Bloody Aussie humour. 'Well, the guy's not called Roxie Lawless.' Mike Carney, the comedian looked to be a man in his late forties. Under different circumstances they could be good mates.

'You taking the piss, officer?' Don's leg had been giving him gyp. 'What's the name on his passport, the name he used to enter New Zealand?' His patience now wearing thin.

'Constantine Marcos, the same guy who ID'd a certain handless corpse as Matua and gave you the DNA of the killed -to -order dude complete with the spiderweb tattoo.' Listening, Don sucked air in through his clenched teeth. Mike Carney went on, 'these people mean business and until we wrap up this investigation, you two will need to be placed in protection.' Barbe gasped.

Don grabbed her hand and squeezed it; he could see the emotion flooding her face. Having been there before, he reassured her 'the Police on both sides of the Tasman, and Interpol, are all working to accelerate this investigation.'

Looking him straight in the eye Barbe pragmatically pointed out, 'this could change things between us.' She ignored Mike Carney and the other Federal Officers around the room.

'Not if we refused to allow it,' Don said, about to elaborate when Mike Carney added.

'We're going to split you up to make things harder for whoever wants you out of the way.' Don still held Barbe's hand and squeezed it again.

'Over my dead body. We're an item, family, sorry mate but it's not happening.' He stuck his chin out and pursed his lips. Mike Carney's irritation bubbled to the surface.

'I hope your remark isn't a Freudian slip, mate, because over your dead body is exactly what they planned.'

'I take my orders from New Zealand, Superintendent Tim Paxton. Let me talk to him – in private.' Somebody handed Don a land line which he pushed away. 'Barbe stays with me. Give us alone please.' They cleared the room and Don stood up in pain rubbing his knee.

'Bebe, stick to me like glue I don't trust the Aussies.' Punching the Super's name in the speed dial of his cell phone, he waited. 'Super, did you know the Australians want us in witness protection? You did? When were you gunna tell me?' He raked his fingers through his hair, frustrated. This would be his worst nightmare.

'We're coming home. I'll get legal advice. You're putting me under undue pressure, I don't need this, Sir.' He complained. the muscles in his jaw twitched, he looked ropable. 'No Sir, I would never put her in danger, Barbe's safety is paramount. Why can't we come home?' He barely got the words out before he had worked it out, 'your gunna keep this from Matua and the rest of New Zealand, aren't you? I get it. Well, there is no reason to split us up. Surely, we can just be holed up out bush somewhere?' Barbe watched Don's face, trying to glean something, anything.

'I know we aren't married Sir. Is marriage your gold standard in these cases now?' Tim Paxton didn't answer for a few seconds. 'Okay you organize it with the Aussies for me to be issued with some personal protection, Gaston G.' He turned to Barbe, 'Bebe, get the goons in here. Paxton wants a word.'

Only a matter of hours later Don and Barbe were airborne in a small four-seater Cessna heading in a north westerly direction over the Blue Mountains to beyond the black stump. It looked like late afternoon when they finally landed at a remote property somewhere in the Australian outback. Don had noted a small town about fifty kilometres back. He felt sure the plane had done a complete three sixty as the crow flies, because the sun had been on their left at the start and now it shone on their right. They hadn't done as many kilometres as it appeared. The pilot told them the property they were headed to was called Home Valley Station; the name told them nothing. At the Station air strip, they were met by a bandy-legged stockman name of Jamie who drove them to the station settlement - of a couple of dwellings and a number of outbuildings. Jamie helped with their luggage and gave them a landline number.

'No cell coverage out here, mate. If yer need anything just use the landline phone. Someone will answer. Linda will come and see ya later.' Don thanked him and Jamie left.

The house appeared to be no more than a small wooden cottage, a good few hundred metres away from the main homestead. The black painted front door opening divided the small area in two, dining and living. A pot belly stove appeared to be the only heating. Don opened the door of the pot belly, commenting that the fire had been set. A good size bedroom at one end housed an average size double bed, with an adjoining toilet, shower, and vanity. In the dining end of the living room sat a small rustic oblong table and four director's chairs. The back featured a small kitchen and laundry area.

Checking the fridge Don sighed, the contents offended his Mediterranean roots; margarine, plastic looking over-processed cheese, no wine, sliced thick white bread and a plastic bottle of homogenized milk. No fresh greens, no tomatoes- he never kept tomatoes in the fridge anyway. A great lump of red meat and some anaemic looking sausages. Outside the front door stood a single veranda with two comfy-looking chairs and a small table. The whole structure elevated on the nub of a hill looking down towards a substantial homestead. The living area housed three pieces of nondescript furniture; an 'L' shaped grey lounger in segmented pieces, one coffee table and a bookcase. A wall mounted television dominated the whole room. Barbe said nothing, relieved it looked clean and smelled fresh. She noticed the only piece of art in the entire place appeared to be an old Pears soap poster of a little girl and her foxy dog circa 1900's set a thick wooden frame. Don caught her eye.

'I'm sorry' he said.

'What for? What passes as art or getting me into this mess? You're not responsible for this that. I quite like the nostalgia of the poster. I always wanted one,' she said wistfully.

'Poster or dog?' Don said curious.

'No, I always wanted to have a daughter. I love my boys but a little girl ...' she sighed.

'Been there done that, I'm too bloody old...' A sudden thought struck him 'Oh Lord this is a conversation we haven't had, you're on the pill, aren't you?' panic stricken.

'No, but don't panic I think I'm probably past it too. Peri menopausal symptoms, got the curse this morning, first time in months.' She said embarrassed. He usually took care of contraception.

'We'll just have to pray...' Hearing him say those words she burst into laughter.

'Adonis, a Catholic praying his sins do not find him out is an oxymoron.' She grinned and he pulled a wry face.

'Catholicism is a culture and we're all sinners.' An interesting concept, she had felt constrained by the patriarchy of the church, men dictating the terms. She had no say and often felt undervalued. Sitting down on the lounger she felt powerless.

'You know growing up, my parents encouraged me to pray for a good husband and I did religiously, for years.' Don watched the pain in her expression. 'Technically I got one, but I was not good enough for him to love me.' She shrugged, she knew he did love her but define love, he had not been capable of husbandly love with a woman.

'Bebe, I love you you're my forever woman. The Church has got to get its act together and get into the twenty first century.' He pulled her close enveloping her in his arms. 'We're going to make the best of this time together. I'll get us some food. You're a list writing woman, go for it, After dinner we'll plan our time.' He kissed her lovingly. 'Tell me what your goals and aspirations are, oh, and the conversations we should have.' he rubbed his thigh, it ached.

'Okay, but you will have to do it too,' she told him.

After a feast of bangers and mash, 'needs must' he told her. 'The only tomato I could find happened to be tomato sauce.' Don wrote two lists; one a shopping list the other a 'to do list' with his goals and proposed conversations.

Chapter Twenty:

F rank Taylor and Tim Paxton had discovered Detective Hellen Couch had been married at one time to a senior corrections officer based at Tararua Prison. Her new partner, also something at corrections and Hellen had friends at numerous prisons throughout the country. For various reasons there is always movement of prisoners between the prisons. Like cops, prison officers gossiped. Some of them also had legitimate relationships of sorts with prisoners, dealing with their needs, remand prisoners as well as convicted prisoners. Frank felt convinced the leaks were haphazard, unintentional leaks which had escalated. Tim had been less convinced.

'They know the things they learn in the execution of their duty must be strictly kept inhouse. So why would you give your husband or partner information meant to stay in-house. Were they swapping information for ultimate financial gain? Corrections and Police are two different departments. What we need to do is leak some information not in the public arena and see where it goes.' They decided to bring up the fact, Carlos Matua's partner Constantine Marcos had been killed in a gunfight in Sydney at the weekend. They talked about the fact Barbe Anderson and Don Lancini were there too. Both agreed it would add more to the story if they casually mentioned Don had been shot in the same incident. Both agreed to leave Barbe out of it because she was a civilian. Superintendent Tim Paxton decided,

'I'll deliver the news after prayers (their daily meetings) on Monday, when the others have gone, and Hellen Couch will be the only one present with you and me.' Tim planned to stress this police business they discussed should stay inhouse and between them. After they laid the bait, they simply needed to wait.

Frank needed to inform Hunter Anderson his ex-wife was in police protection in New South Wales. He phoned Hunter who realized that at noon on a Sunday the police did not make social calls. Hunter suggested Frank call at forty-three Latta Crescent, Kelburn where he and his sons were home this weekend. When Frank arrived, Hunter ushered him into the formal living room, one of the very few times it had been used in months. Calling to Ryder he asked him to make them a coffee.

'What's happened? Detective' he wanted to know thinking it maybe something to do with his client, Matty Thomas.

'Mrs. Anderson has been involved in a shooting in a carpark in downtown Sydney last night. She's fine' he added hastily, 'but the detective with her copped a bullet.' Hunter processed the information in silence.

'You had a detective protecting her in Sydney?'

Frank gulped, shit trust Hunter to get to the crux of the matter. 'We never planned it, but she has once again been lucky, the detective took the hit protecting her.' Frank didn't want to get into this, did he need to know? He is her ex.

'Well, how did you plan it? Did you know she would be in danger in Australia?' He cross examined the detective. Frank couldn't lie, Hunter Anderson would never trust him again. 'We had no idea she was in Sydney; she had been working there for a few days apparently. But you would know her work schedule Sir.'

'Where did your detective fit in to this scenario?' Hunter asked curtly while Frank sat in silence wondering how to tell him and cursing Don Lancini for landing him in this invidious position. In came Ryder with the coffees. Hunter held up his hand to stay Frank from speaking in front of his young son.

'Thanks Ryder, you can go and play Fortnite, Detective Taylor and I have business.' Hearing the magic word Fortnite uttered, the boy didn't need to be told twice.

'Are the detective and my wife...?' Hunter seemed clearly surprised and annoyed.

'I don't know any details; you'd need to ask your wife Sir. I mean ex-wife and it is clearly her business you know. How many years is it since you divorced?' Frank did not appear at all surprised by the miffed expression on Hunter's face. You did not cross this man, but they were divorced, why couldn't he let go? Now Frank could feel how annoying it must be for Don and Barbe. Hunter poured their coffee, his peeved expression giving way to hurt.

'When we had a drink a few weeks ago, I told you I had holiday hopes,' he gave Frank a conspiratorial look, 'there has never been another woman for me. I love Barbe, always will.' Passing a mug of coffee to Frank he asked, 'what's he like, this man?' Frank sat stunned; the guy had a softer, vulnerable side. The blokes Frank knew didn't talk about their feelings.

'He's a good man, Don Lancini, well liked and a good copper.' Perhaps he'll finally let her go, Frank wondered.

'Lancini, does he have a brother?' Frank nodded 'I went to school with a Tony Lancini, possibly his brother. Shot you say is he all, right?' he sounded concerned.

'Fortunately, just a flesh wound; they're both in a safe house till the Australians have finished their investigation.' Frank watched Hunter's expression change, barely disguising his anger, they finished their coffee and Frank left, adding 'The department needs you to keep this strictly between us. The cover story is simply she is back in protective custody, no details.' Hunter agreed. He knew only too well how dangerous it could be for her.

AS DON AND BARBE SAT down to discuss their lists, a knock sounded at the door. Don opened it.

'Hi, I'm Linda,' the tall blonde woman introduced herself. 'I'm a profiler with the Federal Police, on maternity leave at present and this is my husband's family farm.' Don invited her in and introduced himself and Barbe. 'If there's anything you'd like just let me know.' He handed her the shopping list which she perused.

'Cripes you'll be lucky; I'll do my best. The local supermarket is getting better but...' Barbe offered her a cup of tea. 'Thanks, great. I believe you two are a couple.' She frowned waiting for them to elaborate.

'Yes, both divorced with kids. We haven't moved in together formally, if you understand,' Don said with candour. 'It's all very new so having to hide out is a bit of a strain.' Barbe handed her a mug of tea. 'Milk? How old is your infant?' she asked, curious.

'Seven months, our daughter is just seven months. I agreed to do some work from home I still have a few months maternity leave. Then my mother will mind Jacinda while I work. Mum lives quite near the office in town and Gavin's family live down the road. As far as the locals go, I'm just a civil servant.' Linda smiled.

'Thank you for allowing us to use your cottage.' Don felt relieved now he knew some of their host's details.

'Pleasure's mine and they do pay me for my trouble, so don't feel indebted to me.'

'I still do actually, and I'd love to meet your daughter, bring her down some time.' Barbe fizzed, loving the idea of having a cuddle with Linda's baby. 'I need to dress Don's leg tomorrow. Do you have a first aid kit?' Don flashed his charismatic smile and Linda left armed with his shopping list, saying her husband would drop off the first aid supplies tomorrow morning.

'Bebe, what would you like to do tomorrow?' Facetiously she answered him teasing him with her face about two inches from his.

'After a trip to the beauty parlor and a bit of shopping, I'd like to take in a movie and then find a new personal trainer and get an exercise regimen and if you're lucky I'll cook you a gourmet meal after I've had a long soak in a very warm tub.'

Without missing a beat, he replied,

'Gee you're good at this game. Only three things we can't arrange, the beauty parlor, shopping, and the soak in the tub, it's a shower. The rest is doable' he smirked.

'Your list is so long, I only have three things on my list; breakfast in bed, a back massage and someone to read to me something of my choosing.'

'What about the conversations?' she asked as he pulled a silly face while combing his fingers through his hair. Something troubled him. He always did the hair thing when he had something on his mind. She had been right being locked, away together like this felt difficult.

Thoughts of her boys continually filled her with anxiety. Not so much her job when push came to shove a job is a job, but Nicholas was at a difficult age and could so easily become anti his mother. Ryder would fret, he sensed things and what would Hunter say to them, how much would they be told, 'your mother has been meeting a man in her hotel room in Sydney, and he spent the weekend with her.' Great role model. To Barbe's surprise she helped Don,

'Let's set some ground rules because this situation of us being locked away together has the potential to go either way. Also, we have no idea how long it will last.'

He agreed, 'Until we've covered just about everything, we'll have a state of the nation meeting daily at lunch time, taking turns at picking the topic or question. Just thirty minutes max. I hate bloody meetings; thirty minutes and we both get to have our say. What do you think?' This man loved to talk; he seemed so much chattier than anyone she had ever met.

'Interesting, it sounds like marriage counselling. We never bothered with counselling.' She gathered up the tea things.

'Neither did we, but we never talked, like you and I do. I would have been lucky to get a text telling me to pick up some milk. If I did get one, it went like 'you've used all the milk. You selfish git,' he put on a high-pitched harpy voice and had her laughing again.

The things Don referred to as the hard conversations came more easily than either of them thought. Often, they agreed a certain position but came at it from different angles, politics being a case in point. They were both right wing, Barbe had caught things from her civil servant father who had been kind but quite conservative. He believed in a hand up but not a handout. He told her, 'Educate the mothers and the children will follow, encourage business with incentives so they will provide work for others. We can't all be the boss, and everyone has a place in the scheme of things, but they must know their place. Don't feel sorry for the poor state of public schooling in this country. For generations, we Catholics, have paid school fees in order to maintain the unique character of our Catholic education and it has been a struggle for many families. If those thousands of children suddenly landed in the state system, it couldn't cope. The Government should subsidize our schools, for generations we have effectively been taxed because of our religion.'

'Of course, my father said this years ago, it's different now for my boys. But we still pay fees and not just for boarding,' Barbe explained.

Don's view of politics seemed conservative. He believed in law enforcement and justice for all. His view was people needed to be responsible for themselves and learn to live within their means. People shouldn't expect the nanny state to take care of their every need. They should stand on their own two feet and thrift and good business should be rewarded.

When they had these hard conversations, which included everything from global warming to consumerism, the 'me too' movement and euthanasia, nothing between them had been taboo. Don acknowledged Barbe seemed softer than him, but Don believed women were meant to have a softer side. They were the nurturers.

As the days turned into weeks, Barbe became fitter and less strung out under Don's fitness regimen. He began to realize there is more to life than work, enjoying the simple pleasures of cooking together. Their routines and daily rituals became enhanced by their dreams of a future together. His leg healed and Barbe removed the sutures. Every day she read him something from the selection of old books in the bookcase. They discussed each piece of writing as they reviewed the work and the writer's intentions. Slowly they learned each other's little idiosyncrasies.

Linda had explained her mother, a teacher, had ensured her love of the classics and good literature which included some Australian writers such as Banjo Patterson, Colleen McCulloch, and Morris West. The ex-Catholic priest's stories they found interesting. Some heated discussions ensued, but their shared values and interests meant they were discussions not arguments.

In the evening they sometimes played board games and cards, but Don usually won at cards. His memory for the cards played seemed phenomenal. He teased Barbe mercilessly when some native Australian scared her, like a blue tongued lizard or a spider. Mostly they had fun together and enjoyed each other's company.

A couple of times Barbe looked after little Jacinda while Linda worked from home and her husband worked out on the farm. Don watched her lovingly care for the child and he remembered his own little girl at the same age and wondered where the years had gone. His love of the urbane would never fit with farming in Australia, however, he helped out on the property once or twice. his love of food and gardening ensured he would be missed by Linda's family who watched delighted as a kitchen garden took shape.

Then one afternoon around five, Linda came and told them tomorrow they would be going back to Sydney.

Chapter twenty-One:

E ach had an acute feeling the worst might be yet to come as they packed their bags. Linda advised them to wait until their debrief before contacting the outside world when they reached Sydney. Detective Inspector Mike Carney of the Australian Federal Police gave them an overview of events in the last month.

'The Griffith gang has morphed into several other groups after Carlos Matua's death whilst in prison in New Zealand. Nobody is likely to be charged with the killing. It was made to look like suicide. The Office of the Ombudsman has furnished the coroner with a report. The findings are still to be presented. It looks like there is insufficient evidence to do anything.'

Don felt completely detached from the proceedings. When he learned Constantine's death as a result of 'death by cop' in the carpark weeks before had apparently put down to the police defending two innocent civilians caught in the crossfire of a gang fight, he couldn't believe what he heard. A phone call to Superintendent Tim Paxton advised him he'd been replaced in Tonga and his luggage and personal effects had been sent home. He was instructed to report to HQ for a debriefing and then he could have some leave.

Barbe phoned her boss Ricard Beauchene, who felt relieved to learn of her safe return. He said he had been in touch with her lawyer Simon Perry and given him some background information,

'Just what Hunter told me. DSS Frank Taylor has been in touch too.' Feeling redundant Barbe insisted she come to Auckland for the staff meeting and get back to work. 'Only when you're ready.' he said adamantly.

'Term break is just a month away and there is much to be done before then,' Barbe told him

On their flight back to Wellington their apprehension became palpable. Don watched as Barbe sat knitting. Linda had supplied the materials as she didn't knit and Barbe offered to make some cardigans for Jacinda. He sat thinking, cripes I hope she's not clucky or nesting. We just skimmed over the 'babies' conversation, both saying they were too old. Plenty of women have babies at forty and plenty of men father babies at forty-six. He relegated those thoughts to the less visited parts of his mind. Barbe had simply thought she better get the garments finished and posted because she would soon be too busy.

Coming into land at Wellington, Don watched as Barbe sat chewing her lip. Covering her hand with his he whispered. 'Don't fret Bebe, we're together on this, side by side we'll do it.' Don knew Barbe had put off the uncomfortable situations in her life and just been pushed along by the events and then became unhappy with the results. Their 'hard conversations' went so well Don didn't understand why she had put up with Hunter's rigid terms and conditions for their divorce settlement. Still, he'd fix her situation.

They had not even passed Customs when she received a text from Simon Perry, *please skype me after hours and text first to check time is right, SP.*

In the taxi on the way to Latta Crescent both felt a little awkward.

'You sure you're okay with this Bebe?' She sighed.

'Well, we need to get a place of our own. We can't very well move in with your mum. Does she even know about us?' Don knew he had put his job ahead of his life. He had rented out his house to cover expenses. Frankly it needed to be refurbished according to his construction entrepreneur brother, Tony.

Carla Lancini, the matriarch of the family, knew nothing of her baby boy's new love. Also, they needed to consider Hunter. As far as he was concerned 43 Latta Crescent had been the matrimonial home he owned it and he provided for his family to live there. Hunter always got what he wanted.

'We'll regroup at my place, then you can go to Headquarters while I get dinner. After dinner we can skype Simon Perry together.' She advised him. Thinking about his debrief at HQ began to cause Don some anxiety, plus he would have to deal with her ex.

'Bebe, we should have the conversation with Hunter tonight, too.' The look she shot him said it all, another tough conversation. Why did life have to be this hard, he wondered? Thinking about their time in hiding at Linda's family farm, it had turned out to be something special. This time would be too, once they had everything out in the open.

At Latta Crescent, Barbe became furious when she let them in. Hunter had never been a housekeeper and the place looked like a bomb had gone off. Shoes, clothes, sports gear and take-away boxes littered the rooms. Dishes filled the sink and covered the benches.

'If I didn't know better, I'd swear he already knows about us and this mess is just defiance,' she harrumphed. 'He couldn't even turn the dishwasher on.' She had no sooner put on the jug to make a hot drink and Hunter called on the landline.

'Barbe, how are you? I intended to send Mrs. Nelson over to clean before you returned, but they just told me you were back in the country already.' He sounded like it was a very minor thing, but not to Barbe, it was a big house to keep clean. She pressed the speaker so Don could hear their conversation.

'I'm not impressed, I could do without this mess right now. The boys don't leave this mess when I'm home. I can't cope with this on top of everything else.' Barbe's voice terse, a long silence stretched out before Hunter cleared his throat.

'Barbe, I need to talk with you... alone.'

Don wrote on the on the phone pad, arrange it for after we have skyped your lawyer.

'Okay, tonight, but I need to skype Auckland first, so I know what's happening.' She knew he would think she was talking about work.

'You phone me as soon as you're done, and I'll drive over.' He sounded miffed and hung up.

'Take no notice of him wanting to talk alone, he obviously knows, so he can deal with it.' Don sat up on a stool at the island bench. 'I could buy an apartment or a townhouse, and then, when everything is settled, we could find our forever home.' This sounded like another conversation they had never really had. 'I'm not completely irresponsible with money. It's never been my number one motivator. I loaned my brother money to expand his company a few years ago and I didn't want interest just shares in his company. We do have a legal agreement. I should have bought another place but I'm rarely home.'

Impressed with his honesty and his simplicity Barbe walked around to him and put her arms around his neck.

'Adonis, I'm not concerned about money. Simon Perry reassured me I would be okay, and he's meant to be the country's top divorce lawyer. Ricard told me Simon's itching to take on Hunter if he gets difficult with me.' She kissed him, drinking in his special fragrance. He responded, leaving her in no doubt he wanted her as he hungrily deepened the kiss. Gently she pushed him back. 'The thing is, I've never challenged Hunter on anything until now.'

TIM PAXTON SAT WAITING for Don to arrive. All things considered he seemed surprisingly pleasant. The Superintendent claimed the team were grateful for Don's input into the investigation. Most of the loose ends were now tied up.

'Naturally, the war on drugs particularly amphetamine is ongoing and reaching epidemic proportions in some places. You may be required to give evidence in the Matty Thomas case. It would simply be about the background drug trade in Tonga and the tip-off leading to the Navy intercepting the Indonesian fishing vessel and finding the cargo of amphetamines. But then again, you may not be called.'

Don sat quietly listening and to his surprise, the Superintendent actually apologized for any offence he'd caused when he referred to the association between him and Barbe.

'I felt concerned about the fiduciary relationship. I know bonds can develop in these situations. Fair enough you were both free adults on your own time in Sydney, but this business is bigger than you. You'll be required to have counselling or at least a psych test. We can't have a claim of PTSD down the track because we didn't follow protocol. Particularly, now you're up for promotion. But we'll get the medical and psych tests completed first.'

Don sat there amazed. He had just been given a slap on the wrist with a wet bus ticket and now he's going to be promoted.

'I'd like a change of scene Sir. Anything on offer?' In for a penny in for a pound.

'Funny you should ask; we have an opening in the ISG (international service groups) in the Pacific again.'

'No thanks, I'm talking here at home in the Investigation section. No hurry, I have another option I'm considering.' He thought. Well, I will be now; I don't need the aggro. 'Training or investigations, they interest me.' The pair chatted and Don asked, 'what became of the internal investigation into the leak? Did you find anything?'

Tim stood up and gazed out of the window admiring the Wellington skyline from his tenth-floor office.

'You were right in one matter and wrong in another. We had a leak, Hellen Couch, and her partner with their pillow talk. Trouble is they were both as bad as one another. She gave us prison gossip which at times had been useful. In turn she gave her partner, and her husband over the years, police information. She is only a detective, but her ex-husband is something in the chief executive's office of the prison service. Her partner is a senior warden. We fed the story about Marcos Constantine being shot dead and you also being shot. Whether it was careless talk or not, Carlos Matua knew about it within forty-eight hours. He became distressed, disruptive and a general pain in the arse. Three weeks later, they found him dead in his cell. There were several breaches of protocol apparently. We didn't put the hard word on Hellen Couch until Matua had been found dead. She freely admitted telling her partner. Hellen knew she had been responsible for the leak because she had been the only person we told about Marcos Constantine. We told none of the other staff members. She'll be disciplined if she doesn't resign before. It looked sloppy, however, there appeared to be no intent to commit a crime. As I said pillow talk between two gossips, sloppy policing and potentially dangerous.' The pair chatted along those lines and Don suggested,

'DSS Taylor could easily run my team Sir. As you will have seen over the past few months, he's the ideal person for the role. Don noticed the wry expression Tim Paxton gave him as he left.

'Your car's in our car park below,' the young detective constable gave him the keys. 'Pleased to have you back Sir. How's your leg, you're not limping?' she observed responding to his infectious smile.

'All healed, thank you Detective. I had a great nurse.' He didn't even flinch, he knew the bush telegraph had been working and he would not deny the truth. 'DSS Taylor about?' He thought he'd catch up with Frank.

'He's gone for the day Sir, it's after six.' Don sighed and bid the young woman good evening. He could see Frank Taylor would be better in the job than him. Frank understood work-life balance.

Arriving back at Latta Crescent he phoned Barbe who opened the gates and the garage door. He looked around him impressed. Order had been restored to the interior of the house and the glorious smell of tasty food cooking welcomed him.

'What's cooking?' he smelled the air.

'Guess.' She grinned, putting the final touches to the creme custard for her Neapolitan pastry.

'Are you sure your Baba wasn't Italian?'

He nuzzled her neck as she stood stirring the custard.

'No, I told you she came from the Dalmatian coast, not too far from Italy as the crow flies. My mother is there at present, her sister still lives there.'

His reply sounded like a deep groan.

'Mmm.'

After dinner Barbe cleared the table as Don sat, motionless, hand on his stomach.

'Bebe,' he whispered. 'Don't ever cook your lasagna again, please because I'm in danger of not fitting into my flash suits,' he slowly took her hand then his trademark smile evinced itself.

'Believe me, I loved my Nonna's lasagna too. The only problem is my childhood photos prove it. Boy, your lasagna tasted so good.' He pulled her towards him 'thank you.' He gave her a look of pure love and she trembled with delight.

Don made coffee while Barbe set up her laptop on the dining table. Simon Perry sat ready to skype.

'Evening Mrs. Anderson.' From the look of his room, he appeared to be still in his office.

'Call me Barbe, please' she insisted. He nodded in agreement, telling her he had studied the file and already made representations to Hunter on her behalf.

'He is bound to want to discuss this with you and cut me out of the loop. Don't sign anything and don't be bullied. Discuss it by all means. Remember you are entitled to stay in the family home until Ryder turns sixteen, but whether you want to do that is another matter. Your situation is somewhat unusual.' A noisy clinking of coffee things sounded as Don set down a tray on the table behind the laptop, out of range of the camera.

'Are you not alone?' he seemed surprised.

'No, Don is here with me. Don meet Simon Perry.' Don moved around the table to stand behind Barbe who pulled out a chair for him.

'Don Lancini,' he introduced himself. Things appeared awkward for a moment, then Simon Perry gathered his thoughts.

'Good to meet you Don, er have you moved in or are you just visiting?' The man shot from the hip. Don liked him.

'No, I haven't moved in, but I'm staying over. Is it a problem? Simon raised his eyebrows.

'Not for me it's not, but it will be for Hunter, I'm sure.' Tough titty he'll have to get used to the idea.

'I don't know how much you've been told. I've been on deployment in Tonga and my house is rented out. I plan on getting something short term, we want to look for our forever home in due course.' As Don spoke, Simon nodded in understanding.

'Good, because Hunter might not accept you being there when his boys come home from boarding school.' Simon watched the pair together and noted Don seemed quite unafraid to show his feelings, touching Barbe's arm and smiling at her affectionately.

'I understand what you're saying, but in his case, it may be the pot calling the kettle black. What I hope, is Barbe will move in with me, and Hunter can have his home back. Surely, a trust to which he is the sole beneficiary is hardly an equitable arrangement as a family home, especially in light of the fact Barbe had fewer options than he did. It was never a marriage of equals. He saw to it. I'm sure the family court would see it, too.' Don needed Simon to know he was serious.

'I can see you've read the document.'

Don told him he had then he went on to say, 'did Barbe tell you she had to use her inheritance to keep afloat and to maintain this place in the years when she couldn't work?' Surprised, Simon said she hadn't told him.

'Are you familiar with Catholic Marriage?' Simon asked Don.

'If you mean Catholic annulment, I know they're as rare as rocking horse shit, I told Barbe. I'm divorced but as a Catholic who never married in the church, it's not something I have to contend with. I'll support Barbe in whatever she wants to do in this situation. I agree with your comments, the circumstances are not common and please God the church sees it the same way.' Simon Perry smirked at hearing Don's words. Spoken like a true lapsed Catholic he thought, Don stood up and excused himself and taking his mug of coffee left them to speak in private.

Simon commented, 'he cares about you' and Barbe agreed.

'It's mutual.' Then she went on to say Hunter wanted to talk to her in private tonight.

'Do you think you can handle him? I'm not saying the man is a bully, but he definitely has a way about him.' Barbe let out a bit of a chortle, saying Don agreed and he would be present. Simon asked what he did in the police. Barbe told him what she knew, then Simon felt sure Don could defuse any escalation of tension.

'Have the discussion and get to the nuts and bolts. It's not called 'splitting the sheets' for nothing.' Barbe appeared horrified but agreed to speak with Simon again the next day.

Hunter arrived fifteen minutes after she called him. he used his electronic gate opener and then his garage opener only to find a strange car in his park or what he perceived to be his car park. Leaving his black Mercedes four-wheel drive parked in front of the garage he wandered through, annoyed, yet somehow a little apprehensive too.

'Barbe,' he called as he strode down the hall walking towards the family living area. Barbe pushed aside her laptop and Don busied himself making more coffee. Hunter stood for a few seconds surveying the domestic scene.

'Don,' Barbe called to him, 'this is Hunter' immediately Don smiled his warm disarming smile and put out his hand.

'Don Lancini.' Hunter took his hand a little uncomfortably. Don saw him for the first time in a different light, as a self-conscious man impeccably dressed in grey pinstriped trousers, white shirt with a black jacket, as he would wear in the High Court. His tall, lean, normally formidable bearing looking tired and his thinning hair appeared greyer as he adjusted his horn-rimmed spectacles. He looked out of his comfort zone.

'Don Lancini,' he repeated. 'It's Inspector Adone Lancini isn't it? We've met in Court.'

'Would you like a coffee? Barbe asked, thinking he looked tired. He thanked her saying it had been a hard day. 'Have you eaten? It's lasagna.' His face lit up in a half smile.

'Thanks, I haven't had anything since luncheon recess.' The kitchen clock read eight o'clock. Don poured him a coffee and Barbe heated a generous helping of lasagna in the microwave.

'Sorry, there's not much salad left, but there are some Sfogliatelle for after.' Hunter sat at the head of the table in his usual spot.

'She can cook,' he sounded sad sound as he said the words. Don felt sorry for him but still he reserved his judgement, the man had a formidable reputation. 'This is not what I expected. I thought we would talk alone.'

Barbe set down the meal complete with serviette. Don watched Barbe's reaction, she treated Hunter with dignity and respect. Although he could clearly see her apprehension, she made no smart-arse comments or cheap jibes. Don could only see sadness in Barbe's expression.

'Enjoy your meal,' she said.

'I'll finish my coffee, then I'll leave you, if you're completely comfortable Bebe.' Don suggested, waiting for her to agree adding, 'I'll do a load of washing.'

Hearing his words Hunter thought, more domestic bliss, he does his own damned washing so he's not a mummy's boy.

'I had some correspondence from Simon Perry and Associates. What is it exactly you want?'

Barbe wondered how long he would stay reasonable.

'Hunter, I don't want to live here anymore. I just want my share of the family finances, what's fair, and I want to move on.' Hunter breathed deeply, sipping his coffee and looking restored now he had eaten.

'You do know you can live here until Ryder is sixteen? Possibly even longer if the Courts agree.' Don watched for her reaction. Instead, she stood up, fetched a plate of his favourite creme pastries and put it down on the table. Don immediately helped himself to another one.

'Delezioso,' he winked at her and left them to talk.

'No, I don't want to stay here. While I live here you still control my life, because you would argue a good catholic mother would not be living with a man other than her husband. But God knows what you get up to,' she said firmly. Hunter knew exactly what she alluded to.

'I'm sorry Hunter, I do understand. I want an honest relationship with my sons, so they in turn can be honest with me. I love Don and I'm applying for an annulment.' A mixture of fear and anger flooded Hunter's face.

'You're very unlikely to ....' she cut him off.

'My Catholic lawyer believes I have a very good case. I don't do this to hurt you. God knows I love you but no longer as my husband, wifely love went years ago. You need to face the facts, be honest and move on.'

Hunter sat seething, he didn't want to talk in front of Don and waited for him to move completely out of earshot. He would never admit his sexuality to Barbe, he couldn't even be honest with himself. Hunter breathed deeply as though preparing to deliver one of his court addresses.

'Listen to me very carefully. I have never in my life done anything with the intention of hurting you. I don't believe you truly grasp what you're doing here. Think about how your sons, our sons are going to react to your new situation.' Barbe felt strong knowing Don would be close if required.

'I will choose the time I tell them and what's more I think they understand more of your situation than you know.' Hunter frowned at her curiously. 'It's just from remarks they have made which I ignored, because of the elephant in the room. It doesn't matter to me what you or what anybody else thinks because this is what is right for me. The boys will understand in time. No matter how much you undermine my position with them. You can use whatever religious diatribe you choose because what Don and I have is, by your own standards, the natural order of things, and the boys will understand. I will allow them to be whoever they are, and I will love them for it, so we can be honest with each other and rest easy.' As she spoke Hunter appeared frozen rigid. The time for honesty seemed overdue.

'I understand you don't choose to be homosexual, but please be honest with yourself, even if you cannot be honest with the ones you love. They will accept you. Even the Pope accepts these things now.' Hunter sat feeling battle weary and defeated, still his voice sounded strong.

'I can't seem to get you to understand, I'm not homosexual. Do you think I could love you and our sons our babies if I were...that way?' His argument sounded hollow. He knew he enjoyed a lifelong attraction to men, but he would never admit it. How many times over the years he had acted on it? Still, he did love Barbe, but not quite the same way.

'Yes, I believe you are 'that way' as you put it and I believe you love our sons; they could never have a better father than you. You're warm, loving, caring and in most things an excellent role model, but sexuality is an instinct. All your life you have been told how you must behave and how you must react. Just because you're told you must do something diametrically opposed to your natural instincts does not mean you can sustain the behaviour forever. Love is so many things. If you really do love me, be honest please Hunter. Don't condemn us all to live out this farce.' For one brief moment his sad, grey eyes held hers. Each could feel the pain of the other. If he refused to admit his homosexuality, then how could she ever convince the Catholic marriage tribunal and Barbe knew she would be guilty of living in sin with Don and deep down she felt Don didn't want to feel the pressure of Catholic guilt either.

'My behaviour on one particular occasion may have given you the idea I had been deviant but if all men who had experimented sexually once, were accused of deviance, then there would be few of us left. I'm not homosexual. It is the truth I'll give the tribunal.' His sad grey eyes turned cold as he watched the silent tears roll down her cheeks. 'And you're right I will argue in the family court you are not a fit mother, if you live with that man. Not fit, because it goes against the grain of everything, we have brought them up to believe. It goes against the very fabric of our faith. Next weekend I'll have the boys at my apartment until you sort yourself out. Think very long and hard before you drag my family through the Courts and Catholic Marriage Tribunal, because it will be a very cold day in hell before they'll grant nullity on the flimsy say so of a neurotic woman who has an ulterior motive.' He stood up, pushed back his chair and strode down the hallway to the front door slamming it on his way out.

Chapter twenty-two:

Hearing the front door slam Don came quickly to see what had happened. Barbe sat at the dining table sobbing into her folded arms like a child. Sitting down next to her, he tried to comfort her. She looked distraught. He had never seen her like this before.

'I'm sorry. If I'm honest I should have known how he would react.' she told him.

He leaned over and picked up his phone which sat beside her laptop at the other end of the table. Don had set it to record. He would play it later and get a handle on their conversation.

'Come and sit next to me here, so I can hold you.' Taking her hand, he sat her down on the settee.

'Do you feel like talking about it?' She shook her head, and he held her close, whispering softly,

'We'll deal with this together, side by side, remember.' After a few moments she calmed down.

'I think I'm going to have a soak in the tub.' She sighed.

'Good idea, I'm going to nip out to the supermarket and see if I can get a copy of the paper. I missed it at the airport, and I'd like to catch up. She smiled weakly at him.

'And to get the crossword,' she whispered. He agreed, having completely forgotten about the crossword.

'Okay, see you in half an hour. I'll make the hot chocolate,' he said, putting his phone in his pocket, and taking his new gate and garage opener. Once in the car he played the conversation back through his Bluetooth as he drove down the road to the supermarket. Don realized Hunter sounded desperate. Why else would he be so dogmatic? Getting milk and the paper he slowly returned, having thought of the solution to the situation. But would Barbe buy it?

HE WANTED QUICK SHOWER. First, he made her a hot chocolate. Barbe finished her bath and seemed a little subdued. Grateful for the drink, she picked up her mug and started sipping. Don strode out of the shower wrapped only in a towel.

'Bebe' he whispered as she turned to see him down on one knee. He held out his hand to her. 'I love you, Bebe. Please will you marry me?' Seeing him naked except for the towel, she laughed.

'Marriage won't solve anything Adonis but thank you and I love you too.' Stunned by her response he knelt on both knees and pulled her towards him.

'You don't want to marry me?' he feigned hurt, 'you don't know what you're passing up.' He stood up and sat down on her bed next to her. His voice changed. 'When the time is right will you marry me?' She sat silently. 'I have to admit something. I recorded your conversation with Hunter, I heard his threats. If we marry now in a civil ceremony, if and when the Catholic annulment comes through, we can do it again in church. But no court in the land will think you a bad mother, a bad example to your boys, if after all this time being divorced, you marry because you have met this handsome Adonis,' he grinned. 'We're not starstruck kids. I suggest we marry as soon as possible and then throw a party and invite our families and friends. They can all be shocked and surprised together. We will tell them we are going for an annulment, and they'll be invited to the church wedding in due course. Our legal commitment will show everyone we are not a bad example to our children. Also, I think Hunter will eventually come around.' He took her mug and set it down.

'Please Bebe, what do you say?' he asked. Her sad face said it all.

'I love you but I'm so scared. Hunter will never admit his sexuality. How can I possibly move forward? Also, I can't expose him publicly; it would be a huge betrayal.' Listening to her Don closed his eyes. He had painted himself into a corner. If she did not agree to marry him, where would it leave him? he wanted her as his wife, and he knew when families blend there is always baggage, but this was huge, and they would both need to work together.

'Don't give me your answer just yet, sleep on it. I'll be on the couch downstairs.'

Cold and uncomfortable, he tossed and turned on the couch. Going over and over the facts like a policeman. If he could gather evidence Hunter kept company with other gay men, maybe the tribunal would need nothing more than that evidence and Barbe's testimony. From the words Hunter used calling Barbe a neurotic woman with an ulterior motive, Don wondered if her mental health might be the direction his counterclaim would take. Barbe had told him she had been very lonely and depressed after she had demanded a separation from Hunter, because she felt unable to talk to anyone. Not even her best friend Kate who now lived in Perth. She simply told Kate, 'Hunter is having an affair' and Kate accepted what Barbe said. Kate, herself, had just gone through a relationship breakup and she and her then fiancé had gone their separate ways. Kate went to Perth to become the director of a large art gallery.

It had taken Barbe a long time to get to the point of demanding a formal separation. Hunter went out all hours, sometimes away overnight at times. There were all the hallmarks of an affair Barbe had told Don. If she had not seen the young man naked in her bedroom with Hunter, she would have been sure he had another woman. Hunter had ignored them all back then, including his young sons. He had seemed preoccupied with his own secret life.

Don had watched Hunter 'perform' in the high court. He had seen him decimate the evidence and character of an otherwise competent complainant in a rape case and make her look so bad. He feared for Barbe. Surely, he would not treat the mother of his sons so badly. In the recorded conversation Don heard the malice in Hunter's voice at times and realized if the man were cornered or felt trapped, he would lash out at Barbe regardless of any feelings he might have had for her. Don's head throbbed and he couldn't get comfortable, so he got up and drank a large glass of cold water. Trying to settle back on the settee, for the first time in many years he prayed consciously. Regardless, he still justified to himself his decision to marry Barbe. If she would have him, he desperately wanted her, but worried the strain of the circumstances would tear them apart. In his honest view of things, marriage would be the sensible solution.

UPSTAIRS BARBE, UNABLE to settle, also hashed over the evening's events. When Hunter became confrontational using his silver-tongued rhetoric to argue his case, he had always been a force to be reckoned with, awe-inspiring, intimidating, and formidable. She'd heard the adjectives used to describe his magniloquence. She'd been on the receiving end of his sharp wit and tongue. Older now she felt more confident and mature. Hearing him call her a neurotic woman had been the last straw. Lying there thinking about it made her furious. If his plan was to undermine her confidence with his less than subtle put downs, then it wouldn't work anymore.

For the last eighteen years he had controlled her, not loved, or cherished her. She could see it now. She should have found a decent lawyer when they divorced instead of allowing him to convince her, his way would be best for everyone, but Hunter did convince people of his argument.

Thinking about Don made her sad. She loved the man. He was everything Hunter is not and more besides. The simple things in life filled him with joy. If she were abstruse in her explanations, particularly about her family dynamics, Don would say, 'bloody hell woman spit it out. I'm just a

simple copper,' even if deep down he clearly understood, he wanted her to tell him clearly, so there could be no room for misunderstandings.

Would marrying him right now in these circumstances be the answer? She didn't know. However, she did know he filled a huge void in her life, he made her laugh, they shared the same basic values (church doctrine aside), his honesty disarmed everyone and most of all she loved him and all aspects of their relationship. Making love to him felt like nothing she had ever experienced He took her to a whole other dimension, she felt complete. Thinking about her failed marriage she felt totally let down by the church, not by God but by the patriarchal fathers who had not supported her when she desperately needed it. Several times when she had tried to discuss her marriage in the confessional where she felt she had the undivided attention of a priest, they had never truly been able to grasp what she had been going through. It became obvious from their comments they were unable to understand.

Looking back on her marriage she now understood true intimacy had never been there. Hunter never really wanted her as a woman. Now she had the love of Don the difference proved obvious and compelling; hindsight was twenty-twenty. It felt very demoralizing to be wedded to someone who just did the expected as though they were simply going through the motions, sometimes enjoying it and yet often not interested. She remembered with nausea the way he always wanted to sodomize her, she didn't understand it and felt worn down and tired with two little boys. Sometimes she didn't have any fight in her either. She felt tears on her face, she had never told anybody about it, how could she? It disgusted her.

Remembering her wedding night, well lots of people don't consummate their marriage on the first night, but he never seemed interested in touching her either. Life is not all about sex, it had been one of the things that endeared her to Hunter in the first place. He had never been all over her like a rash. Thinking about other guys she had dated before Hunter; their wandering hands presented a continual struggle. Then she thought about her Adonis, he had been gorgeous, and very intuitive. Would she let her disastrous marriage ruin the rest of her life? Earlier in the day she and Don had one of their famous 'hard conversations.' She had been busy knitting baby things for Jacinda, while they watched the news as their Lasagna cooked. He had looked at her in his quirky way.

'I've told you before, you know I'm too bloody old for babies, don't you?' Remembering he looked at her almost as though he felt scared, he'd not meet her expectations.

'I always wanted a couple more, but I think I might be past it too. Oh, gee what if it happened?' she wondered aloud. He went quiet for a moment.

'Then we'd be older parents, and wouldn't my mother be thrilled.' Then he laughed and told her he'd deal with it as she would. Slowly as sleep claimed her Barbe knew what she had to do.

Chapter Twenty -Three:

S howered and dressed in her jeans and a merino jersey she went downstairs to talk to Don. The kitchen clock read eight am and he had gone. After a quick check, she noted his car had gone too. However, his bags were still in her room. It seemed obvious he had taken some clothes, showered downstairs and disappeared somewhere. They were both upset the previous evening, but they were not starstruck kids, his words. She felt confident he had something important he had to do. Making herself a morning cuppa she found his note on the bench.

Bebe,
I have some business I need to deal with.
I'll phone you this afternoon.
D.

Just as she had thought. Checking her calendar, she noticed her mother would be due home from Europe next week. What had Hunter told her, if anything? Barbe had only just sat down with her fruit and yoghurt when the phone rang. The caller, old Mrs. Percy, her mother's neighbour, a spritely woman in her eighties sounded upset.

'Barbe, I'm sorry about old Chester, he took ill last week, I had to take him to the vet, and she advised me to make the hard decision and have him put down.' The woman sounded upset but then Chester had been more her cat than her mothers.

'I'm sorry you were left to make the tough call. I've been in Australia, did Hunter tell you?' Barbe agreed to drive over to Khandallah later in the morning. Normally she would have visited the woman a few times, she usually did, when her mother went away visiting her sister in Europe.

She powered through her chores, baking for the boys and even Hunter. She always had. She knew it could hardly be called necessary, but she worried about him. Taking some baking and a few lemons she drove over to her mother's neighbour. Driving back to Kelburn she realized they were coming to the end of an era. Mrs. Percy and the cat had been in her life for years. Now the cat had been put down, and Mrs. Percy said she'd sold her home, with the intention of going into a retirement village. Barbe dreaded the thought but knew she would have to phone her mother to tell her the news. Her real news however would be Don Lancini. What would her mother say? Jovana Brunner, an old-world Catholic. She would not approve she would curl her lip and tsk-tsk, Hunter could do no wrong. Jovana or Jo as she preferred, looked, and sounded English having been born there. Her family originally came from the Dalmatian Coast of Yugoslavia and her younger sister Katarina had moved back after marrying a Croatian doctor thirty years before. Barbe procrastinated, she'd put the phone call on her to do list. Next stop today, her hairdresser; it had been months since her last appointment.

IN HIS OFFICE AT POLICE Headquarters, Don had a few loose ends to tie up before he returned to Latta Crescent. He had called Simon Perry's secretary and arranged for Simon to skype him at his earliest convenience. The call came at barely eight-thirty.

'Thank you for taking the trouble with this, I wanted you to hear a conversation I recorded yesterday evening after you skyped Barbe. Don watched the expression on Simon's face as the conversation played out. When it had finished Simon spoke.

'Is that the first time you met the man?' Don replied apart that from meeting him in court, yes it had been the first time.

'You can see what we are up against. The financials are straight forward, and trusts can be unwound if the Court sees fit. But I don't understand why the man would go to these lengths to deny his sexuality when the world is embracing diversity.' Simon said.

'I do,' Don replied sardonically, then told him plainly. 'Your family must be particularly accepting and forgiving. Mine are a bunch of hypocrites. While they openly accept anyone else's son or daughter being gay, if it were one of their own, their heads would be buried in the sand, and they would deny it. If one of us 'came out' then all I can say is God help him. So, on the one hand I have sympathy for the man. On the other hand, I can see what it's doing to Barbe. After all these years she is still torn, still caring and yet she .... I'm glad we found each other. I have asked her to marry me as soon as we can legally do it. But she will still apply for the annulment so we can marry in the Church down the track.' Don waited for his reaction.

'Interesting, the courts will be sympathetic to Barbe I think, and I have found something I believe may help with the Catholic Marriage Tribunal. The thing is, Hunter will make a plausible statement. He does it in court all the time.' he paused. Don asked what he thought maybe useful, because he had his own ideas but needed to ensure they were on the same page.

'Social media, I have had my young experts trawling through video footage from gay bars in Wellington and from there following some of the characters on social media. There are no laws against any of it, but it definitely goes to show a certain state of mind, spending hours in certain bars.' Simon held up his hands. 'I hate this kind of thing, but it's simply a matter of profiling the character. Don nodded his agreement; they were on the same page.

'Barbe wouldn't have a bar of this you know. She calls it character assassination and she's right, but then you may just need the ammunition for any annulment.' Don advised. Simon insisted they keep this to themselves, and Don agreed.

'Just one thing, when you explained sexuality to Barbe she felt she had a better understanding not only of herself but also of Hunter. Is there something I can read so I can get a more compassionate understanding?' It became obvious to Simon that Don Lancini was a special kind of man.

'I'm taking it you've done a bit of online research.' Simon watched Don's little smirk. 'You probably won't find a lot there because it's really quite complex. I did tell Barbe, sexuality is on a continuum, however it is not simple. It has depths and segments like a Rubik's cube. Simply put there are three major areas to understanding sexuality; desire, behaviour and identity.' Don listened fascinated.

'Who they want to have sex with, is desire. Who they actually have sex with is identity, and who they tell the world they'd like to have sex with is their behaviour and often with very sad consequences' Don said he'd like to speak with him again down the track, maybe in Auckland.

CARLA LANCINI LOOKED surprised when her baby son turned up at home with a bag of hot pastries for morning tea.

'What are you up to heh?' The curvy seventy-three-year-old hugged her son.

'When you bring food Adone, you're up to something.' She patted his cheek affectionately.

'Yeah, okay Mamma, got me first time. I suspect Tony has told you already I've met someone. It's serious and yes, she's Catholic, but don't get excited. She's divorced like me but she's going for an annulment. Regardless, I'm going to marry her,' his fingers crossed in his pocket.

'You've been on your own too long. It makes me sad; I'd like to meet her.' Don wished he could tell his mother all the details so she could better understand, but as a man of his word he had promised Barbe he would keep her secret.

'Michelle tells me you two went to the food fair at the weekend. Did she enjoy it?' he said, curious. Carla rolled her eyes, shaking her head and poured him an espresso.

'What do you think? Her mother doesn't eat, she picks and pushes food around. The woman has never been a cook. Michelle doesn't mind eating but she'd prefer to order it in.' Tsking, she sighed. Don grinned, asking why she took his daughter to the food fair then.

'I live in hope, I live in hope,' she repeated. Mother and son chatted about family and Carla reported Tony had a small bowel resection and required no further treatment. Then she added, 'he works too hard you know.' Don agreed.

'I'm looking for a change within the police department so I can get better work-life balance.

'I look forward to meeting her.' She said, giving her son a wry look.

Chapter Twenty -Four

A s Barbe came out of the hair salon her phone pinged a text. *'Will be at Latta Crescent in half an hour, okay? D'* She replied, *see you then* and checking her hair in the rear vision mirror she set off home with a satisfied smile.

On the short drive, she remembered the conversation she'd had this morning with Simon Perry, he had told her to go around her home and list the items she wanted to take with her when she moved as they would need to be considered in their chattels list. Hunter played hardball and it had come to this. The list looked very small and when she emailed it to Simon, he called back on the phone asking, 'surely there is more after all this time?' She reminded him she had been divorced for years, but it was still Hunter's trust's furniture. He suggested he would approach this from another angle. He would ask Hunter what he wanted from the house because it had been her home for eighteen years. Thinking about it made her uncomfortable, but she barely had time to dwell on the matter when Don arrived back.

From the internal garage he walked hesitantly back into the house. 'Bebe,' he embraced her.

'Your hair, it's gorgeous, very flattering, loved it before but wow! The dress is stunning too. Hey is this all for my benefit?' She kissed him and just as it started getting hot and heavy, she pulled back.

'Don't you ever spit the dummy with me and sleep on the couch again. I couldn't sleep a wink,' she protested.

'Well may I ask the question again?' She pursed her lips nodding at him.

'Will you marry me as soon as we can arrange it, please Barbe?' They were both smiling; he knew her answer but stood waiting for it.

'Yes, I will. Right this minute.' to which he laughed.

'I'm good but it will have to be Friday, I've booked the registrar, and the licence will be through by then.'

'Really?' she gasped. 'Mr. Confident, but where are we going to live?' Ever practical, he thought as he raked his fingers through his hair.

'I'm working on it; we have an appointment with a real estate agent tomorrow.' He told her he didn't feel comfortable in Hunter's house and suggested they stay over in a hotel.

'A colleague of mine, who's on deployment in Tonga, has offered us his place till we can take possession of our own home. I just need to pick up the key from his neighbour.' Barbe suggested they go immediately and dispense with the hotel.

'I'm over hotels,' she told him.

LOADING THE FRESH BAKING into her car she drove to Saint Benedict's College. The boarders' house master had allowed her to meet with the boys in his flat. They were both very keen for their lives to go back to the routine they enjoyed prior to their mother being a witness to murder. Nicholas wanted to go back to being a day boy, insisting he could live with her, and it wouldn't matter when she went away on business, because at seventeen he could take care of himself. Poor Ryder looked lost. It took all Barbe could muster to keep herself from tears.

'Our lives are going to change for sure but one step at a time. First, I need to tell you I have met someone.' Watching their faces, she felt surprised. She expected more but she saw very little of anything, except nervous apprehension. 'Don is a good man; he is the detective on the team who kept me safe.' The boys stood in stunned silence. 'You know I have never had a boyfriend since your father, and I divorced. Don is more than a friend, I love him.'

'Are you sleeping with him?' Nicholas said. Furious, he didn't wait for an answer. 'Gross.'

'Don and I are getting married.' She hadn't expected his comment. But she should have realized it is typical, she is ancient after all. Seeing Ryder looked confused she pulled him to her and hugged him. 'I wanted you to meet him first, but your father....' her voice trailed off.

'I'm not surprised, I don't need a stepfather, he won't be anything to me.' Nicholas spat.

'I'm simply telling you this good man will be my husband. Hunter will always be your father, but I want Don to be my husband.' Seeing the look of contempt on the boy's face she added firmly, 'I don't need your permission Nicholas, all I ask is for you to be courteous.' This had all the hallmarks of a hard road to hoe. She felt anxious.

'When can we meet him?' Ryder asked he too, looked uneasy. Barbe asked if they would like to go to a restaurant for dinner on Saturday and they could meet Don at the same time. Remembering Hunter, she added, 'If your father agrees, because he insists you stay with him at the weekends till things are sorted.' Ryder looked at her sadly and it suddenly occurred to Nicholas things really were changing.

'He's not moving into our house, is he?'

'No, we are going house hunting tomorrow. In the meantime, we have the use of a house belonging to a friend of his, who's overseas.' She stood up to leave knowing they had homework to complete, and that dinner is always served early at school. 'Text me the details of your games Saturday, I'd like to come.' Hugging each of them she left, knowing things were going to be difficult.

On her way back to Latta Crescent she dropped three containers off at Hunter's office, not waiting to speak to him. She explained to Stephanie Maxwell, his personal assistant,

'This is just some leftover lasagna; he likes it. The rest is his usual baking.' Naturally, the woman wanted to know what had been happening. She knew Barbe had been Barbe had been the victim and witness to another crime. Barbe insisted she could not stop.

'I'm parked on a delivery spot and Hunter can give you the details.' The woman knew she was being fobbed off.

THE DAY FELT COLD, blustery and wet.

'Ideal for house hunting, everything will look at its worst,' Don went on as he drove them into the city. The previous evening when Don had discussed the budget for this house Barbe thought it a fortune. Soon she would learn just how expensive Wellington was to live in. Don had suggested they look at four bedrooms, two bathrooms and some off-street parking.

'Don't you mean garaging' she naively corrected him. He simply smiled. By lunch time she felt wretched, the cost of anything remotely like Latta Crescent appeared well beyond their budget. Don knew it would be but waited for her reaction.

'Adonis, this afternoon why don't you look for a house without me and I look without you, then choose two to show me and I'll do the same.' At three pm she called him, saying she had found the perfect place, refusing to tell him where. Insisting she do the driving she made him cover his eyes. Her excitement seemed palpable, and he reveled in it. When they arrived, she had arranged to drive the car into the single garage and there in the dark she gave him a loving kiss. He just wondered where the hell this house would be. Then she opened the door at the rear of the garage, and they walked towards the front door of the old double bay villa. Don had a sense of deja vu.

'This is within our budget, isn't it?' he asked. The agent stood waiting on the porch.

Immediately Gillian Derwent's jaw dropped.

'You, you and Barbe are... When were you going to tell me Don?' Don shot her his charismatic smile.

'Cat's out of the bag Bebe, meet Gill, my ex.' Surprised Barbe giggled nervously, and looked at Gillian. The two had hit it off earlier in the day when she showed Barbe the house.

'Gillian can keep a secret, especially if you're doing business with her.' Barbe said anxiously. Don appeared amused and he didn't agree but held his tongue, Gillian was a gossip. The house stood seven hundred metres from his mother's home; would it work?

'Before you look inside, I have to tell you when I said it's perfect, I lied.' Barbe bubbled with excitement. 'But it has the potential to be perfect.' Taking him through the house he could see a small older home. The only redeeming feature, it had been well maintained. There were no wardrobes, no storage, a single garage and the old-fashioned dining and living rooms were down the other end of the hall from the newly renovated kitchen. Don breathed deeply.

Listening to Barbe, he realized she and his brother Tony both had the same sort of imagination and vision but at what cost? Gillian's amused skepticism annoyed him. The woman seemed to be enjoying watching him desperately trying to please his new woman, but all he could see were dollar signs the size of telephone numbers appearing before his eyes. He suggested before they committed to anything, she needed to see the two houses he had chosen. Just as they were leaving Barbe said to Gillian,

'I would love to meet Michelle; please can we take her out for an early dinner Saturday?' both Gill and Don seemed surprised. 'Don's been itching to catch up with her. He's only just arrived back from overseas.' Caught completely off guard the woman agreed.

'Only if Michelle wants to, you know what teenagers can be like.' She said then went on making excuses. Barbe forced a smile, changing the subject.

'This house is my favourite, but I'll have to talk about it with his nibs. We'll pick Michelle up at six on Saturday, I'll be in touch.'

Don drove back to his agent.

'Am I missing something here? I didn't think you would be into house renovations; we would need to have your ideas costed.' He combed his fingers through his hair, and she burst into laughter.

'As soon as Gillian saw you, and I learned she is your ex; didn't you notice the dynamics change? The thing is this morning I naively told her things, so she knew who you were all along and never said a word. When you appeared out of the garage door and her game was up, I decided I didn't want her to know my real plans for the house. The few truly necessary alterations could be done within our purchasing budget. The rest can wait.' Sounding organized she elaborated,

'I learned from my parents; you need to live in a place for a bit before you spend money altering it. What I like about the property is, you can walk to the village, it's only ten minutes by car to the city centre and it's on the flat, a great forever home.' Don looked so relieved he drove directly to Latta Crescent. 'I don't think the other places would suit you now, too far from town, multi levels built into the side of hills.' They decided to make an offer on the double bay villa subject to a builder's report.

HUNTER PHONED SAYING he had made a list of the chattels he wanted from the house, and he'd emailed it to her. Barbe told him the property they were moving to was smaller and she would be leaving quite a bit behind. After an awkward silence, he thanked her for the food she left at the office. Then she asked him if she could take the boys to dinner Saturday night. she heard him inhale and before he answered she told him plainly that when she and Don were married, the courts would not buy his unsuitable parent routine so the old custody arrangements would resume unless he wanted to push it, which of course he didn't, because he knew she was right. Both Simon Perry and Don had reassured her.

The house they were staying in belonging to Don's friend was half an hour out of town and over three levels: typical of Churton Park. Don soon tired of tramping up and down stairs and looked forward to being on one level. Gillian telephoned. their offer on the villa had been accepted provided they agreed to an early settlement as it was in a chain. Don pretended to play hardball, but he felt over the moon. Tony Lancini arranged for a qualified building surveyor to check the property so Don could confirm the contract the next day. It all happened very quickly.

On Friday, the day of their proposed marriage, Barbe felt apprehensive. While Don showered his mobile rang, Gillian called saying Michelle had a friend's birthday tea and couldn't do dinner on Saturday night. Immediately Barbe insisted she must do it tonight instead. Gillian could be heard asking Michelle, who agreed, they would pick her up at six.

Don felt a tad annoyed on hearing what she had arranged.

'I thought we would have a romantic dinner, just the two of us all dressed up in our wedding finery.' He stood, checking his appearance in the mirror. '

'What could be better than the two women in your life enjoying some fine dining with you? I want her to see what a lovely man you are.' Barbe hoped Michelle did not favour her mother, the tall blond skinny woman had a hard edge about her.

Then she also hoped Michelle didn't sound like Nicholas, all bulchy and entitled. She prayed he would grow out of it. Listening to her, Don smiled his special heart melting charismatic beam, it would always be her first memory of him.

Chapter Twenty -Five

D on's witness would be Frank Taylor. Elizabeth Martin, an elegant confident woman and good friend of Barbe's, who owned a perfumery on Lambton Quay, would be her witness.

They all met at the Registry Office in Mulgrave Street at fifteen minutes past two for their two thirty appointment. Barbe looked stunning in a cream brocade sheath dress and jacket, carrying a posy of cream rosebuds and baby's breath, with a small clutch purse tucked under her arm. Don in his best Ralph Lauren suit looking like a mafia don, straight from a Sicilian enclave complete with entourage. Frank, his sidekick, in an equally dapper suit and his wife Marion, a warm attractive schoolteacher about Barbe's age, came armed with a professional looking camera. Elizabeth Martin, Barbe's friend brought her partner of nearly ten years, a merchant banker originally from Sweden.

After the brief ceremony, the party drove off in separate vehicles to the Intercontinental Hotel for an elegant and delicious high tea with champagne. The party laughed as Don tried to explain why his bride gave him a ring, yet he had no ring for her. Barbe just giggled, saying the Lancini ring is under construction.

'My Nonna had rings on all her fingers and bells on her toes and she left them to me,' Don joked 'so I offered them to Barbe to choose something. Who knew, she wanted to be like my Nonna only her version, which means all the family jewels are being made into one very interesting multi diamond statement piece, ready next week.' He shrugged and Barbe insisted good things took time. 'I'm not using all the rings, just three of them. We've designed something for Michelle with the rest, for when she's a bit older.'

By quarter to six the little party had dispersed. Don and Barbe drove off to collect Michelle. When she opened the door, his heart melted. His little girl looked all grown up, at fourteen. Her dress of navy blue, covered in tiny silver heart-like spots, had spaghetti straps with an over lay of navy chiffon. A satin sash sat at her waist. Barbe watched as Don and Michelle walked hand in hand to the car. She got out of the vehicle to greet Michelle. The dark-haired beauty towered over Barbe who felt small by comparison to this willowy young woman with her father's charismatic smile.

'Hi, I'm Barbe. I feel I know you already. Your dad is so proud of you, and I can see why.'

Michelle replied awkwardly, 'thank you.' Her father opened the car door for her and soon they were making their way to the restaurant.

'Adonis, she is so like you,' Barbe enthused. Michelle giggled as her father inflated with pride.

Over dinner Don enjoyed watching Michelle and Barbe interacting.

'So, how did you two meet then?' she wanted to know. Don watched as Barbe explained about the shooting.

'Of course, I did see it on the news, but I didn't realize you were involved Dad.'

Barbe calmly told the story and about how afraid she felt and how Don had taken care of her. She spoke about Don being shot in the Australian car park incident. Also, about hiding out in witness protection getting to know each other.

'Now the gang has imploded, we're safe.' Barbe sighed looking at her new husband. Michelle noticed the ring her father wore. 'Are you two married?' her voice a tad accusing.

'Yes, we married today,' Don told her, watching her expression change.

'Today?' she frowned at Barbe. 'Why aren't you wearing a ring?'

'Barbe's ring is being fixed at the jeweller's. Yes, it is quick but at our age we've had time to work out what we want.'

Ignoring his remarks Michelle looked at Barbe's hand.

'You've been married before' she sounded even more accusing this time.

'Yes, I have and so has your father, another reason we couldn't just live together, we needed to be good role models for our children.' Barbe watched the girl's face. 'I have a son your age and one seventeen.'

She had hardly finished speaking when Michelle did the hair flick and said 'cool.'

Don half closed his eyes as he rubbed his forehead and realized they had three teenagers and wondered how it would work.

'You would have met them tomorrow night but ... maybe another time.'

Michelle corrected him saying, 'definitely another time.'

As the conversation went on from there Barbe worried about Ryder. Michelle seemed so much more mature than Ryder. She'd heard the girls today were more mature and assertive with boys than they were in her day.

Don sat thinking he'd need to keep Barbe's two testosterone charged teenage boys away from his darling daughter. He blinked, remembering his randy seventeen-year-old self. He squeezed Barbe's hand hoping she couldn't read his mind.

Like her father Michelle enjoyed her food but had little interest in cooking it.

'Did you have fun at the food fair with Nonna?' Don wanted to know. His mother said she seemed ambivalent.

'The food is always great, but you know I'm not a foodie and mum is so calorie conscious I couldn't get across the harbour on my board if I ate like her. Mind you, she and Da...Wayne drink a few calories.'

Don sat speechless. Gillian's husband of quite a few years was called Wayne, did Michelle nearly call him Dad? Barbe said nothing and Don sat there while Michelle went on, 'they don't drink every single night, well they do, but they only have a session about three times a week.'

'It's just wine though, isn't it?' he asked, recovering himself.

'Bourbon and coke.'

Barbe thought it time to change the subject, knowing kids were prone to exaggeration.

'Do you have any plans yet for when you leave school?' Barbe asked.

'Dad said I should go to University, but I'm not sure.' Don didn't remember even having any university conversation. 'Yeah, he reckons I should do something like web design, because he sees me doing all their online stuff at the Real Estate office, I think it is actually an IT course. It could be good too.' Don bit his tongue, the man had clearly been usurping his place in his daughter's heart.

Barbe saw his angst and realized his plight. Patting his hand, she held it firm, poor Don.

'Michelle, if you could do whatever you wanted, what would you choose?' Barbe questioned as their desserts arrived.

'I've thought about being a cop like Dad.' Michelle hesitated, seeing the look on her father's face. 'But who knows, I'd like to get to the Olympics windsurfing too.' Don's beamed proudly.

As he drove her home, Don could see his little girl is still there under all the confidence and bravado.

'Mum said you've bought a house down the road from Nonna.' Michelle's statement surprised Don.

'Yeah, but your Nonna doesn't know nor does Barbe. I planned on introducing them at morning tea tomorrow. Want to come?'

'I usually sleep in on Saturday mornings but tomorrow won't be one to miss.' Michelle laughed.

'Should I be scared?' Barbe wondered aloud. 'Since you married me before you introduced me to Nonna. The truth is my mother will be the bigger challenge.' Her mother scared her rigid.

BACK AT THEIR TEMPORARY home in Churton Park, Don waited till Barbe climbed into bed before he put out the light.

'Six months ago, I would have looked at your beautiful face in a shop window and I wouldn't have given the woman a second thought.' Barbe sucked in a sharp breath. 'You know why? Because I would have thought she looked unobtainable, out of my league, until we were locked in a hospital utility cupboard. Then when you nearly fainted and I grabbed you with both hands, I told myself, grab her and never let her go. I always do what I tell myself,' then he chuckled.

'So, I hope you are not tired tonight Mrs. Lancini.'

Without missing a beat, she replied, 'if I am, I'll just fall asleep, won't I? listening he groaned.

THE HOWLING SOUTHERLY wind rattled the windows and rain pelted on the tin roof Wellington in winter. Barbe shivered and snuggled up to Don, who opened one eye and checked his watch, eight thirty.

'I remember when the milkman used to deliver' his voice husky. His out of left field statement woke her up.

'What are you going on about? she muttered, aware he had more insulation than her. She enjoyed the heat from him.

'We're going out for breakfast, there's no milk. We'll need to do a shop.' Hanging on to him she had no intention of letting go.

'Only if I get to shower first, because if my hairy yeti leaves this bed I'll freeze.'

His large hirsute chest resonated with his chuckle.

'And no, we couldn't, have you seen the size of the shower? It makes the hospital utility cupboard look like a ball room.'

He covered her lips with his and as his kisses moved to her neck he whispered, 'I had something different in mind, there's a much better way to keep warm.'

THEY NEVER DID GET breakfast. Tt became coffee to go, bagels with cream cheese with smoked salmon and a box of morning tea goodies. They arrived just in time to pick up Michelle for the morning tea with Don's mother. Wayne Derwent opened the door and called to Michelle.

'Don's here sweetheart.' Don wondered why didn't he say your father's here? Gillian appeared behind Michelle; her lip lifted slightly as she tried to smile.

'I believe congratulations are in order.' her voice, saccharine.

Is she congratulating me in that backhanded way she's perfected?

'Your mother's going to be furious.' There was no love lost between Gillian and Carla Lancini. 'She could forgive you once for not marrying in the Church, but not twice. I'd love to be a fly on the wall' she chuckled.

Don controlled his annoyance. Barbe is a completely different woman from Gillian. His mother would see it too.

Michelle stood at the front door all rugged up with a jacket and scarf.

'Call me when you're done, sweetheart. We're going shopping, remember' Wayne the hugely successful realtor, loved to splash his money about.

'What's he talking about?' Don asked when they were in the car.

'Take no notice Dad, he's winding you up. He wants me to help him choose a printer for the home office. It has to have fax capacity for the legal stuff.' Michelle grinned at Barbe.

The Lancini family home stood within walking distance of everything in the village of Island Bay; the sea, the Church, everything. The old villa, of substantial proportions, looked loved and so did the garden. Carla Lancini stood in the doorway, hurrying them indoors so she could shut out the weather again. Once inside, they quickly shed their coats, scarves, and boots.

'Mamma meet my Barbe, my wife.' Don beamed.

Barbe affectionately held out her arms.

'I knew you would be a lovely woman, because your Adone is special.' Barbe ignored the skeptical look, she meant it honestly.

'You love my son then?'

'I do and I pray we can marry again in Church. God understands what we seek.' She imagined her own mother would be harder on them. Carla ushered them into her lounge and told Don and Michelle to make the coffee.

'You know the Church seldom grants annulments especially when there are children. You have children?' Barbe nodded and sat where Carla suggested. 'So, what makes you think your circumstances mean you could possibly get an annulment?' The beautifully tinted dark honey hair on her head looked thick and curly like Don's. Barbe thought for a moment, then she folded her hands in her lap as the woman scanned her.

'I have no idea how these things work. But my lawyer, who is catholic is helping me apply to the marriage tribunal. There are circumstances which suggest I have a case, they tell me. These are private matters and as there are children who will be affected, I can't discuss them with you. I'm sorry my husband, I mean ex-husband, is a good man and he deserves his privacy too.' As Barbe spoke the old woman frowned.

'All I can do is pray and leave it in God's hands,' Barbe added. She started nibbling her lip apprehensively.

'Mmm, so why not wait until the tribunal gives its decision?' Carla pursed her lips and raised her brows.

'I planned to at first. But my ex-husband would not allow me to have shared custody of my boys, if I had been living with Don, or seeing him. He said he would claim I'm an unfit mother. I would be setting my boys a bad example, going against the church. Also, I still lived in the matrimonial home. It's complicated, my ex-husband is a barrister, Hunter Anderson, have you heard of him?'

'Have I heard of him? Everybody's heard of him. Didn't he get that taxi driver off from the charge of murdering the prostitute a couple of months ago, I remember reading something about it. From memory his father, I can't remember his name, he used to be a judge. Isn't Father Jo Anderson a relative of his? He's a lovely man.

How could you possibly get an annulment, those sorts of people never do anything wrong. Their marriages are made to last.' Carla sounded unconvinced until she turned back and saw genuine tears in Barbe's eyes and her sad face. 'So why did you marry my son?'

'Because I love him and in the eyes of the law, we have the protection of a marriage covenant. It tells the world we are committed as a family and although sadly, it's not likely, I would love to have more children.' Barbe wiped away her tears; she didn't want Don to see those. Looking at Carla Lancini she felt the woman could almost read her mind. 'Don't ask me why Hunter and I divorced because I'll not tell you, except to say, I did nothing wrong and I never wanted it, but it seemed imperative at the time.' Hearing noises down the hall she breathed deeply, feeling relieved, she had been saved.

In came Don, with morning tea/come breakfast. Carla sat for a moment thinking. Barbe's honesty had disarmed her although, she still held tight to her principles. She began to wonder what the real story might be. Adone, her baby son, the apple of her eye, under any other circumstances she would be rejoicing because she could see something very endearing about Barbe.

'I'll pray for you, all of you,' she announced as though it would fix everything. Barbe thanked her, hoping to get others on board with the prayer power. Don grinned, recognizing she had just been through the third degree.

'Did you tell her we have bought the house down the road?' Suddenly a commotion sounded, with Michelle, Carla and Don all talking over the top of each other in excitedly. Barbe laughed she would feel very comfortable in this family, they had passion. They ended up staying until just before the boys' rugby games. Michelle's mother came and collected her.

Chapter Twenty -Six:

Don ran up and down the sideline getting into the spirit of the match, yelling his support enthusiastically. The winner of this match would go through to the finals of the college XV games. Ryder's team had finished for the season, so he stood watching his brother play too.

Don came across as friendly and polite to Ryder, however there seemed little privacy for in- depth conversation. Rugby has the ability to bring men, together, soon Hunter joined them. Barbe checked again the boys would be available to have dinner with them.

'Where, at the house?' Hunter asked, reassuring himself it would not be where Barbe and Don were living.

'Wherever the boys fancy eating. Name the restaurant Ryder.' The sooner the custody arrangements were settled the happier Barbe would be.

At dinner in the Tex-Mex restaurant of Ryder's choice, Don said he'd enjoyed the game and congratulated Nicholas, who looked chuffed his team had made it to the finals.

'I'd love to see the match, but your mother and I have to be in Auckland on Friday, and we won't be back till Sunday,' Don said, genuinely disappointed.

The seating in the restaurant was booth style, like railway carriage seats facing one another. The boys sat together facing Don and Barbe. They were well mannered, but Nicholas had an edge about him. Don understood the boy did not like any change to the status quo he couldn't handle and so it made him annoyed. Nicholas wondered why his mother could not have waited until he started at university. Just another year and a bit was all he needed, as though the world revolved around him. The quieter, more sensitive, Ryder wanted to get to know this fellow and he asked the same questions Michelle had asked them the previous evening.

'Were you on mum's protection detail?' Don controlled a little smirk at the influence American television detective programs had on the choice of language. He also noted Nicholas's faint eyeroll, still he answered honestly.

'You could say, but the truth is I had to go into protection too. Head Office instructions after I received death threats. I had been undercover investigating the drug trafficking of an Australian- based gang who were trying to get a foothold here. Unfortunately, I had my cover blown. I had to lay low till the hotel shooter had been arrested.' Ryder wanted to know every small detail. Don quietly told him some of the details were not yet in the public arena.

'Like when you were shot at in Australia?' Nicholas loved to surprise.

'How did you know about the Australian shooting?' his mother asked, wondering what Hunter had told him exactly.

'I heard Dad on the phone to one of the partners from his firm after a detective called one Sunday afternoon. I don't get it. Did you travel with mum to Australia the week she had to work there?'

Don combed his fingers through his hair as he did in these situations.

'No, the truth is we wanted to meet away from where people might know us, so we could get to know one another. After the Australian incident, we were put in protection until the Australians completed their investigation.' Don felt relieved when the server brought their food, thinking the hungry boys would be busy for a while getting stuck into their huge plates of steak and chips. Wrong.

'Oh, like those two French spies who bombed the Rainbow Warrior. We learned about it at school. They were sent to an island

in the pacific she ended up having a baby, but they weren't married.'
Barbe groaned. Ryder was growing up.

'Well, not married to each other.' Nicholas elucidated.

'Your mother and I are married. We love each other and need
to ensure we maintain a strong moral compass, so we are legally
married. We want to do it again in church, but it may take another
year or so.' Don sipped his water; he required a clear head for these
two.

'What's the hurry? Are you pregnant?' Nicholas's derisive tone
annoyed Don who needed him to know who's in charge here.

'What difference would it make?' Don said, as he watched
Nicholas's upper lip lift like a *snirk,* half sneer half smirk. 'It's what
families do; they have babies and don't look at me like you don't
know this. Get used to the idea because the child would be your little
brother or sister.' Don sat squeezing Barbe's hand under the table
and she blushed. 'Would you be having this conversation with your
father if he remarried?' Nicholas remained defiant, but in his heart,
he knew the answer. Don laughed, shaking his head, and the tension
between them eased.

'How old do you think I am? I'm about ten years younger than
your father, and no there is no pregnancy, not that you would be the
first to be told if there were one.' He laughed again. 'Bloody cheek.'
He watched as Nicholas seemed to relax. The boy could see this man
did not look as intense as his father, he might even be fun, might, but
then again, he might not.

'Do you have children?' It suddenly occurred to Ryder he might
already have step siblings. Don said he had a daughter about Ryder's
age. 'Well, why didn't we all meet and go to your wedding?' It
seemed like a reasonable thing to Ryder.

'Because time was of the essence. Your father would understand
how these things work. But we are having a party for family and
friends in a few weeks, and you'll be invited. Then when we renew

our vows in church next year...' he squeezed Barbe's hand and he crossed his fingers.

'You can have a role, altar boy, usher, give your mother away or whatever.'

He had hardly finished when Nicholas added, 'not if she's pregnant, I'm not.' Barbe felt annoyed now.

'What is this obsession of yours about me and pregnancy?' she said, clearly upset. Don leaned over and kissed her cheek.

'Don't worry Bebe, I think your son is jealous,' he smiled. Horrified, she blurted out, 'not an Oedipus complex.' Ryder looked from one to the other, not understanding and wishing he could google it. But the no devices at the table rule stood.

'No, it's nothing to do with Oedipus,' Don chuckled, 'it's just a seventeen-year-old young buck thing. You'll get over it Nicholas, and I hope one day you remember this conversation when you're my age.' It certainly made Nicholas think, his father would never have talked openly like this. Hunter would have shut him down and not addressed the issue. Don Lancini was a senior police officer; perhaps they talked more openly, he didn't know.

Barbe told the boys about the house they had bought, and Don said there would be room for them but not like Latta Crescent. They spoke about alterations in broad terms. Ryder asked if in a couple of weeks when they were back from Auckland he could come and stay with them in Churton Park. Don said it would be fine, but their father needed to approve in the short term, aware the boys would go home and tell Hunter everything he had said, and wishing he could be a fly on the wall.

BARBE HAD BEEN PROCRASTINATING so Don suggested they skype her mother, because in ten days she would fly back to New Zealand. It needed to be done as soon as possible. When Barbe phoned to arrange the skype time her aunt, Katarina, answered the phone. Katarina had always been a much more understanding and realistic woman than her older sister who had been forty when she gave birth to her only child, Barbe.

'You met someone yet, beautiful girl?' she teased Barbe every time they spoke.

'Actually, I have Aunty, but don't tell mum. Just say I have something to tell her. I also need you present, because it's special.'

An hour later they were face to face, Mother and daughter, with Aunty hovering around in the background but in view. Unlike Don, who sat waiting to be called.

'Hi mum. Have you heard from Hunter in the last few months?' she wished she had asked him before now.

'Yes, he's phoned me several times, unlike my daughter.' She glowered at Barbe. 'Don't panic I understand. He told me you witnessed a massacre in your hotel, and you were shot at. Are you okay now? It sounded like a nasty business. Hunter assured me you were fine. There's been nothing on the news here. I would never have known if he hadn't kept me in the picture.' Katarina pulled a face behind her sister Jo.

'Mum, I want you to meet someone, but before you do, I must tell you Chester had to be put down. Old Mrs. Percy took him to the vet, he'd got sick. The vet recommended they euthanize him.' Barbe tried to soften the blow, the vet said it would be the kind thing to do.'

'Enough of the *old*, Doreen Percy is just a bit older than me. In cat years poor Chester would be another twenty years older than either of us. Still, it's the end of an era. None of us lasts forever.' Then Jo suddenly thought, 'you said you wanted me to meet someone. You didn't get me another cat did you because I'm over pets.' Barbe interjected...

'No, he's not a cat.' She motioned to Don who came and sat down beside her. 'Mum meet Adone Lancini, my new husband.'

Barbe could see her mother's shocked face, while Katarina clapped her hands together.

'Lui e bello,' the woman was such a flirt. Immediately Don flashed her his charismatic smile. He'd been told what a handsome boy he was since his Nonna bounced him on her knee.

'Grazie chiamami Don.' He watched as Jo looked him up and down. An elegant older woman with dark greying hair in a chignon at the nape of her neck. Finally, the words registered, and Jo blurted out...

'Your husband... your husband?' It came louder the second time. Her accent had a plummy English intonation. Don said nothing, he simply nodded at her deferentially.

Barbe elaborated, 'Don looked after me in witness protection.'

This did not appear to be going well, skyping never worked well in these situations.

'I'm looking forward to meeting you next week when you get back to New Zealand Mrs... what would you like me to call you?' Like a time, delay, the pause lengthened.

'Mrs. Brunner will do fine, thank you' she did not look like a happy woman.

Katarina spoke over the top of her 'Call her Jo, she likes Jo, she's a bit shocked aren't you Jovana?'

'Jovana' is not a name we hear often over here. Like your daughter, I'm Catholic and divorced, but I'm free to marry in the Church when Barbe's annulment comes through,' fingers crossed. He had to get it out there up front. 'It's what we plan. We've made this known to everyone, including our children.' Barbe felt upset by her mother's coolness and the conversation dragged like pulling teeth.

'Barbe and I will meet you at the airport and when you're over your jet lag, we can talk and get to know each other.' Don tried his best.

Jovana sighed. 'I'm sorry. This is a big shock, something I never expected. I thought from the way Hunter spoke before you went to the Whitsundays, maybe you and he...' Hearing her mother mention the Whitsundays Barbe became furious.

'What exactly did Hunter say to you before we went to the Whitsundays? Because if he had talked with me before we went, I could have saved you all a lot of grief.' Don took Barbe's hand softly, trying to placate her. Katarina helped by passing a few pleasantries.

Then they agreed to talk again, next week, when she arrived in the country.

'You can see what I've been up against. Hunter would talk to my mother before he discussed something with me. How could he do it? It's so condescending, like I'm a child and my opinion doesn't count. No, thinking about it, it's a calculated thing to keep him in a good light with my mother, like he's the one making an effort. As though putting in an effort can possibly change anything.' Don enveloped her with his arms.

'We knew this would be hard, but I thought our kids would be tougher on us than our aging parents.' He kissed her hair, 'you reckon your mother has no clue Hunter's gay? I didn't either. The man is masculine, nothing effeminate like the old stereotypes. I don't understand. If I'm honest, I don't want to, either.'

Chapter Twenty -Seven:

T he following week Don had his psych test. Dependent on the outcome he would be able to return to work. In his mind he had no doubt what the outcome would be. His marriage to Barbe had given him a new lease on life. Previously, he felt a little jaded in some of his thinking, not now, all he wanted is a job far from the front line and he'd be over the moon. Suddenly he had a different lens on life. He wanted the house organized, so their kids could have another home and they could have people around. They both could cook, maybe he'd get a little dog, and every night he'd cuddle up with the woman he loved.

The po-faced psychologist who did the testing said he had just added to his stresses by getting married and moving to a new house. Add the shooting and the stress numbers would be off the Richter scale. Then the woman had the cheek to ask about his finances. He knew they were tight. He would talk with his brother at the weekend, and as soon as Hunter paid Barbe out it would make a big difference. He felt a little niggle in the back of his mind about the mother-in-law from hell, Barbe's description. She told him several times her mother had been beyond difficult and bordered on being a religious bigot. He imagined the scene between his mother and her mother. He wondered how they would get on. When they did meet, he would need all the mental reserves he could muster. Only a catholic family could put on such pressure. If their mothers did not get along, it could well be apocalyptic. They would be damned if they did and damned if they didn't.

The psychologist said she would clear him to return to work on the proviso he took another week off. Don felt relieved. They had plenty to do.

Some smart alec from HR suggested he take his routine fitness level test this morning also. Without thinking, he agreed. Keen to do the test now because he felt fitter than he'd been in years, he needed it benchmarked. There were two other officers also taking their tests at the same time. Don felt really great, especially since he appeared to be older than the other two and his requirements were a little less onerous. He ran his best time in three years. He did the same number of pushups and crunches as the others even though it had not been strictly necessary. He'd been exercising daily. It certainly helped reduce the stress factor and improved his overall performance.

RICARD BEAUCHENE MET them at the airport Friday morning and dropped Don off at Paritai Drive before going into town to their work meeting.

'So, she's your new lady? Can't wait to get to know her,' Beth watched as the vehicle drove off.

'She's very attractive.'

'My wife,' he beamed. 'Mum knows, and she told you too I bet, so why the charade?' He grinned at his sister-in-law, knowing she seemed a little disapproving, but she didn't know the details and he wouldn't tell her. He fobbed her off. 'Barbe and I are seeing her lawyer this afternoon. The paperwork for the annulment application is already completed, it's just a matter of time.' He began to believe his own spin.

The work meeting had been just what Barbe needed; the schedule they set out for her for the next couple of months would give her life structure again. A smart man, Ricard, insisted she reduce her away from home nights per month down to three, except for the winter cosmetic trade fair which always proved an onerous few weeks of working weekends and being home mid-week. The fairs only lasted six weeks each year in the middle of winter. They formulated a simple plan showing her how it could be done. If she worked eight hours per day, including her travel, then effectively she would be free each week from Thursday till Sunday night. However, once a month she would have catch the red eye flight to Auckland for the day and return in the evening. Ricard suggested Don should join her at any time if he had the time available. He had invited them to dine with him tonight so he could get to know this man, if only to meet one of the very few men in the country who belonged to the exclusive group of Pascal Rousseau pour Homme users. When Don declined the invite, saying he needed to catch up with his brother and sister-in-law, Ricard had insisted he bring them too.

'You're not eating in a hotel? My Bebe's off hotels' he joked. They arranged to meet at seven at Pierre's in Remuera. But first, they had a 3.30pm appointment with Simon Perry.

Don drove Beth's car to Simon's office and this time Barbe felt sure she wouldn't need a ream of tissues because she had Don. Last time Simon had caught her unawares. The receptionist ushered them into Simon's office and he and Don shook hands, appraising one another.

'Today we have the application to sign for nullity to be granted. You wanted me to check it. I think you've covered everything. As soon as they get this application, they will decide whether or not the marriage is null. If they feel there may be some questions, they'll be in touch with you and interview you alone.' he looked at Don, 'I don't know how long it'll take. Set aside some time. Then they'll want to interview Hunter and afterwards before any deliberations they may want to speak with you again.' He sighed, 'from there it's a waiting game. If at any time during the process they believe the marriage is indissoluble they will tell you immediately.' Simon paused, asking if they had any questions. Barbe shook her head. Looking at Don, Simon added, 'it can take anything up to a year or so because there are other cases being heard and scheduling witnesses can cause delays.' He handed Barbe his pen and told her where to sign.

'There is some good news on the horizon,' Simon Perry said as he studied Barbe. Whenever she had a business meeting, she dressed to impress, today she excelled. The grape-coloured merino dress flattered her curvy figure, her makeup was perfect for her position as a Pascal Rousseau woman. Her thick dark hair bouncing on her shoulders. The jewellery understated except.... Don watched Simon's face as he noticed the stunning wedding ring; a wide band of odd sized round diamonds set lace-like in a statement piece framed by a thin gold edge, top and bottom.

'Wow, what a beautiful ring.' he took her hand to study it. Don sat amused. Barbe announced proudly, 'Don's Nonna's diamonds, special, aren't they?' Don winked at her, remembering the hodge podge of old rings he had offered her and what she had done with them.

'Barbe designed the setting,' he apprised.

'Spectacular,' Simon said. 'I mentioned some good news on the horizon. Here is the proposed settlement Hunter has agreed to.' He took another folder from his desk and opened it and gave her a copy of the agreement. 'You take any furniture you want from the family home, except the pieces listed there, mostly Anderson family pieces I believe. Hunter will pay three quarters of the boarding fees and expenses for the boys, and you pay the rest. The final figure is your cash settlement. Hunter doesn't want to sell Latta Crescent. Legally you are entitled to half of everything at the value given at the time of your divorce eight years ago. I know it doesn't seem fair, given you were obliged to live there, but I suggest you accept it, simply because the convoluted agreement you had may go against you if you were to contest it.' Don watched as Barbe's face flushed and she looked dismayed. Seeing Don watching she thrust the papers at him, embarrassed. He took them and quickly scanned the pages. He went back for a second look to confirm.

'Barbe, this is very generous, I agree you should sign it,' He glanced at Simon Perry.

'I can't sign it don't you see it's way too much. Why would he be so generous?' her voice quavered.

Immediately Don looked to Simon 'is there another explanation?'

'Don't worry about him, he can afford it. His statement of position indicated old money, inheritances, his alone.' Simon fingered the file on his desk, not telling her about the conversation he had with Hunter where Simon indicated to him at thirty-six years old, when they married, he knew his sexuality. That made the marriage all the more reprehensible.

'I can't accept so much money; it doesn't seem right.' The lawyer shot Don a knowing look and shook his head. He had worked very hard to get her the settlement. Still, to Barbe, something didn't seem right about it. 'Does it come with a gag order, stopping me from talking about him, is it hush money?' her voice full of sarcasm.

'No, nothing of the sort. There is a confidentiality clause, naturally and then there is my ginormous fee to be deducted,' he smiled trying to inject some levity into the situation. 'Hunter can't stop you being honest with the Marriage Tribunal.'

Once again Simon took out his pen and handed it to Barbe.

'Just how much is your fee?' she naively asked.

'A mere one-point five percent of your settlement plus disbursements.' He passed her the documents to sign. Don watched her adding up in her head.

'It's way less than the commission my ex earned when she sold us the house.' Obviously, he'd been thinking about her commission too. That had been two-point five percent.

'Let me assure you Barbe, Hunter Anderson is never going to be skint.' Just wanting it all behind her she happily signed. Simon took back his Waterman fountain pen and capped it.

RICARD BEAUCHENE HAD arranged for his executive team to join them for dinner at Pierre's. Ricard had hired a private room with French Provincial decor. The guests stood around enjoying aperitifs and canapes before they were finally seated. In typical New Zealand style Ricard and Tony Lancini quickly worked out they both belonged to the Ponsonby Yacht Club and had met at various functions.

The party of sixteen wasted little time in getting to know one another. The Lancini brothers proved great fun, with Tony telling them anecdotes of growing up in the predominantly Italian community of Island Bay in the nineteen sixties and seventies. Tony spoke of his father owning the local barber shop and with a café next door there were always groups of men hanging about drinking coffee and enjoying animated discussions in English and Italian about the quirks of life in New Zealand.

'If you tied their hands behind their back, they wouldn't have been able to talk,' he joked waving his hands about. 'Uncle Jo, Dad's brother, was a fisherman and if the weather looked too bad to go out to sea, he would be in the barber shop drinking his espressos and talking to the customers.' Tony appeared polished and suave, but still a laugh a minute with his silly stories.

'When I die, I've left instructions to be cremated and have my ashes sent to the IRD along with a note saying, *"now you have everything"*.' Beth skillfully moved around the table chatting to everyone, she realized Barbe was a quiet self-contained woman, the perfect foil for her charismatic brother-in-law who only let his older brother shine when they were together in public. Although she enjoyed herself, Barbe had been looking forward to some time with Beth and Tony. Being an only child, she had missed out on life with siblings. By comparison, Hunter had been the youngest of a large family and the only child left in Wellington. His brothers, one an academic, on the faculty of the University of British Columbia in Canada. The other brother, an industrial chemist, worked for one of the largest drug companies in America. They seldom saw each other or kept in touch, apart from the usual Christmas letter or occasional post-Christmas holiday in the Marlborough Sounds. Hunter's two sisters were both in Brisbane and their families had grown up. They had married two brothers and were always happy to see Hunter and Barbe but never went out of their way to maintain any closeness. One sister had indicated she had been happy to leave the Anderson's in Wellington, complaining their father had been far too strict, she even went as far as saying Hunter did everything to please the family and still, they were not satisfied.

THE FOOD AT PIERRE'S was outstanding and looked worthy of a cuisine magazine. Lobster thermidor being the most popular main course, and crepe suzette for dessert, brought flaming to the table. Don shared with Ricard his love of cooking, offering to cook for him on his next visit to Wellington, and quietly described the garden he wanted to create at their new home. The evening proved fun, but Barbe still found herself looking forward to Saturday with family. Beth expressed amazement that Barbe enjoyed being a homemaker, especially because she had this very glamorous job, and she looked the part.

'Barbe, I always knew Don would fall for a gorgeous woman. I just never thought the woman would embroider and knit as well as cook and be a mother,' she said pleased.

'What are you trying to say Beth?' Don grinned as she elbowed him. 'You didn't trust my choices?'

'No, she's lovely,' she hugged Barbe 'and I'm happy for you both. We expect to see a lot more of you now, especially with Barbe's company being Auckland-based.'

Chapter Twenty -Eight:

On Saturday afternoon at about four thirty Barbe's phone buzzed, Hunter called, his voice anxious.

'Barbe, I know you're in Auckland, but you need to know Nicholas has been involved in an accident. He's unconscious and in hospital.'

'What happened? not a car accident?' she panicked.

'He and another player collided on the field during the first XV final, a complete freak accident, but Nicholas came off second best.'

'How bad is he?

'It's a nasty concussion; they're doing all the tests. It's just a wait and see situation.'

'I'm coming home, I'll be there as soon as I can.' She killed the call. 'Don, Nicholas is unconscious, he's been knocked out in a freak accident during the game,' Don looked at his watch, wanting to know how long he'd been unconscious, her face crumpled, and Don hugged her.

'I don't know, Hunter just said he's in the hospital and he's unconscious. I need to get back to Wellington, I'm sorry.' Don called the airlines as Barbe packed her bags.

'Only five minutes this time, and no kitchen sink,' he joked about her packing speed. 'The airline said get to the airport and they will get us on the next flight to Wellington.' Tony drove them to the airport and Beth came along to see them off. Barbe sat very quietly on the journey, she had never really enjoyed the physicality of competition rugby at Nicholas's level of involvement. But there had always been an overwhelming pressure on the good players like him to play hard, especially ones who had a family tradition in the sport at the college.

True to their word the airline managed two seats on the next flight to Wellington. It helped Inspector Don Lancini had the gift of the gab and clout. Whatever he used they arrived in Wellington and headed straight to the hospital. Hunter sat at Nicholas's bedside and stood up on seeing Barbe.

'He's come around and they've given him something. He's pretty groggy.' Hunter looked greyer than usual, 'Oh God, it was frightful, the bone crunching noise when they collided. I thought for sure he'd fractured his skull or worse still, broken his neck.' Barbe opened her arms to give him a comfort hug, he gripped her tightly, ignoring Don standing behind her as he stood embracing her. Don noticed Ryder out of the corner of his eye coming up the corridor towards them. He stepped out.

'Give your parents some space eh' he suggested. Guiding Ryder towards the office he asked,

'tell me what happened at the game? The accident I mean.'

'The game looked rough; I don't think I want to play first XV level if it gets so rough. The whole match seemed tight and intense. A real grudge match. The referee decided neither player is to blame apparently. Either of them could have come off worse. The field looked heavy and boggy, and the teams were revved up. There were other injuries, plenty of them actually. Nicholas gunned it the whole match like he had something to prove. I hate it when he gets so competitive.' Don put his hand on Ryder's shoulder.

'Yeah, I know what you mean, I used to enjoy playing the game until I got a nasty hit like Nicholas. Never played again after my accident.' Don's admission surprised the boy. 'Let's get back to see what's happening.'

This time Hunter acknowledged Don, even thanking him for getting Barbe back to Wellington for Nicholas. The high dependency unit staff were still doing fifteen-minute pupil checks and half hourly vital signs. The registrar came and gave them a report, telling Nicholas how lucky he had been.

'You're not out of the woods yet. You need to be monitored in hospital for a couple of days, then if I'm happy with your condition you can go home for a week, not back to school. You might be able to return to school after a week or so,' the neurologist said.

Barbe immediately told Hunter she wanted to look after Nicholas at home. Hunter acquiesced, thanking her, saying it suited him as he had a case he needed to deal with. Don told him he'd be welcome to visit anytime. Then Ryder asked if he could go home with them next weekend too. Barbe agreed, saying she and Hunter would work things out, none of them fully aware of the path it would take them on.

Nicholas's condition showed no improvement, and the medical team said rest was required and no stimulation. He was put in a room by himself, where he did quite a bit of sleeping. His head ached and sometimes he threw up. They all returned the next day, but as Hunter was preparing for his court case, he didn't stay very long. Barbe became the parent keeping the bedside vigil, with Don and Ryder sneaking off for snacks and coffee. Nicholas did nothing much more than lie still, his neck painfully sore and his head still ached intermittently. The only treatment that worked seemed to be rest and Panadol. The regular monitoring continued. Ryder went back to school on the Sunday night.

On Monday, Barbe worked a full day, as the registrar and neurologist said the patient would likely be discharged on Tuesday. Don happily took the extra week's leave he had been ordered to take. Nicholas went home with them on Tuesday to Churton Park. Sometimes Don kept an eye on him while Barbe either packed things at the house in Latta Crescent or worked from home, planning some staff training material for new beauty therapists and cosmeticians.

Don offered to cook dinner and invited Hunter to eat with them each time he visited. Hunter refused on principle but by Thursday evening he felt worn out and gratefully accepted Don's offer.

'It smells too good to turn down tonight,' he said, with a completely straight face.

'My veal scaloppini is world famous in my family.' Pushing the boat out to impress Don cooked the vegetables Nicholas chose, mashed potatoes, fresh green beans with bacon bits. He covered the browned and cooked veal in Swiss cheese and the special sauce of chopped onion and tomatoes, then grilled it till the cheese bubbled and melted. Now sitting at the table Nicholas hoed in. His huge appetite convincing his father he had begun to mend.

'I won't see you now until next weekend, like we used to do.' He directed his firm voice at his son. Then he turned to Barbe.

'Those old arrangements do still suit I take it?' She nodded, realizing Don had been right. Now they were legally married he could not deny her access. Legally, he could not have done even if they lived together, but he would certainly have made life very difficult. He had done it before.

Later when they were alone together, relaxing, Barbe diplomatically spoke to Don.

'Do you think we can wean Hunter away from us. I don't fancy sharing our life with him.' Don laughed; he loved this woman.

'It's not my choice either but you do understand we both have children with other parents, and they will always be there in the background at some level. But they won't be dining with us every night. I think even Hunter made that clear tonight.' He cuddled up to her on the couch. 'I needed to soften him up, especially after our visit to Simon Perry last week.' Don also thought about having a greater input into his daughter's life but, until he knew where his police career was headed, he had no idea of the kind of life they'd lead or how it would work.

Next morning Tim Paxton phoned.

'Sorry to disturb your leave. I thought you should hear this from me first. I'm leaving the unit, not going far. I've been promoted upstairs, Assistant Commissioner.'

'Congratulations Sir, great, who will be replacing you?' The selfish thought crossed Don's mind if it were Bill Powell he'd be resigning, because he didn't fancy reporting to the pedantic pommy prick, as he referred to the man.

'That's what I wanted to talk with you about. The job's yours if you want it. You'll be getting the confirmation from upstairs later today, when I tell them you're happy to do it.' Don's mind began to race. This would be perfect. More structured working hours yet not completely chained to the desk. There would be some out of office stuff when things got interesting, like a big drug bust, or a search and seizure.

'I'd like it very much. I'll come in to see the boss whenever it suits.'

'Good I'll be in touch,' Tim said.

Don desperately wanted to tell Barbe, but she had gone out doing the grocery shopping. Ryder would be home for the weekend and having two teenage boys meant constantly having food handy. Don idly passed by Nicholas's room and saw him working on his laptop. He stood in the doorway for a moment. Nicholas, who should not be watching any screens for two weeks, had not heard Don. Standing behind Nicholas, Don looked horrified. The boy sat watching porn and from the pictures of the nude woman and her male partner's behaviour, it looked hard core.

'Nicholas,' he said, his voice commanding. 'What the hell do you think you're doing?' Suddenly Nicholas snapped his laptop closed.

'Nothing, yeah sorry I know, no screens.' He jumped back into his bed clutching his laptop. Don surveyed the room and chose to sit in the swivel desk chair which he scooted to Nicholas's bedside.

'Give me the laptop,' he quietly insisted. Nicholas knew protesting would be useless, but he felt confident Don wouldn't learn much as he had recently wiped his browsing history. Don insisted he open it, demanding the password or he would have the police forensics team check it and he'd then have to report it to Hunter. Nicholas obliged and as the video clip came up on the screen, Don checked the recent history.

'The number of times you have visited these sites in the last couple of days indicates you have a problem.' Don's voice sounded calm. The short browsing history didn't appear nearly as bad as many he'd seen, but he wanted to put the fear of God and his father into the seventeen-year-old.

'What you see on these sites is not normal sexual behaviour.' Don's voice resonated fatherly concern. 'This is not how normal people behave towards one another.' Don closed the laptop but hung on to it. Nicholas looked confused and annoyed at being caught out.

'What do you mean normal, at least it's a man and a woman, it's what they do isn't it?' This was a difficult conversation Don and Barbe had never had, sex education and their blended family.

'No Nicholas, this is so far from normal it's wrong on many levels.' He combed his fingers through his hair thinking it would soon be grey if there were too many situations like this. He needed to couch his words to avoid gender bias.

'What you're watching is not two adults committed to each other, in love, respecting each other, understanding each other's needs. There is no tenderness there, just a couple of animals on heat, exhibitionists.' Don floundered to express himself, 'look, all I can tell you is people who watch this stuff cannot sustain happy loving relationships. Life doesn't work like porn movies. It's hard enough navigating the rules of normal sexual behaviour without complicating it with this crap.' Don studied Nicholas's face, he looked like a young Hunter, complete with those intense grey eyes, tall and lanky but filling out to match his bone structure.

'Has your father talked about sex with you?' It struck him, while eloquent in the courtroom, had he bothered even with the basics when it came to his sons.

'Course he has,' Nicholas didn't sound quite as confident as he did at dinner the night they first met. 'Well only the nuts and bolts, not the best techniques exactly.' He raised an eyebrow at Don who could see a twinkle in the boy's eye, this lad had something of his mother about him.

'Ah, the best techniques, well they are a bit like food, people have preferences, but I can tell you there is nothing to be gained from this,' he tapped the computer. 'You might start by getting a proper education through literature. Reading will help you learn about women, understand them, and get one step closer... it is women? Oh, I mean it's not my business.'

Nicholas laughed then he stopped realizing Don seemed embarrassed.

'Yes, I prefer women, never men in case you thought otherwise.'

'I just didn't want to presume. Your life is your choice but be honest with yourself. Everyone will accept it.' Don couldn't help himself; he just had to say it, and Nicholas understood but felt irritated.

'It's the truth, for fuck's sake. I should know.' He raised his voice annoyed.

'Well then, read about decent relationships and don't watch this crap or you'll be a sad, lonely man.' Don never commented on his use of the 'F' bomb and Nicholas somehow admired this man.

'I'll not mention this to your mother, except to say I confiscated your laptop to stop you using screens at the moment. But if you ever want to talk about anything and you feel you can't talk to your father or your pastoral carer, I'm here.' Don stood up just as they heard Barbe's car enter the garage. 'Get up Nicholas and take a shower then come down to lunch.'

Chapter Twenty-Nine:

D uring lunch Don got up to answer his cell phone. He walked away and a few minutes later returned.

'I need to go to HQ after lunch. I have a two o'clock appointment with the Commissioner.' He saw the look on Barbe's face. 'It's a routine thing before I start back at work. I think he may offer me something different.' He smiled at Barbe, who wanted to know if he might be transferred out of the district. 'No, we discussed my options when I returned from Australia. I told them what interested me and what did not. He knows I could disengage under section 28D of the Police Act, that's where we resign due to stress. The Police Employment Rehabilitation Fund pays us out.'

'But I thought you passed your psych test?' she protested.

'Yeah, but after a couple of weeks in the old job I might find it too much.' He flashed her his smile this time he looked all-knowing. 'I've had twenty-six years in the job. I could retire soon too. I can't honestly imagine retiring for a few years yet. I have options Bebe.' He didn't want to tell her about the promotion until it became a done deal.

After lunch Barbe did her usual Friday baking and Don left for HQ dressed in a suit and his gorgeous aftershave. Nicholas had been playing patience with a pack of cards at the table, then he sat building houses of cards. He seemed bored rigid, no screens and nothing to do. The neurologist had told Barbe he could go back to school after a week or so if he felt up to it and left her to decide. Seeing he looked bored she suggested he help her ice the baking and perhaps he could return to school after the weekend. He seemed happy to do it, especially when she suggested he go with her to pick up his brother from college later.

At the college Nicholas received lots of support from his friends and teachers. He lapped up the attention. Their team had won the final and everyone seemed happy. The neurologist intimated rugby may not be a good idea for him in the future. On learning he wanted to study law like his father she suggested he coach instead of playing.

'You only get one brain, and it can't take too many knocks. A good lawyer needs his wits about him,' the woman had told him. Firmly adding, 'your life is your choice, but you will not play for the next six months at least.' When the family discussed it, Ryder had told them about Don's similar accident. Then he told them he didn't think he would play next year. Hunter listened and remained very quiet on the subject, but had some sympathy for the boys telling them both,

'Regardless of what the school tells you it is first and foremost your choice.' Nicholas listened to his father, then quietly told him in that annoying way of smart-arse teenagers,

'How come you never said so before? I remember when Anton Lane switched to soccer after his best friend got a neck injury and you said Anton's a sissy and didn't deserve a place in the St Benedict's First XV, even if he is a good player.' To his credit, Hunter simply said he'd rethought the situation after speaking with the neurologist.

BY FOUR PM BOTH BOYS were sitting down with their mother enjoying afternoon tea when Don returned. Barbe could tell from the look on his face it had to be something good.

'You are now looking at Superintendent Lancini, Officer in Charge, of the Wellington special investigations section.' He grabbed Barbe and kissed her lovingly, making a meal of it to get a reaction from the boys. Ryder made a retching noise pretending to put his fingers down his throat. Don looked across, grinning at him. 'Don't mess with me if you want takeaways for dinner, special treat.' he said, still hanging on to Barbe. Immediately Ryder saluted feigning respect, the boy always a real character and endowed with loads of personality. After a round of chocolate cake and orange segments, washed down by tea they all played cards. Nicholas determined to beat them all, he played at his sparkling best. At about five thirty Barbe heard the ping of a text message, at first Don thought it sounded like his phone, she read her message in amazement.

Barbe, I heard about Nicholas's accident, don't bother to meet me at the airport. My plane is now getting in later and I have made other arrangements. I'm staying with a friend; I'll be in touch when I'm over my jetlag. Mumma xoxo.

Having read it, she shot Don a look as she passed the phone to him. Don mouthed the word, *Hunter*? and Barbe said, 'who else?' The next few rounds of cards she brooded over the slap in the face her mother had delivered.

At eighty-one years old, Jovana Brunner could not soften her approach to her only child. Barbe remembered trying to tell her mother about finding Hunter naked with a younger man in their bedroom. Jo had shut her down before she even heard any details. She had referred to it as an 'indiscreet dalliance' saying it would never have happened if her daughter were more available to her husband. 'You promised until death do you part, and you will stick with it come hell or high water my girl.'

Jo's thinking felt so dated, not even in the same century let alone on the same page. How could Barbe begin to describe her marriage with Hunter? Jo Brunner had been pampered by her doting older husband and now he had been dead for years. Hunter could do no wrong and she would not hear a word against him. She believed Barbe showed little gratitude to her husband and her overactive imagination couldn't be healthy for her boys in her mother's view.

JO BRUNNER'S PLANE landed in windy Wellington well after midnight. Because of her age she had taken more stopovers, so tonight she and her sister Katarina had only flown in from Sydney and had no jet lag. The two-hour time difference made them feel not yet ready for bed.

Eventually settled in at Hunter's apartment, the two women sat nursing their brandies regaling him with their skype introduction to Adone Lancini.

'Katarina is incorrigible, she actually flirted with the man in Italian, telling him he looked handsome, from memory.' Jo loved to embellish the details and she loved Hunter.

'Well, it's the truth, he has a beautiful smile, and he answered in Italian. I'd love to meet him in person.' Katarina had always been a little scatty according to her sister. In truth, Katarina could never be called a lightweight. A qualified nurse, she worked with her GP husband all their married life and had always been more fun than her sister, especially in her old age.

'The sad thing is he's actually a good bloke.' Hunter sighed, 'but the pair of them are delusional if they think they'll be able to marry in the church. You know I've tried so hard for my boys to make this work. I really thought after the shooting in Auckland...' he stared into the amber liquid in his glass.

'Do you know where you went wrong?' Katarina queried, she seemed more astute than Jo.

'You said you tried so hard for your boys. A good marriage is between one man and one woman, those boys are teenagers. Sure, they are the product of your union, but to make your relationship work it should have been for the love of your wife, no other reason.' Katarina sipped her brandy waiting for his reply. Hunter simply waved his hand.

'God knows I've tried; a man can only stand so much rejection. It's all academic now anyway.' Jo moved on to discuss the fate of Chester, her old ginger cat.

THE WET MISERABLE WEEKEND gave way to family fun, board games and food. On Saturday afternoon, as arranged, Don went to fetch Michelle. When they arrived back at Churton Park Barbe had a special afternoon tea organized. Don introduced Michelle to Nicholas and Ryder who offered her a high five.

'Does this mean we're kinda related?' Ryder asked, Don answered him quickly.

'Yes, if it means you look out for her, okay? Michelle's the youngest.' Ryder held up his finger to ask a question.

'So how old are you anyway?' She replied telling him, fourteen. He beamed, 'cool you look way older.' Barbe noticed the hair flick and lash flutter so did Don.

'Yeah well, she's not, so remember age-appropriate stuff, okay?' Don shot Nicholas a very intense look, to which Nicholas said.

'Wh-a-t?' Don narrowed his eyes slightly, giving him the policeman stare.

The weekend went surprisingly well. Michelle could hold her own in conversation with the boys and she teased Nicholas. She'd always wanted an older brother. She could blackmail for cash if she ever caught him doing stuff like kissing his girlfriend, or he could bribe her to keep out of the way. Don told her firmly what Nicholas her business did was not; he knew the appropriate boundaries. Michelle would store up that information till she turned seventeen. She and Ryder interacted like siblings; however, she seemed a little in awe of Nicholas. Fortunately, he didn't notice.

The inclement weather proved perfect for board games, and a little screen time had been reintroduced for Nicholas, who watched oblivious to the fact Don had placed parental controls on the internet. Michelle found some posters of Barbe made up for in-store promotions of the French cosmetic products she represented. The girl seemed fascinated. Barbe gave her some samples showing her how to apply them professionally. Don and Barbe shared the cooking, and the family went out for Sunday lunch after Mass. Don chuckled to himself as he entered the church. He knelt thinking it's been a while and the roof's not fallen in yet. He even found himself praying as he sat with Barbe on one side and Michelle on the other. He wanted a fully functioning family. Surely it is not too much to ask after all these years. This is the beginning, he told himself.

By the time Sunday evening came around the newlyweds were pleased to have some privacy again. 'I'm not used to sharing you or being second guessed. Teenage boys are full on.' Don sat yawning on the couch.

'You think? My friends tell me teenage girls can be high maintenance, so I guess we'll see when the novelty value wears off.' She flicked the remote to turn off the TV. 'I can't get over my mother, I have no doubt Aunty Katarina, will sort her out.'

'I'm sorry you're getting the cold shoulder,' Don sighed. 'It's a wonder someone in the family hasn't guessed Hunter's secret,' he suggested.

Barbe turned off the heat pump and the table lamps.

'I'm not really surprised, now Simon Perry explained it a little better, about people closer to the middle of the sexual continuum being able to vacillate either way for short periods of time.' she plumped up the cushions. Don picked up the Sunday papers from the floor.

'Unless they saw someone of their own persuasion,' Don suggested, 'someone tastier. But they're not able to sustain a heterosexual relationship. Well, so I'm told. Cripes you don't think Simon's one too?' He looked at Barbe, slightly amused.

'I simply don't care anymore,' she told him. 'All I ever wanted was honesty. To be armed with the knowledge and the freedom to choose. They call those kind of marriages a Lavender marriage, when you get to choose. But if you don't know and think there's something wrong with you, then it's no marriage at all.' They walked arm in arm up the wooden hill to bed.

Chapter Thirty:

A lthough packing and getting ready to take possession of their home, they developed a routine of sorts. Don largely worked regular hours but when Barbe went away on business he pushed the envelope, working extra hours clearing his desk, waiting for the next big thing. It would only be a matter of time. Policing worked like that.

The Catholic Marriage Tribunal had acknowledged her application and would be in touch in due course. Barbe felt elated, seeing it as one step closer to an annulment. Don on the other hand, felt a little anxious wondering what effect a refusal to grant nullity might have on their relationship and thinking about them more and more, he felt a child might be the answer. However, every time it came to the forefront of his mind, he remembered her remarks about being perimenopausal and dismissed it as unlikely, telling himself, in any event he felt 'too bloody old.'

The more he knew this woman the more he loved her. The way she always had a sympathetic ear for his little rants about work, the way she reminded him gently to text Michelle or phone his mother. No wonder he was a shit father, he just got so engrossed in his work he became oblivious to the world around him. Except when they kissed, then he became totally in the moment. He loved the way she touched him this gentle tactile woman, cuddles, shoulder massages, little affections. How lucky he felt to have a woman who wanted him physically as much as he wanted her. They possessed a secret covenant of unity and oneness which neither of them had enjoyed before.

TONY LANCINI HAD SENT his Wellington team to complete the first stage of their house alterations. The team converted the old hobby room to a fourth bedroom with the addition of wardrobes and storage cupboards. The other three bedrooms were all given built-in wardrobes and storage. A floor to ceiling bookcase with shelving now ran the length of the family room and with a bit of decorating the house would be finished before they moved.

Hunter had received notification from the Catholic Marriage Tribunal, Barbe had applied to have their marriage annulled and they would investigate based on her allegations whether or not the marriage is valid. Furious, he made a point of being at the college careers evening, knowing Barbe would be there too, and he would have the opportunity to speak to her face to face. As Nicholas had decided his career path and looked set to follow it, only the younger Ryder needed guidance. He had no idea what he wanted to do, and it annoyed his father, because with Hunter everything was cut and dried. When Ryder's form teacher had told his parents what a delight he was to teach, his father filled with pride.

'He's such a well-rounded young man and while he'll never be dux of the college, he's a bright boy and a popular student, caring and empathetic.' Listening to the teacher Hunter said quite automatically,

'he's just like his mother.' He gave her a look full of love and Barbe touched his arm, thanking him. Five minutes later the pair were headed in the direction of the car park and like Dr. Jekyll and Mr. Hyde Hunter grabbed her arm and spun her round.

'I see you're still going through with your ridiculous farce with the marriage tribunal. Well know this, since you're intent on causing my family embarrassment and distress and it is my family not just us and the boys or you. It's the Anderson family name. You've got a shock coming to you.' She pulled away.

'Don't be such a dramatist, I'm not married to the Anderson family, it's only you and I who needs an annulment.' Barbe started fumbling for her car keys as Hunter held her arms tightly with both his hands.

'I haven't spent thirty years in court rooms to learn nothing. Wait till they question you because you are wrong about this. Do you care so little about me and the boys that you are prepared to make a spectacle of yourself with these preposterous allegations? How come you waited all these years to dream this up?' He stood inches from her, his grey eyes desperate. 'There is a big difference between proof and truth and the church will want the truth, but they will not grant nullity of a holy sacrament on your say so with no proof. You don't have any proof because there is none.' His intense grey eyes turned cold in the last light of the day.

'Please, let go of me. All I want is the truth. The process is confidential you of all people know how it works.' Her words annoyed him more and he gave her a shove as he let go of her. She stumbled before standing firm.

'You will rue the day you did this to me.' He said maliciously.

'The only day I rue is the day I married you.' Sudden tears filled her, as she realized what she'd said. She broke down sobbing. 'I'm sorry I didn't mean... I love our boys...' He watched as she dabbed her eyes and found her key. Driving off, she looked in the rear-view mirror to see him still standing there frowning. He wondered if there might be trouble in paradise.

ON THE WEEKEND THEY moved into their new home. Barbe felt so excited she woke early on the day. The previous day she had remeasured the furniture and worked out where everything would go, labelling it with the room name for the removal company. Last weekend when the boys were home, they packed their own rooms. Don had taken them to the climbing wall in town and all three, Don included, had great fun climbing the wall then abseiling down. Later when Nicholas had driven over to his mate's place, Don took Ryder out for a driving lesson. He knew all the places around Wellington where a learner driver could have good practice. Ryder, an excellent chess player agreed to teach Don. The two had a great line in banter and a friendship had begun developing.

Don wanted Michelle to join them for the weekend or at least the Sunday, however she had an outing organized with her mates but promised to help with the move. When she saw the bedroom Barbe had decorated for her she became excited, immediately over the moon. She had been allowed to choose her curtains and light fittings; she had only seen the mood board they made together. It all looked so much nicer in real life; she told her father. By the end of the weekend everything appeared in order and the house had Barbe's stamp on it. Stylish, eclectic and home, with her personal touches echoing good taste. Don loved it. what had previously been a separate dining room had become a den full of his personal treasures. Police memorabilia and photos, plus his beloved book collection. The seating, a small comfy sofa in buttoned leather and two club chairs.

'Is this where I sleep when I'm in the dog box?' he asked, pointing to the sofa and grinning with pleasure.

'Adonis, dog boxes are for dogs, we sleep together, every night we are home together till death do us part.' Even as she said it, he noticed how tired she looked. Barbe had not told Don about her contretemps with Hunter in the college carpark. She hated unpleasantness.

Carla Lancini called in with baking and some parsley growing in a pot.

'An old Italian tradition,' she told them as she admired their home. She approved.

In the dogleg of the hall, Carla admired a collection of icons. All good Catholic families have holy pictures.

'You will have to get the priest here to bless the house,' she announced.

BARBE'S INTERVIEW BEFORE the Marriage Tribunal and the defender of the bond had been scheduled. On the day, she dressed as though attending a funeral, plain sombre and black. Her only jewellery, her pearl earrings. Don, seeing she appeared anxious, cancelled his appointments and insisted he take her, so she had support.

In the old wood-panelled hallway of the diocesan office of the tribunal, Barbe nervously waited on a hard chair, to be called. It looked a sombre place. Don squeezed her hand telling her not to worry. Truth be told, he worried enough for both of them. Barbe had not seen her girlfriend for years and she had agreed to be her only real witness and even then, she saw nothing and Barbe gave her no details. The priest she had tried to speak with about her situation had been protected by the seal of the confessional and could not be required to testify. Barbe's mother would have been a hostile witness as she had refused to listen to anything derogatory about Hunter. But Simon Perry insisted she be put on the list.

'She'll be asked direct questions and being an honest woman, she may be more help than she realizes.' Today, only Barbe would be called. They had only been there twenty minutes and already she had made two nervous trips to the ladies.

Finally, ushered in and seated before the panel of four people, three men and one-woman, Barbe appeared nervous. The panel made up of the defender of the bond, plus two other priests, and a psychologist. Barbe didn't know if the woman had been simply a panellist or the Psychologist. In her nervous confusion, she felt unsure.

The first question they asked threw her off balance.

'It is eight years since the final decree of your divorce, why do you apply for an annulment now?'

'Well, I didn't think I had grounds for an annulment. I only learned this when I sought legal advice to get a settlement of the matrimonial property.' Remembering what Simon Perry had told her, she looked the panellists straight in the eye.

'Why was the matrimonial property not settled before this?' the priest asked.

'I had a settlement agreement document I signed at the time, permitting me to stay in the family home. I'm not an owner of the property, it's in a trust. I've learned my husband is the sole beneficiary of the trust. But look, I'm more than happy with the final settlement. I needed to move out of the family home as I have remarried.' Noticing the priest's lips twitch and purse, she added, 'It became imperative I marry because my ex-husband said he would not allow me to see my boys if I lived with 'that man' as he referred to my current husband. At least now, I have the protection of the law as well as a loving man.' Ignoring her comments another panellist spoke.

'you claim in the application, your husband is homosexual. Yet you never told another living soul until now,' he said, looking for comment.

'I felt so ashamed, and bereft, Hunter denied I saw him and this younger man naked at it doggy fashion in our bedroom as I described in my written application. But as soon as I saw him it answered so many questions for me. His staying out all hours, not coming home some nights. The way he never seemed interested in me sexually at all. I can't begin to explain...' her voice cracked. But this time she felt prepared and took out a tissue. 'I saw all around me how my friends' husbands behaved towards their wives, and I can't explain, except to say, he wasn't really interested in me. We had no rapport.' She blew her nose. 'I tried to talk to my priest, he told me I must be mistaken. Homosexual men are impotent with a woman he said. I told him there is a difference between emotional impotency and the physical kind. I went online and learned you don't need anyone's permission to divorce in New Zealand. So, I did it. Hunter became furious. I had an inheritance from my father, in a bank account in my name. I told him I intended leaving him. When he realized I had proceeded with the divorce application he drew up a settlement saying he wanted the boys to be brought up in their family home. Also, he wanted them to attend certain schools I would not necessarily be able to afford. So, we came to an arrangement.

I know he does not choose to be homosexual. Hunter had turned thirty-six when we married. I have read men would definitely be aware of their sexuality by thirty-six. To be quite honest, our marriage worked well for quite a few years. When we separated Hunter had an apartment. It gave him the freedom to live his life as he chose. However, he cut my allowance and when my inheritance ran out, I found myself forced to get a job. So, then the boys became borders at St. Benedicts, that happened three years ago now.' Sitting there she thought for a moment. 'The thing is if I had the slightest inkling, he was homosexual before we married, I would never have married him. There are little nuances between a couple that I never knew about when I married at twenty-one, almost twenty-two. I had no one to compare relationships with. I felt so terribly hurt and ashamed.'

'How would you describe Hunter?'

'There is no doubt he is a good man, an excellent father and a brilliant barrister. But he was never a husband like Adone Lancini. Small thing, but when we were out together as a family, for example when we went to the Whitsundays a few months ago, my sons were checking out all the pretty girls on the beach. I looked around noticing most all of the men were checking out the pretty women. But not Hunter, quite honestly, he just about got whiplash when some tanned young bloke with a six pack of abs strolled along. Apart from one or two girls no men took the slightest bit of notice.' The defender of the bond argued there seemed insufficient evidence to find the marriage is null. He considered one incident insufficient, but it sounded grave enough to hear the respondent's side of the story and possibly the witnesses.

Chapter Thirty-One:

Barbe felt very despondent after her session with the tribunal. Don set about conditioning her to what he perceived as the most likely outcome.

'Barbe, Hunter will drag the chain claiming already booked court cases requiring his input. It will be months before the Tribunal can get to him and besides, they are bound to have other cases. You know he can't fob them off forever and sooner or later they will proceed with or without him. We'll just get on with our lives. God knows what's in our hearts.' Then he'd flash his smile and she would be won over and feel loved and safe.

Even her mother seemed to have mellowed, much to Barbe's surprise. Aware Don had driven over to see her just a few days after her return to New Zealand she wondered what he had said to her because Jovana treated him differently and with warmth. When Barbe asked him, he simply grinned and his dark eyes twinkled; the man had a way about him.

Don remembered knocking on the woman's door. When she opened it and they stood face to face he thought this is what Barbe will look like in forty years; dignified, refined patrician even. the old woman had great bone structure. her welcome was gracious, if a little cool.

'I wanted to meet you face to face and talk to you.' she ushered him into a comfortable living room and offered him a chair. 'I love your daughter and we're a family. You know how you raised her; do you think she moved on from Hunter because she felt happy?' He watched the woman frown, breathing deeply.

'Happiness, is a childish notion, adults must do what they commit to before God.' Don flashed her that smile and then he asked her another question already knowing the answer.

'Were you happy with Barbe's father, your husband. What sort of man was he?' the woman's face changed, although asking a woman her age such a personal question sounded a bit cheeky, her face warmed as she remembered.

'Bernard was lovely, although quite a few years older than me. I said if we had twenty years together then we'd be blessed. We had thirty-five wonderful years.' Don, ever tactile patted her hand.

'Just like my parents, I'm pleased. So, after his death, Barbe and Hunter divorced?' he asked, pulling his chair closer to her.

'Yes, thank heavens it would have caused him such distress.' Her lips pursed again.

'He liked Hunter then?' As Don said the words, he watched her face, with the expert eye of an experienced police investigator. Noting a slight hesitation before she commented,

'He was very impressed with him. He's a brilliant lawyer as you would know.' Jo's momentary hesitation gave Don what he needed.

'Yes, he's a brilliant legal practitioner and quite formidable on the cross examinations.' Once again, he flashed his smile, and she smiled back this time. 'Do you think Barbe's father would have wanted to know why quite suddenly she became so unhappy and why her marriage failed?' His question took her by surprise. She looked uncomfortable, knowing she had refused to listen to Barbe, not wanting to hear anything untoward about her esteemed son in law. Don watched in silence as Jo shuffled nervously in her chair. When she said nothing, Don sighed.

'Poor Barbe, she had no one to confide in until now.' He shot her a sad look and pushed up his lip. 'Something like this can unwittingly isolate you. I think Hunter understands this and perhaps it's the reason he appears, on the face, of it to be selfless.' Jo just listened, hardly moving. 'But then he is the one with the most to lose, sadly. I understand how it must be for him in his Catholic family, mine would be brutal under the same circumstances.' Before he said more Katarina, who had been next door with Mrs. Percy, arrived back and the conversation took an entirely lighter note. Still, Don had sown the seeds of doubt in her mind, and she began to think about things. There appeared to be a noticeable softening of her approach and Katarina may have had some influence there too. Don stood for a few moments at the mantelpiece admiring a great photo of Ryder and Nicholas in the Whitsundays. It had been made into a postcard and mounted he noted the photographer's name, as he fingered it. He thanked Jovana for her time and invited her and Katarina to Sunday lunch in three weeks.

TO BARBE'S DELIGHT Brad Murphy won the Pascal Rousseau Scholarship. Ricard Beauchene felt pleased, telling the team,

'Gender equality goes both ways, and he is the best person for the job. The first man in Australasia to earn such a Scholarship.' When she told Don, he shot her an interesting look.

'Go on, say what's on your mind,' she told him curtly. He raised his eyebrows smirking.

'I was about to say, 'poor bugger' Ricard hit the nail on the head when he called it the snake pit. Those women on the beauty counters scare me spitless.'

'They do not!' she scoffed. 'You love them and all the attention you get.' Barbe swotted him with the fish slice which he grabbed with one hand, holding the utensil above his head out of her reach while he chased her around the bench trying to kiss her. When he finally caught her, she looked breathless and went all faint. He grabbed her.

'Bebe, are you okay? I'm worried about you. Last night after dinner you weren't well either.' He helped her to the settee. 'Sit here I'll get you a cuppa.' He made her a mug of tea. 'Perhaps you should see the doctor.' he sat down and smoothed her face with his hand.

'No, I'm fine. Last night I knew I shouldn't have had two helpings of Banoffee pie, sheer gluttony and the doctor would tell me so,' she said embarrassed. Frowning, he realized this fainting is out of character and he wanted her checked out. He had undergone a complete medical after being shot in the thigh, but not Barbe, she left the hospital without being discharged after the hotel massacre. It had been quite stressful.

The family Sunday lunch loomed. both mothers, Aunty Katarina, and his sister who had come over from Melbourne with her husband, ten of them in total, including their children. Not all the family, just some of them. Barbe had been looking forward to it, but something niggled her. She did not feel quite on her game, she put it down to the stress of the marriage tribunal.

Today, Thursday, she had the day off. Don arrived home for lunch, he never came home for lunch, but today he insisted he take her to the doctor. They sat in the surgery of Barbe's doctor, Maryanne Wade, a woman about her age.

'This is not necessary you know, I'm fine.' The woman ignored Barbe for a brief moment, turning to Don.

'Why did you think it necessary for Barbe to see me?' Don went into great detail about the shootings and their adventures. Then he said, 'I don't believe it is PTSD because she has quite physical symptoms, like tiredness, throwing up and frequency ...cripes you couldn't be pregnant, could you?' He looked at Barbe, who shook her head and laughed then immediately burst into tears.

'I hope not, not on top of everything else.' He put his arms around her and comforted her. 'We had this discussion Barbe. Don't worry we'll cope whatever the situation.' After a thorough examination and a urine test Doctor Wade wanted an immediate ultrasound, which they did at the same clinic.

'Barbe you are fourteen weeks pregnant,' the radiographer announced.

'Don't tell me the sex of the child. It's all too much' she groaned.

The doctor explained the irregular periods, plus putting any symptoms down to stress; the shootings, the change in family dynamics, the marriage tribunal, all meant she missed the fact she was pregnant.

'It's not uncommon under the circumstances, when you miss the early signs and symptoms. It's usually down to lower hormone levels at your age. But thanks to your husband being concerned you may have had PTSD and bringing you here, we are now on to it.' None of this felt helpful to Barbe, except at least she had a few months warning. The doctor said she would see her again in a month.

They drove home shell shocked. Don sat thinking; I know I said it would be fine but... He looked across at Barbe, her face now buried in her hands as she sat saying nothing. Leaning over he patted her knee reassuringly, but he didn't trust himself to speak lest his voice gave him away and conveyed the wrong message. He drove into their single garage and opening her door he mustered his strong voice,

'go have a lie down I'll bring you a tea.' The cure for everything a cup of tea and a lie down. It looked like a miserable spring day; she climbed under the covers hibernating. When he returned, he stripped off to his underwear and snuck between the sheets, enveloping her in his arms. He turned around to face him.

She whispered 'I'm sorry, if I'm honest I know you didn't really want this, I'm sorry' she kept repeating.

'Bebe every child is wanted at the moment of its conception. I know I definitely wanted it, and I wanted you ... like now,' he kissed her, she burst into tears, again.

It looked almost dark when she became aware he lay still, holding her with his big hand gently rubbing her stomach. Yawning and stretching he said he'd been doing a bit of thinking.

'I know.' she replied, 'I felt sure I could smell wood burning.'

'You can but it's not me, you've been thinking too, so share.'

'You go first.' she said, and he groaned.

'Third week in March, the doctor said. We've got work to do. Just as well we never did the major alterations, we need another room,' he told her.

'No, we don't I've worked out how to make it work. Our walk-in robe becomes the nursery annex for a year, then Nicholas and Ryder can share because the hobby room is huge, and they already argue over who should have it so they can share...'

Don got up suggesting he cook them some dinner.

'It doesn't matter Bebe, we'll work it out,' he called from the hall. 'Wow, now I've got a chance to redeem myself and lose the shit father moniker.'

Chapter Thirty-Two:

S unday lunch came around far too quickly. The pair had agreed to keep the pregnancy to themselves for the time being. Lunch would be a potluck affair, Barbe had made her famous lasagne and creamy potato bake, Don made a chicken and mozzarella dish. Carla, always afraid there wouldn't be enough food, produced two main dishes and two desserts.

'Well, if your sister were still living here, she would have brought something too. So, I did it for her, besides have you seen her kitchen? She's messy, I didn't want her cooking in my kitchen,' she harrumphed looking up at her baby son.

Teresa, Don's sister, looked to be a curvy fashionable woman, her husband, Nico was short and stocky, a typical Australian of Greek and Italian extraction. He fitted well with the Lancini family dynamic. The man seemed a hard case with a great sense of humour, He enjoyed winding Nicholas and Ryder up about everything, from who would win the World Cup to his intimations he was mafioso. Don didn't help.

'I'm okay, I'm family, but you two watch your back.' Don whispered conspiratorially.

Barbe listened to Nicholas talking with Nico.

'Is Nico short for Nicholas?' he asked, staring in amusement at the man's abundance of gold jewellery and his thick greying hair all spiky with way too much hair gel.

Ryder whispered to Michelle 'This will be the clash of the aftershave lotions,' and she giggled. Nico picked up on it telling him with a smirk, 'you hurt her, I hurt you, I don't mind going back to jail.' Ryder knew he joked but he said it with such conviction. The boy simply raised his eyebrows. Aunty Katarina became the link between the families, having spent the last thirty years in Croatia during some of the worst conflicts of modern Europe.

'You don't know you are alive in this country,' she told them, her accent thick as she pushed a huge dish of her Croatian goulash in front of Carla.

'Yes well, I'm certainly glad to be alive and what's more I've got a huge scar on my backside to prove it,' Don regaled them all.

'It's on your thigh,' Barbe sighed at his exaggeration. At home he never let the facts get in the way of a good story. Then he kissed her, Ryder did the fingers down his throat thing. They laughed. Don insisted she had tomato sauce on her chin, and he had been fixing it. There were about six different conversations going on around the table and the decibel rating varied depending on who happened to be talking.

Jo surprised her daughter by admitting, 'I think this family have more fun than the Andersons.' Barbe remembered while Hunter's family did have fun, it had been very different. Sunday lunch would have been much more sedate; silver service, matching fine china, speak when you're spoken to and more traditional English food.

'Katarina's at home here,' Barbe said in case her mother's remark had been her way of insinuating they were not up to the Anderson family's standard.

'You're right, they're not as uptight as the Anderson's. The thing I really love is their passion. I think your father would have enjoyed them too.'

It turned three in the afternoon before anyone moved from the table. The boys and Michelle went down to the media room to play video games. Don made copious pots of coffee and tea. The savoury dishes had been replaced by more desserts and sweet treats. No one noticed Barbe had not been drinking wine.

The older women were learning they had quite a lot in common. Three elderly convent- educated ladies of the old school, all mothers and grandmothers. They delighted in telling anyone who would listen what life had been like in a convent school in the fifties and sixties.

'The nuns were strict, but it didn't do us any harm did it?' Jo sipped her wine.

'You speak for yourself; I've still got scars on my legs from the cane,' Carla gave a wry smile looking at Don.

'Are they from the nun I called Darth Vader?' Don asked, amused. 'We called her, Sister Aida Darth Vader.' The old nun had taught him in primary school too.

Teresa and Nico whose adult children lived in Melbourne insisted Barbe and Don come and visit sometime. Now Michelle had left the room, Teresa felt she could tell Barbe that Don's ex Gillian, never had been a fit with their family.

'You have it Barbe, beliefs, culture and history. You two will be just fine. He used to be a workaholic, but I think Gillian had to accept some responsibility for that.'

Barbe felt horrified. She thought Gillian had been okay, apart from her lack of domesticity and tact. Don had definitely felt her put downs regarding his parenting skills. Barbe tactfully changed the subject, suggesting Teresa check out their new home.

Nicholas and Ryder were driven back to college by their great aunt Katarina and grandmother. As usual they took their airtight containers of baking and snacks.

By the time the kitchen had been cleared and all the family gone, it approached six pm. Don and Barbe both agreed the day had been fun and each confirmed a busy work schedule for the coming week. Barbe received an email from her girlfriend, Kate, in Perth. The Perth

Catholic Diocesan office had asked her to give evidence by video hook up. She promised to get back to Barbe afterwards to let her know the details.

Kate added, 'ring me. I have something important to tell you.'

Barbe phoned phone her immediately.

'Kate, how are you? Thank you for doing this for me. I've got something to tell you too, but you go first.' Barbe chatted away but, within seconds she realized something did not feel right. Kate told her she and Graham, her partner, of almost eight years had split up.

'Kate, I'm so sorry but you don't sound particularly upset.' Kate actually laughed.

'I've been more concerned about what you would think, I mean I don't have a good track record with men, as you know.' Barbe asked if she had any regrets.

'To be honest, I'm ticked off with myself for letting my biological clock tick by while I wasted my time on the bastard,' she sounded so Australian. 'The big thing is I'm coming home as soon as my house is sold. I've landed a great job as curator of the Hobson Gallery in Wellington.

What's your news?' Kate asked. Barbe inhaled sharply, what should she tell her, well, not the pregnancy not yet?

'I'm married.' this time Kate gasped.

'You didn't wait for the church thing? Then why bother with it?' Kate seemed surprised. Barbe explained Hunter would not allow her to co-parent if she were living with Don, 'it would set a bad example and go against everything we believe.' She breathed deeply.

'Oh, for god's sake Barbe, who's Hunter to bloody talk. We all know what he got up to, and I bet he still does.' Kate didn't know the whole truth and Barbe had not told her, she simply couldn't. Kate would never understand why she protected him.

'I'm going through with the annulment application because Don and I want to do it again in church. He's lovely, my Adonis.'

'Yahoo! listen to you girlfriend.' The pair chatted about Ryder and Nicholas and agreed to talk again after Kate gave her evidence.

SIX MONTHS EARLIER, Hunter and the Crown had both submitted their management memorandums in relation to the 'Crown versus Mathew Thomas, in the case of murder on the high seas and the importation of over 100 kilograms of methamphetamine.' (Defendants are not required to appear in court at that stage in the proceedings.) The registrar held the case over till the Jury trial callover.

The trial callover memorandums had been filed by both sides and each side knew of the evidence to be presented. The court dates for the trial were set. On the one hand, Hunter felt annoyed Barbe had got him involved in this case. It had all been her fault. It would do his career no harm, quite the reverse. The media were amping up the whole saga.

Don had been right about Hunter in regard to the marriage Tribunal sitting. He would not be free to give evidence just yet. Hunter had written to them, 'I view the matter most gravely and will endeavour to avail myself as soon as possible.' He gave them two dates in the future. Regrettably, both clashed with their other cases and Hunter had then been given a date to which he reluctantly agreed. It would be another month.

DON HAD A BUSY WEEK ahead, with several of his team giving evidence in the High Court in respect of a drug bust which ended in one of the offenders being shot and wounded. Fortunately for Don, it didn't happen on his watch but still meant more paperwork for the people who were involved. As a result, the team was several members down. Add to the list a series of 'bloody meetings,' Don hated meetings.

'Biggest waste of time,' he told Barbe, who felt grateful for the time to herself. After spending most nights alone for almost ten years the two of them hadn't been apart since the carpark shooting in Sydney. She enjoyed her own company and wasn't fazed by his working late to catch up post meetings. Barbe looked at her list, wrote a few things on it then left it, in favour of knitting some baby clothes. As the little garments took shape the truth struck her, she wanted this pregnancy and Don's baby. The only thing she didn't want to think about was work. She couldn't traipse around the country with a new baby or even hugely pregnant. After all the leave she'd been forced to take, it seemed wrong to take maternity leave. It would not be a job she could go back to with a young infant either. The situation required another one of those hard conversations they'd never had while laying low in the Australian outback.

In his office, Don made some progress on the mountain of emails he seemed to amass daily and the ever-growing files. As he worked away, the satisfaction of a job well done washed over him. Meetings with outcomes were good. It occurred to him the best outcome for him and Barbe would be to have a child together, even though, when he learned of her pregnancy, he felt like a stunned mullet. Now the more he thought about it, the more relaxed he became. Now he actually felt excited at the prospect of a second chance at fatherhood. He dismissed the fact he'd be sixty-six when the child turned twenty. It is not unheard of Barbe's father had been around sixty when she was born, and it never bothered her.

DON SUGGESTED THEY work out the school holiday arrangements with Hunter and plan ahead for Christmas. Barbe and Hunter had always done things together so it would need addressing,

Don told her kindly. Barbe asserted herself saying she would speak with Hunter. In her heart she knew Don was right, while she and Hunter supposedly co-parented, it had always been Barbe who minded the children most holidays except January. It had been Barbe who changed her weekends to suit him, but then she really didn't have another life until now.

Sunday evening, Barbe phoned Hunter to discuss the school holiday arrangements. He was busy and suggested he buy her lunch tomorrow. They planned to meet him at his office on the Terrace. Don simply asked that she phone him afterwards and let him know the arrangements.

When Barbe arrived at Hunter's office his PA Maxine came out to greet her. Barbe had always liked Maxine who seemed to understand Hunter completely. She felt surprised when the woman seemed a little cool towards her. Maxine did find Hunter's empty food storage containers and gave them to Barbe. Barbe never said a word although she had decided she would no longer bake for him. She needed to move on.

Hunter shrugged on his suit jacket as they walked towards the lift.

'We won't eat downstairs, let's go further afield.' She watched him press the button for the carparking floor. He turned to look at her. Pregnancy became her; skin and hair glowing, eyes bright, dressed beautifully. He almost felt uncomfortable at how happy she looked. The boys had reported back about life in the Lancini household, and he had been struck by a strong twinge of jealousy.

'How are you Barbe?' Before she could answer, he asked, 'treats you well, does he?' She noted a kind of arrogance in his grey eyes. Barbe looked up at him, realizing he was way taller than Don.

'Yes, he's lovely.' As soon as she had said it, she realized it seemed like rubbing salt into the wounds and wished she hadn't. 'I'm sorry,'

she whispered. 'I never wanted us to end like this ...' She stopped
short of reminding him his dishonesty had been the killer with them.

'I never wanted us to end like this either,' he told her. With one
hand on the close-door button he grabbed her with the other and
pulled her close. He could feel her body, closer to him than it had
been in years, bosoms fuller and tummy rounded. His face inches
from hers, her eyes widened in surprise.

'I'm sorry you didn't want me' he said his breath on her lips. She
pushed him back.

'What are you talking about? You know it has never been a case
of me not wanting you. The complete opposite is true with us, and
you know it,' she said, annoyed. The door opened into the car park;
it looked dark below ground. 'Otherwise, we wouldn't be in this
situation. why would you wait until now to make a move on me if
you really wanted things to be different?' He took her elbow and
steered her to his vehicle and clicked opened the doors.

'Get in. I'll tell you why we were happy the way things were,' he
told her sadly.

'It may have suited your lifestyle but not mine. You had years. It's
over. I'm Mrs. Lancini and I'm pregnant.'

Of course, she is. He had felt it, the little pumpkin between them
she's pregnant.

'You stupid woman, so now you want an annulment so you can
marry in the Church. Well forget it, you have no grounds,' he hissed
at her as he started the vehicle and drove out of the car park. Quickly
doing up her seatbelt, she suggested they just stick to discussing their
sons. The rest was not your business.

'I'm busy with cases for the next three weeks so I can't have the
boys these holidays.'

'Fine,' she told him. 'What about the Christmas holidays?'

'I'll have the boys from Christmas to Wellington Anniversary Weekend at the end of January. Oh, and you are no longer welcome to join us,' he said they pulled into the café at the Botanical Gardens.

'Why, is your boyfriend going?' She had no idea why she said it. She actually hoped it might be true.

'Bitch,' he lashed out, raising his hand as if to slap her. He froze. This time, she deflected his hand, shocked. Immediately he leapt out of the vehicle and ran around to her side of the Mercedes. he looked really upset, realizing what he had almost done.

'I'm sorry I didn't mean...' It was too little, too late. It all felt too much for Barbe, she burst into tears. This had to be the last straw. He'd forgotten about pregnancy hormones. Unable to placate her he drove her home. When they arrived, she got out of the vehicle, slammed the door and left him.

AS SHE LAY ON THE COUCH with her stocking feet up, she mulled over what happened with Hunter earlier. She had just flopped down, cried those hormonally driven tears she couldn't explain then fallen asleep in the sunshine of the afternoon. Barbe heard a noise and turning her head Don stepped into her line of vision. He stood there.

'Bebe, what happened?' her mascara and eye makeup had run, and she looked a fright. 'What the hell happened? Did Hunter upset you?' He watched her touch her face, it felt hot. Enveloping her in his arms he tenderly kissed her cheek, asking her to tell him what had happened. Slowly she told him what had transpired with Hunter.

'I inflamed the situation with the boyfriend remark. I couldn't help it. He'd never hit me,' she protested 'he's never done it before... well once when we were in the Whitsundays. I forgave him. I knew it had just been a frustrated slap. Do you think I should apologize to him?' Shaking his head, Don kissed her again nuzzling her neck.

AFTER REASSURING HIMSELF Barbe felt okay, Don returned to HQ, wound up his business for the day and left to call in on Hunter in his office. Maxine went out to reception to check him out. She had heard him speaking with the girl on the front desk.

'Do you have an appointment, Mr. Lancini,' she asked becoming his gatekeeper. Don flashed her his disarming smile.

'It's Superintendent Lancini, I don't believe I require an appointment under the circumstances.' His tone told her he was the one in charge. A few seconds later she reappeared.

'Mr. Anderson will see you now Sir.' He thanked her as she opened the door to Hunter's office. Hunter gazed over the top of his horn-rimmed spectacles as Don spoke.

'Please tell me why you upset my pregnant wife?'

A supercilious sneer covered Hunter's face, 'I bet she couldn't wait to tell you about it.' Hunter rose from his chair, like a peacock, showing off his six foot four inches of height. Still, he looked smaller than Don who stood only five feet eleven inches, but with big broad shoulders and stocky frame Don looked more imposing.

'No, but she did say she may have inflamed the situation with her 'boyfriend remark' and asked if I thought she should apologize. Whatever she said didn't justify your raising your hand to her. Even if you never hit her, raising your hand is assault under the law, as you well know. If you thought about her comments hard enough you would realize she cares about you still.' Don saw the little sneer disappear from Hunter's face. 'Sadly, you're changing how much she cares, with your attitude.' Don shook his head and Hunter stood strangely silent.

'For God's sake man, you have two children together. You will both be there at their school and university graduations, not to mention other family highlights, weddings and grandchildren. Life is not all about you. Just because you're a bloody good trial lawyer, doesn't mean the world revolves around you.' Hunter opened his mouth to draw breath and comment, but Don wouldn't let him get a word in edgeways. He pulled up a chair in front of Hunter's desk, while still talking.

'Here is how it's going to be from now on. You will speak civilly to her on the phone, and you will meet her halfway in the co-parenting arrangements. We respect the fact you have a busy work schedule, but family comes first.' Did I say that me, the shit father? 'Your boys are going to have another sibling, a half brother or sister. Whenever possible we would like to share holiday time. It won't be long before those boys will be wanting to do their own thing,' Don paused.

'Have you finished?' Hunter narrowed his eyes, readying himself to launch into his own diatribe.

'No, I haven't. I caught Nicholas watching porn. I know it's not the first time he tried to wipe the history. The forensics indicate it's too often for my liking, as a parent. I've introduced numerous parental control apps on the devices and on our internet. I've had the conversation with him, but I suggested he talk to you or his pastoral carer, should he want to know anything.'

Hunter looked gob smacked. He completely understood the ramifications. But because Nicholas had wiped his viewing history, his father naively had no idea.

'I'm sorry, I didn't realize.' This came out of left field, but he trusted the Superintendent.

'What do you suggest I do?'

'I recommend the college invites this woman to speak to the boys and their parents.' He scribbled a name and a web site on the back of his business card. 'Jenny McDermott is an ex-Police Officer who specializes in this whole net safe business. She is a leading authority.'

Hunter gave him a dismissive look, as though to say what difference could one woman make.

'I'm serious Hunter, this woman takes no prisoners and she's amazing. Also, she will spell out quite simply how watching porn can impact your child's life and future relationships. Jenny can read men really well, so any fathers who watch it will feel their ears burning when she highlights the way it has already impacted them adversely. Their women will pick up on it too. It's not like reading a Penthouse or Playboy, this stuff is toxic. If you want your boys to enjoy healthy relationships, you can't leave it too long.' Don relaxed a bit now he'd said his piece.

'I expect the woman charges like a wounded bull.' Hunter, commented, fingering the card.

'No more than you do, and those boys are well worth it.' Don stood up and moved towards the door where he remained for a moment. 'Barbe cares about you and loves her boys. Don't make this any harder than it needs to be.'

Chapter Thirty-Three:

After Kate had given her testimony to the marriage Tribunal, she phoned Barbe, at three in the afternoon New Zealand time.

'Kate, so what did they ask you?' Barbe said, anxious to know.

'Oh, you know,' she giggled, 'name, address, phone number and bath night. Look the one fact they kept coming back to is around the time you caught Hunter and .... you never did tell me who she was,' Kate trailed off.

'I never did know who it was, or I guess I would have told you. What exactly did they want to know?' Barbe asked, a little anxious.

'They asked me how I could be so sure, and I told them Nicholas was just about to start school, so I could be specific about dates. Plus, you looked like a stunned mullet. Wham! All over rover.' For a minute Barbe said nothing, Kate spoke first.

'I have an offer on my house, it's unconditional. I'll be over in three weeks.' Barbe invited her to stay while she found somewhere to live.

With only one more week of school holidays Don had hired a police house, beside the lake at Taupo for some family time and they were driving up at the weekend. Michelle would join them, delighted she would be able to windsurf on the lake. Don looked forward to the trip, they could all sleep in, play board games, go fishing and windsurfing, well the teenagers would. Barbe said she looked forward to reading and knitting and the company of her blended family who all seemed to be getting on fine.

The weather looked great for the drive up north, the vehicle and roof rack were laden to the gunnels. They had food enough to feed a small nation and everyone buzzed with excitement. The drive felt smooth with good weather. The kids were a laugh a minute on the journey. She and Don often found themselves grinning at one another because of the teenage interactions in the back seat. The police house looked comfortable.

They arrived after dinner having stopped on the way for a meal to save cooking. As they sat around in front of a great log fire reading and chatting, Don decided to make the big announcement.

'We're expecting a baby, at the end of March next year.' Suddenly dead silence prevailed. Don never seriously thought the reactions would be what they were.

'It's pretty obvious Dad,' Michelle said looking at the boys. Ryder looked at Nicholas who had made his feelings felt before.

'You're not gonna pick us up from school when it's more obvious are you?'

'Why not?' Barbe asked, concerned where this might be going.

'Everyone will know...' he felt embarrassed in front of Michelle. Don immediately recognized where this came from.

'You and I need to have a talk, Nicholas. I thought we'd covered this before. Children are not just the result of sex they are an integral part of the marriage covenant,' he quietly informed the embarrassed seventeen-year-old.

'Mum and Wayne didn't have kids,' Michelle piped up.

'Yes, I'm sorry they were not blessed with children.' Don didn't want to badmouth Gillian, but her idea of family and his were never the same. The reason he didn't marry Gillian in the Church in the first place had been because he did not feel confident it would last. But he did want his child to have his name and Gillian had been pregnant.

'Why don't you all give us a list of names, boys and girls names. We're not sure we want to know the child's sex just yet,' he told them grinning.

'They have a parenting course at college it runs over a weekend. You get to mind a real baby overnight, change its nappies, feed it and stuff.' Ryder seemed quite keen on the idea, 'Maybe we can use our own baby.' Wondering how it would work using their new baby concerned Barbe.

'Maybe, we'll see I'll be breast feeding.'

Nicholas groaned complaining, 'too much information.'

Barbe produced a large box of chocolates and changed the subject. she knew this discussion would not go away. Interestingly enough, over the course of the week Ryder and Michelle began to accept the idea of a baby in the family. They heard less and less from Nicholas on the subject.

As the week progressed, the planned activities were covered, with quite a lot of wind surfing. Michelle proved very skilled at the sport and patient enough to teach Ryder.

Nicholas and Don went fishing almost every day. Barbe thought Lord knows what they talked about on the dinghy but suffice to say Don seemed to be winning over the petulant seventeen-year-old. One night she asked Don what they talked about.

'Man stuff, I remember I how scared I felt at his age, with no father and no godfather,' Don said simply, and shrugged. 'Tony tried to help but it wasn't till I joined the job. met Shep and later Frank Taylor, that I learned it's okay to be scared. Things get easier when you can admit you're scared,' he said, wistfully. Even after all their fishing the only seafood they consumed had been served in a restaurant. Barbe felt happy to bring out the small garments she busied herself knitting, and no one took any notice. When they arrived back in Wellington after their week away, they seemed like a more cohesive group.

A WEEK LATER, THE THREE family Matriarchs were treated to Sunday lunch with Barbe and Don.

Once again Don made the big announcement, 'we are expecting, end of March next year.' Carla shrieked in delight, over the moon, but she still complained,

'you only tell me now, it's wonderful, why you no tell me before?' normally she spoke with a kiwi accent unless it suited her. Carla had been born in Wellington. Now it suited her to be the Italian Mumma. 'I knew you were pregnant; I give you the parsley plant after all,' she insisted. Katarina too, looked excited, however her older sister Jo sat quiet. She made the right noises, but in her heart, she realized this baby really did herald the new family and the end of the Anderson line.

'So now we have another little Lancini.' Jo said.

Before she could say more Carla added, 'my eighth grandchild. We are truly blessed.' Don knew as soon as she left them, she would be on the phone to the rest of the family with her exciting bit of news.

BARBE AND DON MET KATE at the airport. She guessed Barbe was pregnant as soon as she saw her looking so well. She positively glowed. Don noted with interest that Kate appeared quite different from Barbe. Kate, a tall thin dizzy blond, enjoyed a drink and seemed a little jaded by her lifestyle and age. Naturally, she hyped up her new position, but Don guessed her life had not been moving in the direction she desired and sadly it seemed unlikely, ever. Openly she admitted to Don and Barbe she envied them. Their lives had direction and purpose.

Barbe had always wanted to enjoy the kind of fast life Kate talked about, now she could see through fresh eyes just how shallow it looked. Still Kate seemed to be a good person who genuinely cared for Barbe, and she spoke about how years ago they had always talked of opening up their own gallery. Maybe in a few years they could do it. Barbe mooted it might be just the opportunity she needed, doubting she could travel for work with her new baby. Don encouraged the idea.

Kate had bought a house, sight unseen on the other side of town, and she would be waiting a while for her household effects to arrive so she could then move in.

Katarina confided in Barbe, that Jo had been called to give evidence before the Catholic Marriage Tribunal. Later Jo told Katarina she felt quite strange about the whole business. Barbe had definitely changed when Nicholas went to school, she confirmed when asked. Everything had been rosy in the garden of Hunter and Barbe until then. She had no idea what had happened.

'Did she try to tell you what happened?' a panelist asked.

Jovana was unable to lie and for the first time in many years she felt ashamed of herself. Especially when they asked about it. She had to justify dismissing her daughter's anguish she shed tears admitting Barbe had tried to talk to her, and she had shut her down because she knew her son in law was a good man.

'Your daughter has never disputed her husband's character, and she also agreed he is a good father.' Jo felt confused, admitting she had no idea why they split up and her daughter's behaviour had frustrated her because Hunter went out of his way for Barbe. One of the panelists asked her to explain "how he went out of his way for her." It transpired to be purely material or financial support. Jo said this changed when the boys were about twelve and fourteen, and their father had taken more interest in spending time with them.

'You mean when your daughter started work?'

Jo agreed, saying Hunter worked really hard. Before this his late father had been ill and his mother too and all his siblings were overseas.

'Where did Mrs. Anderson get her support from?' one of the panelists asked.

Jo answered, a tad miffed it had not been obvious to them, 'from me, she got her moral support from me,' she said, irritated.

'Did your son in law ever date other women?' another panelist asked. Jo's back straightened and her lips pursed.

'No, he did not and what's more my daughter did the decent thing for him and accompanied him to the Law Society's annual ball.' She said it as though it had been an expectation of Hunter's. One of the men commented it was good of her and then asked, 'how did she present herself?' Nonplussed, Jo asked what he meant adding 'Barbe is an attractive young woman. She always presented herself well.' Having answered she began to wonder at the question, maybe the answer they were looking for was something else, like her behaviour?

'And your daughter, did she ever date other men after their divorce?' A very direct question.

'No, she did not and for years I lived in hope they would get back together again.'

Somebody asked her, 'when did things change between them after their divorce?'

'Yes, until the shooting, when she met Adone Lancini. He comes from a Catholic family, but I don't think he was practicing when he met Barbe. They both go to church together now.'

The Defender of the Bond pointed out that what Barbe and Don do has no impact on the facts of the matter. Hunter and Barbe were still married in the eyes of God.

After Jo had been dismissed, some discussion ensued around unanswered questions. They still had another three weeks before Hunter would be called to give his evidence.

POLICE HEADQUARTERS was a hive of activity. Finally, the Matty Thomas case would be heard. Hunter and his second chair, Emily Dickenson, were defending. The Crown versus Mathew Thomas in the case of murder on the high seas. Plus, importation of a class A drug in this case, amphetamine, for the express purpose of dealing in it, in return for money.

Don had decided he could not spare the time to sit in the Court room for the whole process, but he did intend watching the defense case. Wondering how they could possibly get creative with the facts, he felt quietly confident of the outcome. Detective Inspector Frank Taylor would keep Don apprised of the proceedings so he would know when the defense case would start.

When Hunter opened his argument for the defense, no one had been prepared for the direction he took. Although, he had disclosed it in the pretrial information memorandum. It had not actually registered until he enunciated the words in his inimitable fashion, that everyone in the courtroom became struck by his talent at putting the human elements together in such a convincing manner.

To begin with, the defense maintained Matty Thomas went to Tonga alone for a holiday. He had been recovering after an appendectomy. Yes, he had met the late Carlos Matua in a bar and the man had invited him to visit his boat with the idea they may do some fishing. Thomas felt anxious when he boarded the vessel because he could see it looked like a small commercial fishing boat. He had been expecting something different, more up market, a luxury vessel he could relax on. Thomas claimed he had been held on board against his will at gunpoint. Matua left the vessel and went ashore. When the ship had been out at sea Thomas feared he would be tossed overboard so when an opportunity presented itself, he had overpowered the captain and wrestled the gun from him. Then the captain's second in command later shot the captain with yet another weapon. Hearing the gunshots, the crew appeared, and

Thomas watched as the crew tossed the dead Captain overboard. They headed for a remote rural coastal area off New Zealand. Days later they were intercepted by the New Zealand Navy and a huge cargo of amphetamine had been found. Thomas claimed he knew nothing about the cargo of drugs. Hunter never called the cunning Thomas and so the prosecution could not cross examine him.

The prosecution had the entire crew of six give evidence through an interpreter. Hunter claimed they were complicit in the illegal amphetamine importation and therefore could not be trusted as competent witnesses against Thomas, who had never been one of them.

The trial was set down to last six weeks. Little wonder Don could not afford the time to sit every day in the courtroom, listening to the masterful Hunter Anderson eke out each cross examination, with an interpreter getting to the minutiae of life on board the fishing vessel. The defense uncovered disharmony and distrust amongst the crew. They had appeared to present a united front to the police against Matty Thomas. During Hunter Anderson's cross examination, cracks began to show in the crew's story. The captain's second in command had never been a popular man and under Hunter's relentless questions, discrepancies appeared in the crew's evidence. The afternoon the last of the evidence had been presented, Frank Taylor returned to head office and spoke with Don Lancini.

'You should have seen him man, the guy is like a steamroller in slow motion. Relentless and unforgiving, a real pain in the arse. I couldn't imagine living with somebody so bloody minded.' Don chuckled as Frank slumped against the door frame.

'Welcome to my world.' He said. 'Summing up is tomorrow, is it?' Frank nodded.

'Okay come on upstairs and I'll shout you a beer.'

Next morning, a small but notable police presence appeared in the court to hear the final summations. Don and Hunter eyed each other without acknowledgement. The prosecution took all morning to sum up, carefully going over all the evidence.

When they returned from the luncheon recess, Hunter stood cautiously aware he had the awful afternoon timeslot he called the graveyard shift, where tummies are full, and minds are drifting. There were only twelve people in the room Hunter needed to convince, and the judge was not one of them, nor was Don Lancini. Standing up, his tall imposing frame bowed slightly, acknowledging the judge, Hunter pushed his horned rimmed spectacles back on his nose, as he began to address the jury.

'Ladies and gentlemen considering the length of this trial I assure you I will not take very long to sum up on behalf of my client, Mathew Thomas. In regard to the charge of murder, I respectfully say you must dismiss, finding my client not guilty. There is nobody, there is no forensic evidence pointing to my client and as I showed when the crew were cross examined, there were no real witnesses to the murder. Therefore, the Crown has not proved, beyond reasonable doubt, my client murdered anybody.

In respect of the second charge of importation of a class 'A' drug for the purposes of dealing in it. Let me ask you this. What evidence proves beyond reasonable doubt my client imported this amphetamine? He had been a hostage on board the ship.

You have heard the various testimonies of the witnesses who could not agree on anything, including what Thomas had actually been doing there? The crew all knew and understood they were in possession of an illegal substance, drugs. It is the reason they were not charged with the more serious crime of importation. They made an agreement with the Crown. How can such men be trusted? Matty Thomas is the only one on the ship who says he was not involved in any way, shape or form with those drugs. He had been held there against his will. Members of the jury, some of the crew, gave evidence under oath saying my client had been held at gunpoint. Others were less reliable but could not dismiss it, they simply chose to stay unsure. You cannot convict a man on the evidence of a witness who is simply unsure. Therefore, you must find the defendant 'Not Guilty.'

The judge summed up, defining the law as he went along. However, in one matter he pointed the jurors towards the defense counsel's summing up. He agreed with Hunter Anderson there had been nobody body and no forensic evidence and no witnesses to the murder.

Then he said, 'however you must decide what it is an ordinary person might reasonably expect to be a true account of the facts given, in light of the statement the crew have made admitting they carried and knew about their deadly cargo of amphetamines. But remember, the burden of proof remains the same. Has the Crown proven beyond reasonable doubt, the defendant killed the Captain, Mr. Haris Megawati. Was the defendant, Mathew Thomas, a party to the importation of this cargo of amphetamine with a street value of over 100 million dollars?'

As soon as Don heard the judges summing up, he felt defeated. It sounded like the Crown had failed to prove their case. Six agonizing hours later the jury returned their verdict, finding Mathew Thomas not guilty of murder but guilty of importation of the drugs.

The judge thanked and dismissed the Jury. Hunter looked around satisfied with his effort and Frank nudged Don, 'let's get a drink.'

Chapter Thirty-Four:

Today Hunter Anderson would be required to give evidence before the Catholic Marriage Tribunal. All his childhood he had been comforted in the knowledge he had been loved and nurtured by his large extended Catholic family. He took so many things for granted. His parents unconditional love, the support of his church community and his Catholic faith. He remembered a particular priest from school days who often used to say, 'you cradle Catholics don't know what a gift you have. I pray your faith will never be tested.' Regrettably, Hunter was only at puberty when his faith had first been tested, by his overwhelming desire and attraction for other boys and men. Countless times he'd been told sex and marriage could only be between one man and one woman for the procreation of children.

Whenever sexuality came up in conversations, he had heard his own family speak with a definite homophobic bias. While a student at university, homosexuality was still illegal in New Zealand. No Catholic law student would ever want to be known as homosexual. Fortunately, by the time he had been admitted to the bar, the Homosexual Law Reform bill had been passed. A date firmly fixed in his mind, *July 1986*. It was still something his devoutly Catholic family did not understand. It isn't natural, it's deviant, and for any Anderson, totally unacceptable. Hunter remembered some very unhappy years, where he felt like God had dealt him some cruel blow. Unable to talk about his feelings with anyone, he suppressed them and at one point he could so easily have slipped into some dark place where black thoughts made him wonder if life was really worth it all.

Fortunately, he had been saved by the friendship and love of another man like him, who later left New Zealand to escape the unhappy trauma of coming out to his family. Hunter once again threw himself into his work and study, the one area of his life he could openly talk about and enjoy his own success. His parents were so happy when he finally married, nearly ten years after his siblings, at the age of thirty-six. They loved Barbe, she was perfect for him, a real homemaker and quite beautiful. They told him he had been very lucky she took him on, although Barbe thought it the other way around. For the first few years they were the perfect couple, but Hunter found it unfulfilling and struggled at times. Barbe sensed his unease but never understood it. How could she? To start with he never told her he had difficulty admitting it to himself. When the boys were born, he loved fatherhood but felt like half of his personality was missing. Barbe wanted more children, still he struggled to be a husband. She never guessed and why would she? Hunter was masculine, strong, and autocratic Barbe is gentle compliant and the little woman he began to resent.

Today, he admitted to himself he felt nervous. Sitting in the wood paneled hallway of the Tribunal offices waiting to be called, he decided he would hold his life together for the sake of his boys. In his heart he knew he could not face the truth and he would not. How dare Barbe do this to him now, just because she wanted to justify her own behaviour. Thinking about the time he tried to speak to his godfather, the Reverend Father Joseph Anderson, Hunter remembered how they chewed the fat about everything except what he really had on his mind. Jo Anderson loved his nephew and accepted the confident façade he presented to the world, missing the clues Hunter purposefully gave him. Perhaps the Reverend Jo had been a little naïve, whatever the reason, Hunter never had the courage to spit it out and tell him plainly what worried him.

Chapter Thirty-Five:

S eated before the Tribunal of two priests, a woman and the Defender of the Bond, Hunter wondered what they had in store for him.

'Thank you for coming to speak with us Mr. Anderson.' The grey-haired priest spoke softly. 'We have your written statement, and we have a few questions. 'You were thirty-six when you married Barbe Anderson,' the man paused. Hunter's experience told him you do not answer unless you are questioned, so the pause hung in the air.

The priest clarified, 'you never met a woman prior to your wife who interested you?' Hunter controlled a quirk of his lips but relaxed and let the smile cover his face.

'No, not one I fancied enough to marry. I've always said there is only really one woman in my life, Barbe,' he said with honesty. It seemed to resonate with the priests, but what did they know he thought.

'So, you never dated other women?' the woman asked.

'I dated a string of other women, but none I had a real connection with. Barbe was the one.'

'What went wrong then?' the woman asked him. She must be the psychologist he remembered.

'Barbe struggled after Ryder's birth, just little things at first, anxieties. I thought she possibly suffered baby blues. Nothing significant enough to suggest she seek treatment until... years later she had a huge meltdown. It seemed quite random, but she became fixated on the whole thing and blew it out of all proportion. Things simply went downhill from there.'

'When was this exactly, do you remember?' the woman asked.

'Oh, I remember precisely, because Ryder was only three and Nicholas had been about to start school.' He waited for further questions.

'Tell us what happened exactly.' One of the priests wanted to know.

'As I said it was much ado about nothing. I had just finished researching for a big case. I had worked extra-long hours as Barbe and the boys were away at her mothers. This particular day I received a call from a fellow harrier. We were training for a marathon, and I needed to get some more hours training in. This fellow, Barry Hamnett, who worked shifts as a fireman, asked me if I wanted to go for a run after work as he had the day off. I decided to take the rest of the afternoon off and go for a run. We planned to run as far as we could from my place in Kelburn for one hour and then back and see what distance we covered. Barry had been a lot of fitter than me because he had more time to train. But I'm bloody minded so I would endeavour to keep up with him. To cut a long story short we did the run and returned to my home to take a shower. Barry used the main bathroom, and I used our ensuite. In those days I wore contact lenses. I had showered and had been attempting to put in a lense when I dropped it on the bedroom floor. I felt ticked off with myself and let out a string of expletives, Barry heard me and came in to see what was wrong. I told him what happened, and we were both on our hands and knees looking for my lens when Barbe appeared at the door wanting to know what was going on. Barry got a huge fright, when she spoke, we weren't expecting anyone and suddenly it was like Worth's circus. He stood up and his towel dropped to the ground I pushed the bedroom door shut and snipped it to give the man some privacy. I felt so embarrassed, my wife stood pounding on the door and yelling at me, kicking up a fuss. I simply got dressed and went with Barry downtown to the pub. I told him I'd deal with her later. Nothing I could say would placate her. Then she started trawling through the minutiae of our intimate life, second guessing everything I had said and done or not said and not done. Frankly, I couldn't handle her hysteria. I found myself avoiding coming home. I didn't want the daily drama. I found excuses not to go home, probably exacerbating the whole fiasco. But really, she seemed to spend all her time trying to rationalize what she believed she saw. I told her the whole situation would be laughable if it were not so serious. I explained how Barry felt totally embarrassed and she simply made the situation worse for everybody, including herself. After months of carping on about my behaviour as though I'd been deviant, I simply couldn't stand it any longer. She wore me down.

I suggested we take some time apart and I got an apartment in the city, but we didn't tell our families. I went home as much as I could to be with my sons. Barbe seemed to calm down a little and after our Christmas holidays; a month as a family holidaying in the Marlborough Sounds, she seemed more amenable towards me. Every time I thought we were moving forward in our relationship; things took a step backwards. A year after her father died, she insisted we separate, telling me she had applied for a divorce. Of course, she didn't need my permission for a divorce. I wanted my sons to stay in our family home, believing and praying we might get back together again. Once I suggested counselling. Barbe wouldn't hear of it saying it would simply be papering over the cracks. When family or friends visited, she would insist I join them for the weekend. But it seemed hopeless, things never really improved, and the divorce went through.

Barbe did not have the resources to give our sons the kind of life I had planned for them even if I paid more than half of it. I drew up a contract to co-parent and provide for the boys while they and their mother continued to live in the marital home. I paid her an allowance because I didn't want her working. I wanted them to have their mother home with them, especially while they were young.

Three years ago, she had a rush of blood to the head and went off and got a job. The work took her away from home about one or two nights a week. Honestly there was no way I could just have the boys on a whim or the vagaries of her part time job selling overpriced cosmetics.

They needed continuity. Boarding school seemed the only option. I was happy with the arrangement it didn't do me any harm when I was a boarder at the college. I have to say our eldest complained most.' Hunter sat back, taking a breather from his telling of the events.

'Did it work for you both, Mr. Anderson?' one of the panelists asked. Thinking for a moment Hunter considered the question.

'To be honest, I think it had been good for Barbe. As a result, I thought we were closer than we'd been in years, we had our rituals and routines, and we did things for each other.'

'Like what exactly?' one of the panelists asked before he had a chance to explain.

'When Barbe did baking for the boys to take back to college she would make up a care parcel for me. She became much more flexible if I needed her to pick up the boys from college on a Friday afternoon, or heaven forbid I needed to swap weekends. We would attend school events together, not separately, until the hotel massacre when Barbe went into police protection. I honestly believed we had a good chance of getting back together. Before we went to the Whitsundays we even touched on the subject of our futures. But when we were on the island, and I tried to bring it up she pushed me away and the next thing I know she is with this police officer and applying for an annulment.'

'This Mr. Barry Hamnett, do you have his address? How can we contact him?' the Defender of the Bond asked. Hunter gave an apologetic smile.

'Sadly, he was killed in New South Wales ten years ago. He went over to help with a bad bushfire but was killed in a car accident.'

'Have you ever had a sexual relationship with a man?' The woman asked. Immediately Hunter's hackles went up and he protested,

'no, I have not.'

The older looking Priest thanked Hunter for his time, and he announced he would shortly be notified of the outcome. Hunter acknowledge the panel with a nod, stood up and left.

The panelists launched into a discussion on Hunter's testimony.

'We must decide who is telling the truth here. Who has the most to lose? On the face of it, it would appear the wife who wants to remarry in the church, has the most to lose. If Hunter Anderson truly loved his wife as he claims, and he were homosexual, we would be understanding of the struggle such a man would have maintaining the role of husband within the bond of matrimony. If he had ever truly been able to undertake the role in all honesty and therefore commit to the sacrament.'

The psychologist argued the huge pressures of a judging Catholic public, including his own family, could easily cause a man to deny his sexuality. Without evidence of more homosexual liaisons, they had no real proof of the man's sexuality.

'There is no evidence of any homosexual liaisons, only the word of his wife and she could be the one mistaken as her husband kindly put it. Regardless, does the possibility of one incident prove there is an impediment to the bonds of the sacrament? I believe not,' the Defender of the Bond said, adamantly.

'In my professional experience,' the psychologist said, 'one incident, whether proven or not is only the tip of the iceberg. Homosexual men tend to be promiscuous where they are not out and openly committed to a significant other of the same sex in marriage or a civil service. So, there would likely be more liaisons and it is only his word against hers.' The psychologist shuffled some files in front of her, concealing her irritation. Sometimes she found dealing with the patriarchy insurmountable.

'I understand what you are saying, however I have known celibate men to admit to an attraction for men only. They have nothing to do with this couple's sad plight. This marriage covenant is indissoluble,' the Defender of the Bond announced.

Chapter Thirty-Six:

B arbe had been looking forward to the big charity bash this evening. The invitation said formal. She couldn't fit her evening gowns. So, she bought a navy velvet three quarter sleeve gown with a sweetheart neckline and ruched gathers flatteringly down each side. It hugged her voluptuous figure. She arranged her thick dark hair in an elegant updo with soft tendrils artistically escaping. Her make up was picture perfect. She glowed. Don stood behind her admiringly as she put in her diamond stud earrings. He nuzzled her neck affectionately, something he loved to do.

'How lucky we are; me to have such a beautiful wife and you to have such a ...' he grinned raking his thick dark hair and checking himself out in the mirror. He looked handsome, especially in a smart dinner suit. Barbe laughed.

'Come on Adonis, we don't want to be late do we, you gorgeous boy.' The three teenagers sat watching sport on TV and they checked the pair out as Don gave them their instructions. Nicholas eyed his mother up and down and to her very great surprise, he stood and put his arms around her, towering over her.

'I love you mum, you look good.' For a few moments he became her little boy again, he looked so much like his father.

'Thank you, Nicholas, I love you too. In fact, I love you all.' Don watched as she hugged Michelle and Ryder. Driving along towards the venue Barbe commented.

'Is it my imagination or do you think something happened at Hunter's place last weekend? Nicholas appears to have done a complete three hundred and sixty degrees in his attitude.' Don raised an eyebrow, then narrowed his eyes in thought.

'Who knows, he could have heard something, seen something or even at school something may have been said. Just enjoy it. If it's important we'll find out when he's ready.' Don pulled up under the portico of the Duxton Hotel. The venue for tonight's Gala awards Dinner, 'Community Gold', where various groups sponsored innovative community projects every two years. He gave his keys to the parking attendant and took the attendant's cell phone number, flashing his ID and saying, 'just in case I need to get my pregnant wife out of here in a hurry.'

He opened the door for Barbe. The foyer buzzed with the glitterati of the capital, politicians, actors, television personalities, and various Wellington businesspeople. The police had a small contingent who gravitated towards each other, all smiles and introductions. The only person Barbe had not met before had been Tim Paxton and his wife Jan, who put Barbe at her ease. She caught Tim studying her intently on more than one occasion, the kind of intense gaze she had become accustomed to from certain men since her role with Pascal Rousseau. Once his wife distracted him saying, 'Tim we should go in and get seated at our table.' He agreed, suggesting it to the others. Superintendent Mary McKay and her husband Luke, a Naval Officer, sat to Barbe's left and on Don's right sat Marion Taylor and her husband Frank. Next sat Joy and Noel Watson, he had the role of Association president. Joy happened to be another schoolteacher like Marion Taylor. Marion asked Barbe how she had been keeping, her pregnancy obvious.

'We'll have an eighteen-year-old and a newborn,' she advised, then grimaced. Don kissed her cheek.

'It definitely keeps you young,' he flashed his charismatic smile. Becoming aware of someone standing behind him, he turned to see Hunter Anderson and Emily Dickenson.

'The partners have a table,' Hunter offered by way of explanation. Don stood and made the introductions. Hunter stooped down to kiss Barbe on the cheek speaking quite audibly.

'Pregnancy always did become you my dear.' Don watched her wince.

'Hunter Anderson, from Holmes Anderson Chapman and partners and Emily Dickenson.' Don's introduction was simple. Emily Dickenson appeared tall and opinionated, the antithesis of Barbe, her slim, angular figure had a boyish, sporty quality. A brilliant lawyer in her mid-thirties, tonight she looked very elegant in a black straight gown, her hair in a short blonde bob. After the introductions they moved off towards their table. Don recognized an awkward moment had been averted and smiled knowingly at Barbe. She hadn't spoken to Hunter since their lunch altercation.

The evening proceeded pleasantly enough. Barbe had not been keen on continually moving around meeting people between courses. Don said they'd leave as soon as the formalities were dispensed with. At one point, Frank and Marion Taylor sat down beside her saying how much they had enjoyed their wedding and the high tea even though it now seemed like a lifetime ago.

'It's just as well you and Hunter get on so well as he seems to be at everything these days,' Marion added. Barbe ignored her at first.

'Yes, well needs must, we have the boys school prizegiving next week,' Barbe said politely. People were milling about chatting while a piano soloist played in the background.

Tim Paxton passed the table.

'Have you seen my wife; she's always disappearing?' He sat down and then Frank Taylor stood to mingle and soon after Marion joined him. Tim seemed to stare at Barbe, before remembering himself.

'You're keeping well? Mrs. er uh?'

'Barbe, call me Barbe.' Where's Don when she needed saving. 'How many children do you have Tim?' He seemed relieved he could speak about himself.

'Jan and I have two daughters.' Noticing the dessert, was being served he asked, 'may I take you up to get some dessert?' Food, something else he could talk about. She stood and took the proffered arm. 'I'm so pleased the dessert menu is a buffet,' she said. 'I have enjoyed some peculiar food preferences lately,' she laughed and looked him in the eye. He put the fingers of his free hand inside his collar as though it were a little tight, he looked away and then back at her.

'When Don told me about you and him, I didn't know quite what to think.' This time he looked her in the eye, his comment, honest.

'I can see he is a very lucky man to have met someone as special as you. Mind you, Shep had already told me,' he chuckled. 'Shep told me you called Don on his vanities and affected mannerisms.'

Barbe gave him her dessert plate.

'As the mother of son's, I understand how he got those vanities. It's a joke in the Lancini family. Adone's the youngest, he's mummy's little darling, his Nonna's little prince and all the old aunties used to tell him "you're soooo cute" and as you know, he is Mr. Personality.' She said smiling as she spoke, but still, he didn't get it. 'He's a lovely man really.'

Don sat down beside her at the table as the others joined them.

'Only ice cream, no pickled onions?' he smiled inches from her face, and she teased him with her spoon. Their own private banter sparkled between them. Laughing, she put his hand on her stomach.

'Move over Andrew Mehrtens,' he announced with pleasure referring to the All-Black boot of the day. 'We may have a Lancini in the role soon.' It didn't go unnoticed. Several others wondered, with a twinge of envy, were they still in the honeymoon phase?

After coffee and tea had been served at the tables, the award winners featured on the big screens. Hunter's firm had sponsored the winning 'Big Buddies programme,' for the second time in a row. He went up to receive the award taking with him the 'long legal streak of opinionated opportunism' as Don thought of Emily Dickenson. Sure, she may be a good lawyer and not bad looking, but he felt sure she had another agenda when it came to Hunter Anderson. His cop's instinct told him so. He knew she would be disappointed, and it wouldn't bode well for Hunter. The woman had always been indiscreet about her bedroom conquests according to police gossip. Hunter had no clue about women and Emily Dickenson would chew him up and spit him out like other cold blooded leggy insects did with their mates. Another reason he felt sorry for him, he believed the man had become imprisoned by his instincts and his catholic guilt made him vulnerable.

Don texted the car park attendant and by the time they arrived at the hotel foyer their vehicle waited for them.

'I'll drive Bebe, I've only had one glass of wine.' He thought of her as his precious cargo with a new Lancini on board.

Chapter Thirty-Seven:

B arbe fancied bagels with cream cheese and smoked salmon and lots of tea for Saturday morning brunch. Michelle and Ryder had been dispatched to the supermarket with a list, while Don taught Nicolas the intricacies of making real coffee, aka his Italian espresso. He suggested Nicholas become a barista ahead of his entitled school friends, so he could get a 'real job' making coffee in the holidays. 'Something to put you in touch with 'real people.' Interestingly enough Nicholas seemed keen. He could see the value in working for someone other than his father.

Coffee made, Don went outside to retrieve his copy of the Saturday Dompost from the front lawn and checking the letterbox, he grabbed the mail, a letter for Mrs. B Lancini. Turning over the white envelope, he saw it came from the Wellington Catholic Diocesan Office. Immediately his fingers froze. His heart racing, he entered their bedroom, he kicked the door closed with his foot.

Emerging after her shower, pink cotton sloppy jersey covering the baby bump, maternity jeans, and bare feet she looked up at him from under the towel she used to dry her hair. From the look on his face, she knew something serious had happened. He held up the envelope. Staying her hand as she reached for it, he reminded her,

'Whatever the outcome, we're a family. We all have a stake in the outcome. This is not medieval England or Rome. The Church must embrace diversity whilst protecting the sacrament.' To his surprise she stood grinning at him.

'Off yer soapbox Superintendent.' this time she grabbed the envelope as he lowered his hand. Sitting on the end of the bed she quickly tore open the letter and read the last line. 'Therefore, having reviewed the case and the evidence, the Protector of the Bond finds the marriage indissoluble.' Her voice cracked, 'I thought this would be the outcome. I know truth and proof do not go hand in hand. I know compared with Hunter I made a feeble witness.' Don encircled her in his arms.

'I'm sorry, I know how much you wanted this. But as soon as they didn't call Simon Perry as a witness, I began to lose hope.' Pulling back from Barbe he could see her tear-filled eyes.

'Ah there you have it. Although I prayed for it, I never truly held out any hope. Do you know why?' He listened to her. 'All my life all the important decisions have not been up to me. I have been loved and nurtured and been dependent upon the men in my life. They have all been good men, but fallible. I didn't expect this decision to be any different. In the last three years I have met three men who have allowed me to grow; Ricard Beauchene, who inspired me to be confident again and believe in myself, Adone Lancini, with whom I fell in love and who loves me back and protected me with his life.'

'And limb,' he added sardonically.

'And makes me laugh, took my family and gave me his and now we are building our own family, our home and we're doing it with the traditional values of our faith, albeit on the fringes.' She kissed him lovingly and the pumpkin between them started beating a tattoo. 'Let's get brunch. I'm dying for a cuppa.' Standing up she pushed him gently.

'Hang on, who is this third guy? You said three men had allowed you to grow.' He followed her down the hall handing her a pair of pink sneakers. 'We don't want the bump getting cold.'

'Simon Perry's the third, he seemed to understand I needed to challenge the system. Just because we do what we've always done, and we get what we've always got, God knows, it's not always right.' Nicholas had the table set for brunch. He stood wearing Don's black apron and had a tea towel draped over his arm dramatically. Don watched him, still frowning as he dragged out a chair for Barbe, she pulled the hair scrunchie off her wrist and tied back her hair.

'Don't baffle me with the science of fancy words Bebe, I'm just a copper remember.' Nicholas poured her tea, Barbe grinned at him. He did what Don referred to as playing silly buggers, then it struck her.

'I'm surprised you didn't actually pull any old copper stunts with Simon Perry; you know offering to garner evidence for him.' Don smirked; heaven forbid.

'It wouldn't have worked would it, as they didn't use him?' She shrugged as the noisy duo of Ryder and Michelle arrived with bagels and croissants.

Chapter Thirty-Eight:

T he brown manila envelope fell out on to the desk as the receptionist at the Catholic Marriage Tribunal sorted the canvas bag of mail. Three times a week an elderly priest collected the Diocesan mail from the Wellington mail centre and distributed it around. Today Father Appleton had other duties and left the bag at reception. Teresa Halligan quickly sorted it out and noticing the bright Australian island tourism stamps on the manila envelope she decided to take the mail into her boss, herself. Knocking firmly on the solid wooden door she heard 'enter' as though it were a clinical waiting room. The Reverend Father Robert Brougham, Doctor of Cannon Law nodded as she held up the mail and he motioned for her to set it down.

'Please may I have these stamps for my son, father? He collects stamps.' A considered man he made no quick reply. Instead shuffled through the mail ignoring her. He muttered.

'Possibly in due course, we'll see.' Then he waited till she had left the room before he curiously opened the envelope noting the Whitsundays Resort address on the back. Inside were a few photographs between two sheets of stiff cardboard and attached 'with compliments' note. The note had been left blank save the photographer's contact details. On close inspection he recognized one man who appeared in all of the photographs. The first photo of two men, one older, one younger the older man had his hand around the neck of the younger man, the look on his face sheer unbridled joy. But then something else, something knowing, lustful and intimate the faces of both men are clearly seen. The next shot shows the older man has taken off his spectacles and his thinning hair is seen from behind as he kisses the younger man on the mouth. The date clearly visible on the photo rings alarm bells for the priest. The older man is Hunter Anderson the well-known criminal barrister and the date is Barbe Anderson's 40th birthday. The priest had a thing for numbers and remembered her birthday. The clock behind the bar read ten thirty. In the next shot, a telescopic lens has been used. The pair are together again and this time, possibly poolside in a private area of a 'guests only' sunbathing space. Both men are naked, bare bottoms seen in one shot, then another shot where one is applying lotion to the other with palm trees and sea in the distance. The final three shots are a little grainy, also taken with a telescopic lens. The same two men feature they are on the balcony of a seaside apartment, and they appear to be arguing. The older man is sitting sipping what appears to be a cold drink, brows furrowed and the same younger man, recognizable, although with his back to the camera has his hands on his hips, he's wearing only swimming trunks, tight like budgie smugglers. The next shot showed his annoyed accusatory expression and he's saying something. His top teeth are quite firmly over his bottom lip. The priest doesn't recognize the expression but then why would he? He doesn't use 'fuck you' as part of his everyday vernacular.

The next picture features the two men almost nose to nose, both looking hostile. There are no more pictures. He can only assume the men take their argument inside. Rechecking the photographs, he notices there are three different incidents on three different dates over the period of five days, from the dates on the film and the clothes the men are wearing and the settings.

The priest felt ill. Sometimes the greatest disappointments come from those we trust the most. He needed to think, to pray and consider what he had been sent. Taking the photos, he put them in a new envelope and folding the old envelope in half he slid it into the new envelope. Then he went to speak to Teresa

'Sorry, I can't give you those stamps, they're evidence.' She frowned but the look he shot her brooked no challenges.

EPILOGUE:

'Poor little Donna, your Mamma woke you just to put on a fussy christening gown?' Don held his little daughter while Barbe put the finishing touches to her makeup. 'This Baptism is a much bigger affair than either of our weddings.' he kissed his little daughter.

'You speak as though neither wedding was to each other,' she laughed. 'Although my mother was scandalized by the fact her only daughter walked down the aisle with her sons either side of her and she was the size of a house and scared her waters would break.' They both laughed.

'Yeah, we truly are blessed.' Don said on a sigh, 'you my little princess, are the only person I know who has four godparents.' He thought it a great idea. 'Your aunty Beth and big brother Nicholas, and big sister Michelle and your next big brother Ryder.'

The infant's tiny hand gripped her father's index finger trying to put it in her mouth.

'Hey, I think she's hungry. Again!'

'She's always looking for food, it doesn't mean she's hungry, she's a Lancini.' Barbe grinned.

The End

"In Truth the Church is too unique to prove herself unique
For most popular and easy Proof is by parallel: and there
Is no parallel"
G.K. Chesterton.

www.ingramcontent.com/pod-product-compliance
Lightning Source LLC
Chambersburg PA
CBHW050719180626
46814CB00002B/518